THE LIFE OF
AN AMOROUS MAN

by Saikaku Ihara

translated by Kenji Hamada
illustrations by Masakuza Kuwata

TUTTLE PUBLISHING
Boston · Rutland, Vermont · Tokyo

Library of Congress Catalog 63-21505
ISBN: 0-8048-1069-9

Distributed by

North America
Tuttle Publishing
Distribution Center
Airport Industrial Park
364 Innovation Drive
North Clarendon, VT 05759-9436
Tel: (802) 773-8930
Tel: (800) 526-2778
Fax: (802) 773-6993

Asia Pacific
Berkeley Books Pte Ltd
5 Little Road #08-01
Singapore 536983
Tel: (65) 280-1330
Fax: (65) 280-6290

Japan
Tuttle Publishing
RK Building, 2nd Floor
2-13-10 Shimo-Meguro, Meguro-Ku
Tokyo 153 0064
Tel: (03) 5437-0171
Tel: (03) 5437-0755

06 05 04 03 02 01   9 8 7 6 5 4 3 2 1

Printed in the United States of America

IHARA SAIKAKU (1641–93) was undoubtedly one of the most uninhibited writers that ever published a tale. Critics of the more sensitive school of belles-lettres have downgraded him as "vulgar" because of his unabashed preoccupation with life in the gay quarters. Others, concerned less with moralistic judgments than with technique and objectivity in the storytelling art, have acclaimed him as a great "realist" writer—largely, it would seem, because of his minute, true-to-life delineation of characters, customs, and events of his day.

Saikaku belonged to the classical school of novelists and poets. The term classical, as here applied, refers to that priceless bulk of indigenous literature, both prose and verse, that had accumulated since the dawn of articulate history until the introduction of Western literary forms in the 19th century, which brought about a complete change in outlook, technique, and style upon the native pattern.

What distinguishes Saikaku from the other two prose writers who share with him the pre-eminent niche in the "classical" firmament is the fact that whereas Lady Murasaki dealt with the ancient nobility *(The Tale of Genji)* and Kyokutei Bakin with feudal lords and the samurai caste *(The Eight Retainers of Satomi)*, Saikaku was concerned solely with life among the common people.

In particular, Saikaku depicted in his writings the pursuits and follies of the most glamorous period in medieval Japan—the dawn of the Genroku era—when the hitherto oppressed commoners first enjoyed the fruits

5

of untrammeled security and ease. He was thus the first vital exponent of the democratic spirit in the annals of written Japanese literature.

Consider the times. The reigning Tokugawa dictatorship, with its sumptuary laws and outspread strategy designed to discourage rebellion among ambitious princes and lords, had brought prolonged peace to a land hitherto wrecked by civil war. Samurai swords now rusted from disuse. The commoners had no part in government, but merchants, craftsmen, shopkeepers, moneylenders, and innkeepers in the great burgeoning cities began to thrive as never before. They were the men with the goods, producers and sellers of services. The samurai warrior caste produced nothing, but, with steady income from feudatories, they became lavish spenders and fell into a state of innocuous desuetude. The merchants set the pace of progress, literally thumbing their noses at the ruling class.

This spectacular rise of the common people ushered in an era of unprecedented prosperity, colorful luxuries, and irrepressible gaiety. Theaters, the arts, and the entertainment quarters flourished. Freedom of expression in the world of art and a new zest for living gave birth to a great number of talented artists, writers, poets, dramatists, and sundry entertainers. And Saikaku was one of the forerunners of this genre school. Thus, what such famous ukiyo-e woodblock color print artists as Hokusai, Utamaro, Hiroshige, and Kiyonaga expressed in pictures, Saikaku told in prose.

Himself originally a thriving merchant in the up-and-coming plebeian metropolis of Osaka, Saikaku lost his wife and daughter long before his prime. The tragedy moved him so deeply that he turned over his business to his manager and led the life of a roving Buddhist monk. He traveled extensively, returning to Osaka once every six months or so.

6

For some twenty-five years he devoted himself to the writing of haiku verse, producing at about the same time a prodigious amount of prose work. As a poet, Saikaku first studied under the aged master Nishiyama Baika and soon started his own avant-garde school of haiku poetry. It was then that he adopted the pen name Ihara Saikaku (his real name was Hirayama Togo). Possibly the most prolific versifier of all time, he is said to have once composed as many as 26,500 poems at a single day's haiku competition. He probably merely recited them extemporaneously, with someone else writing them down simultaneously for the record.

A contemporary comment by Ito Baiu on Saikaku's prose work pictures him as a man of deep understanding and sympathy. Saikaku, the comment says, had a refined, romantic-looking head and a figure that never seemed to age.

The present volume *(Koshoku Ichidai Otoko)* is Saikaku's first major work in prose, published when he was forty-one years of age. It is remarkable less for the gay adventures of the protagonist (a fictional composite of the many *daijin,* or men of wealth, who visited the gay quarters) than for the superb character sketches of the women he dallies with. It was Saikaku who immortalized the famed *tayu* (courtesans) in entertainment houses, the prototype of the modern geisha.

Moreover, he combined in this tale the ups and downs of human experience—good and evil, luck and misfortune, misery and pleasure, stark realities and the mystical, sin and repentance, the sordid and the beautiful. As such, the book is an excellent commentary on the times—how prosperity and corruption went hand in hand among the rising commoners.

Saikaku wrote about what he saw, heard, or experienced without mincing words, in a picturesque prose characteristic not only of his sensibilities but also of his outspokenness. His narrative is interspersed here and there with serious introspective moods, like conscience sitting in judgment. As such, this is not just another medieval tale but a powerful social indictment.

Translating Saikaku's archaic prose, with the ornate idioms, cadences, and stylistic literary norms of a vanished era, and with no punctuation or paragraphing so necessary for clarity and comprehensibility, is an enormously difficult task—a challenge to modern linguists, if not to the Japanese themselves of today.

The method which I have used is, therefore, a departure from the conventional way of rendering word for word, phrase for phrase, line for line. For the most part, I have tried to convey the gist of his narrative, thought for thought, in modern English, without unduly sacrificing the flavor of the original.

Honolulu, Hawaii   KENGI HAMADA

PART I

EVEN THE moon sets all too soon, beyond the shadows of Mt. Sayama. The cherry blossoms were dead, suggesting to him the evanescence of human life and filling his heart with a vague sense of grief. There was the silver mine. It was his. But he was already a man of means, and wealth, as such, held no fascination for him. The drab empty life, here in the province of Tajima, left his irrepressible yearnings unfulfilled. Overwhelmed at last by all this bleakness but hopeful of the joys to be found in romantic old Kyoto, he set out for the imperial capital. Ah, he mused expectantly, *there* he would pursue the charms of beautiful women and the pleasures of wine!

Yumesuke, "the Man of Dreams," they called him in Kyoto. For his sober, hard-working neighbors never saw him otherwise than sleeping or just awaking. Nightly he frequented the gay quarters of Shimabara with such fashionable, if dissolute, men about town as Nagoya Sansa and Kaga-no-Hachi.

In the dead of night, as Yumesuke staggered homeward across the bridge on Ichijo-dori, his aspect was frightful to behold. Sometimes he disported himself in the manner of a young dandy, raucous and maudlin. At other times he wrapped himself in the black long-sleeved robe of a woebegone priest—a man transformed. Or he would wear a long tapering topknot upon his crown, looking for all the world like a foppish rapscallion. If ever a noisy ghost was seen prowling through the night, this was it!

But when the keepers of the Shimabara teahouses

tried to admonish him, Yumesuke would insist with a twisted grin that nothing on earth—not even if the devil himself were to tear his flesh to shreds—could deter him from pursuing his heart's desires. Willy-nilly, being innately kind and business-minded to boot, they tolerated his excesses. They could not very well bar him from their establishments. Nor could they abandon the rambunctious scarecrow on the wayside.

Now, among the Shimabara courtesans there were, at the time, such particularly well-known women as Kazuraki and Kaoru, and Sanseki too. And soon, to each of these lovely women, each of the three cronies became amorously attached. With hearts all willing the men duly paid the ransom asked to secure the courtesans' release from their contracts. Yumesuke took Kazuraki along with him. Each retired with his concubine to a house in Saga or led a secluded life in the shadows of Higashiyama or dwelt unknown in Fuji-no-Mori.

In time, insofar as Yumesuke and Kazuraki were concerned, the ties of domesticity became daily more pregnant with obligations, and a son was born from their union.

Yonosuke, "Man of the World," the son was called. Really there should be no need to dwell so overtly on this, for everyone knows what such a name implies. The mother's affection was pleasant to behold as, fondling the child on her lap, hand tapping hand, hand tapping lips, she mumbled sweet nothings and the child gurgled gleefully. And the days passed and the years too. And then came the month of the frost when the boy, now four years old, went through the customary head-shaving rites. In the spring he wore his first broad *hakama* trousers over his tiny robe. But then he had a touch of the deadly smallpox. The gods, however, answered prayers, and not a trace of the illness remained to mar his face. The fifth year passed and the sixth.

One summer night when he was seven years old, Yo-nosuke got up from his bed and left his pillow. He fumbled with the door catch, and the noise awoke a maid of the household sleeping in the adjoining room. She knew what the boy was bent on doing. Lighting a candle, she walked beside him down the corridor. The corridor squeaked loudly and eerily in the quiet night. Another maid followed them hurriedly.

Out in the yard, beyond the densely spreading nandin trees, the boy performed his pressing task on a pile of dry pine needles. Then, while he stepped back onto the porch to wash his hands at the basin, the first maid held the candle close lest the boy tread on the nailhead protruding from the bamboo flooring.

"Blow out the light," the little boy commanded.

"But it's dark here, at your feet," the maid replied in a scolding voice not unmixed with concern.

"Don't you know that love is made in the dark?"

This was a broad allusion to Tanabata-sama, a festival derived from an ancient legend depicting the tryst of two amorous stars, the one "male" and the other "female," on the seventh night of the seventh month.

The second maid, who carried a short sword, blew out the light.

Yonosuke seized her sleeve. "Isn't my nurse around?"

That sounded exceedingly funny. And it was then that the maids knew he was re-enacting the make-believe of stars a-wooing on the dark heavenly bridge. This seemed incredible in a child so young; he could hardly have comprehended the amorous doings of men and women. It showed nevertheless that the boy was precociously gifted, alas, for sensual things. Yet it was a gift, however singular, and the maids reported the incident to his mother as something rather to be complimented on than scorned.

Gradually, as the days went by, this preternatural tendency grew apace. Yonosuke developed a predilection for amusing picture books of human figures that revealed more than they should. So much so, indeed, that most of the volumes he collected on his small bookshelf began to seem progressively repulsive to the adult eye. He must have known there was something detestable in all this, for he ordered the servants: "I forbid anyone whom I have not summoned to enter this chrysanthemum room."

At one time he fashioned a pair of birds with folded paper and gave these to them, saying: "This is the image of birds making love."

At another time he made a pair of paper flowers attached to stems, and this he also gave to them, saying: "Behold the twin trees of love!"

It seems, moreover, that no matter what moved his fancy among the thousand and one things that stir young minds, little Yonosuke never overlooked sensual nuances or suggestions. Never would he permit the servants to help him with his underclothing. He tied his own waist sash over his robe, making the knot in front and swinging it to the back in dandyish fashion. There was perfume on his sleeves, absorbed from the smoke of an incense called *hyobukyo*. All these things he did with a fastidiousness which even a male adult would ordinarily shun but which nevertheless gave heartthrobs to women and girls.

Even while flying a kite with youngsters of his own age, he would give no thought to skies becalmed or rising clouds. He would muse, recalling that legend of the cloudland bridge: "I wonder if the heavenly beings of ancient times ever stole into the houses of others to see the women they loved."

Then he would sigh over these imagined doings in regions remote and celestial, and he would say regretfully: "The stars met but once a year. What if the rain hid the clouds on that one evening of love and they could not meet?"

14

THE SEVENTH day of the seventh month came around again. It was time for merry festivities. Iron lanterns covered with a whole year's accumulation of dust were lovingly cleaned and filled with oil. Desk drawers were cleaned out and their contents rearranged and put meticulously in order. Ink slabs were washed and polished. It was time for verse writing too.

But then the rains came, as they always did. Streams limpid in the sun and cataracts white with foam turned overnight into muddy swirls. From the north the temple bells of the Konryu-ji broke the evening silence. They brought back acute memories of a love poem, "I Long for Thee," said to have been composed by the eight-year-old scion of the exiled Emperor Godaigo.

It was time, also, for Yonosuke to begin his formal education. Now it happened that he was staying with his aunt in Yamasaki, a few *ri* west of Kyoto. In that quiet village resided a Buddhist scholar who kept alive the traditions of the Takimoto school of poetry and learning and conducted class in the hermitage of an illustrious forebear—a place known as Ichiya-an. To this priest, then, the boy Yonosuke was attached, under a duly negotiated contract, as a disciple in the art of calligraphy and reading.

One day Yonosuke submitted writing paper to his tutor.

"Please, *sensei,* will you write a letter for me?"

Amazed that one so young should wish to dispatch a formal communication, the tutor asked tentatively: "And what, may I ask, do you wish me to say in the letter?"

"Just this," Yonosuke replied, and the following was what the tutor wrote—in his own words of course—after listening to the boy's facile outpourings:

"It may seem rather presumptuous for me to write to you in this fashion, but I can no longer remain silent. You must have known how I feel about you from the look in my eyes. Some two or three days ago, while Aunt was having an afternoon nap, I stumbled upon your spindle on the matted floor and broke it. You did not complain about it then, saying you were not angry with me, though you should have been. I felt therefore that perhaps there was something you wished to convey to me secretly. If there is, please do not hesitate to tell it to me . . ."

Aghast over the adroitly importunate nuance in the drift of this letter, the tutor abruptly stopped writing. He said shrewdly: "There is no more space on this writing paper."

"Then fill in the space between the lines, please."

The tutor was adamant. "This is enough for today. We shall write more some other time."

He wanted to burst out laughing, but this was no laughing matter. "Now let us get down to practicing calligraphy," he urged.

The sun vanished over the edge of the mountain range. Presently a manservant from the household of the boy's aunt came to fetch Yonosuke, and the two walked home together in the half-dark.

Harsh winds were rising. The sound of maidservants beating clothes over washboards in the yard could be heard. Other maids were stretching over drying boards the washed sections of silk robes that had been taken apart for the purpose.

"This beautiful robe here," one of the maids was saying, "is the master's, for everyday wear. But that other one, with the orange-red chrysanthemum design around the hips—I wonder whose it is."

"That," said another proudly, "is Yonosuke-sama's sleeping robe."

"Well, then," a temporary hireling put in rather sarcastically as she folded the dried things here and there, "then it should have been washed in the pure waters of Kyoto!"

Hearing this slur, the boy Yonosuke said sternly: "There is such a thing as sympathy for a maid in need of a job. That is why you, a stray menial with dirty hands, have been allowed to help with the washing here."

Plainly that was adult language, spoken with contempt. Only the voice was that of a child.

The transient maid, feeling the sharp sting of rebuke, could only mumble humbly: "Please forgive me." She tried to move away quickly, but Yonosuke caught her sleeve.

"You shall be forgiven if you will hand this letter secretly to Osaka-sama."

When the maid obediently delivered the letter to the daughter of the house, Osaka became angry and embarrassed in turn as she read it. She could recall no such incident as described therein. Naturally it was unsigned. The sentimental insinuation horrified her.

"Who gave you this letter?" Osaka demanded roughly.

The maid, foreseeing further trouble, shook her head. "I . . . I don't know. I really don't. It was slipped into my hand in the dark."

Osaka's mother said: "Here, let me see the letter."

She examined it carefully, studying with a suspicious eye the exquisite brushwork in the handwriting. In the end she decided grimly that the letter could have been written by none other than the calligraphy priest-tutor himself.

Later the tutor, caught unwittingly in a preposterous scandal and called to account, tried to explain the whole matter in honest detail. Anyhow, he contended impatiently, the contents of the letter were trivial, silly, and absurd. Ironically enough, the more he tried to absolve himself, the less he succeeded. He seemed almost ludicrous to Osaka's mother, if not downright cowardly, to try to foist the guilt on her innocent little nephew.

"No one will believe you," she said acidly.

Finally Yonosuke confessed to his aunt: "It is true. It is really I who am in love with Osaka-sama."

His aunt stiffened. She thought to herself with some degree of alarm: "I was greatly mistaken to have regarded him as an innocent child. I must let my sister know about it tomorrow." She shrugged inwardly: "They probably will have a big laugh over it in Kyoto."

Aloud she calmly told Yonosuke: "My daughter is betrothed to another. She has average looks, and I might have thought of giving her to you as your future bride if only there wasn't such a vast difference in age between the two of you."

Thereafter she watched him carefully, keeping the boy's strange proclivities in mind. The more she watched, the more convinced she became that the things he said or did—so witty, so conceited, so impertinent—could not possibly be the expression of a mere child. He was in every respect adult-minded. She was exasperatingly and uneasily sure of it.

THROUGH A SPYGLASS

STRANGE to relate, it was in music that little Yonosuke exhibited a spark of genius. Quite audibly he excelled in beating the elbow drum. And he sang with a great deal of emotion in his young voice. He sang—or rather chanted—in unison with the hollow throbbing of his drum. Wonderfully good it seemed, and good reason why. He liked the lyrics of a dramatic passage in *Wind among the Pines* that wailed ". . . tormented later by the pangs of love."

He liked the sentiment so much that he kept repeating the line and pounding his drum night and day, savoring it with uncommon delight. Exasperatingly enough, his interest here was anything but aesthetic. Abruptly, therefore, his parents ordered him to give up altogether any further pursuits in "music."

Yet they had to think about a manly career for the boy. Now it happened that his mother was related to the keeper of a moneylending shop called Kasugaya on Ryokai-machi in Kyoto. To that shop Yonosuke was sent as an apprentice, to be initiated in the technique of trading in gold and silver coins.

No sooner, however, had he started working than Yonosuke displayed superior gifts for this trade. He promptly secured for himself a silver loan of 300 *me*. Interest on the loan was fixed at 100 percent, but the boy outdid his adult employers in shrewdness by signing a promissory note payable from his inheritance upon the death of his father. What if his father were to leave him nothing? Say what you wish about the cupidity of moneylenders, but there was something inordinately puerile about this transaction. And it wasn't Yonosuke's fault.

Yonosuke was then but nine years old. On the fourth day of the fifth month—the eve of Boys' Festival Day when irises symbolizing the event would be in full bloom —a waitress living nearby prepared to take her bath in a wooden tub beneath the overhanging eaves of her home. Dusk was falling, and the drooping leaves of a willow tree gave the spot the appearance of a dark and hidden nook. A high bamboo screen-fence skirting it afforded the necessary privacy.

The waitress, taking off her linen robe and dainty

underwear, threw them upon this fence and slipped into the tub. She was quite sure that no one was about. If there should be any sound at all, it could be nothing but the sigh of evening breezes among the nearby pines. Only the walls would hear it. So thinking, at any rate, she started to rub herself vigorously with rice-bran soap and a towel. The water was pleasantly hot enough. Tomorrow would be the iris festival, and she needed a thorough cleaning of her plump warm torso. She took particular relish in removing the dirt from the lower parts of her body. Soon the water in the tub became thick with little bubbling balls of body oil and soap.

Suddenly, as though by instinct, she looked up. And there, on the tiled roof of the Azumaya teahouse next door, she saw the crouching figure of the boy Yonosuke leveling a long spyglass at her.

A mere boy watching her bathe—the idea seemed to her innocent enough and comical. The spyglass aimed at her was the sort used at country estates, summer houses, and pavilions overlooking a lake, undoubtedly an import brought in through Nagasaki by Dutch traders. Evidently he had been observing her for some time.

On second thought, since the boy seemed much too intent with his spyglass, a sense of feminine shame descended upon her. Now speechless with excitement, the waitress put her hands together in the attitude of praying, dumbly beseeching Yonosuke to go away and let her bathe in peace.

Yonosuke pointed at her naked figure, laughed, and frowned. "You're clumsy!" he called down.

Embarrassed but resentful of the ridicule, the waitress stood up, fumbled with her wooden clogs, and was about to flee indoors without even drying her body when Yonosuke slid down the roof and called to her through a wide slit in the screen-fence.

"Come back here tonight through the fence gate," he

said, "when the bell of the first watch rings and everyone goes to bed. I shall tell you something. You had better come."

"Absurd!" the waitress cried angrily.

"If you don't, I shall tell the other waitresses all that has happened here."

For a moment the woman hestitated. She seemed to be in dire confusion. "What did I do?" she asked herself. "What did *he* see me doing to myself while bathing that I should be ashamed of its being reported to others? Oh, botheration!"

"Well, anyhow . . ." she answered back, and dragging her robe and underwear from the screen-fence, she fled into her house without finishing that sentence.

Later that evening the waitress combed her hair as though she were expecting guests, yet not quite so smoothly as to suggest that it mattered to her how well she looked. Suddenly she sat listening with bated breath as wary footsteps sounded outside. And there, at her door, stood Yonosuke.

After he came in, there was nothing she could do, the waitress thought, but to purchase his silence. Ransacking a box, she took out a "mustard" doll, a bamboo lark whistle, and a bouncing clay figure that had been so moulded as to recover its upright position when rolled on the mat.

"To me these are precious things," she told the boy, "but to you I shall give them as playthings without feeling any regret."

Yonosuke showed no sign of pleasure or of accepting them.

"You will need them when you have babies," he replied dryly. "These toys will be handy in quieting little crying tots."

Then he picked up the bouncing clay figure and rolled it on the mat. It sat up facing her.

22

"See," he said with a tantalizing grin, "the doll greets you. It must be in love with you."

Quickly he pillowed his head on her lap and lay there quietly. The waitress reddened. "What would others think if they saw us in this position?" she thought.

But she steeled herself. Slyly she caressed his side, near the armpit, and said: "Last year, on the second day of the second month, when moxacautery was performed on you, I helped pour some salt on the burned spot. You did not behave amiably then. But tonight you seem very amiable indeed. Come here."

She picked him up, tucked his head into her bosom and held him there tightly for a moment. Then she dropped him roughly, ran out of the house, slammed open the door of the home of Yonosuke's parents, and called: "Oh, wet nurse! Wet nurse!"

When the boy's former wet nurse, now personal maid, came to the door, the laughing waitress shouted acidly: "Could I borrow some breast milk from you? Yonosuke-sama still needs to be wet-nursed!"

And when she told the maid what had happened, the two laughed and laughed until the tears came to their eyes.

KNIGHT-ERRANT

TOWARD evening on the tenth of the ninth month Yonosuke persuaded his adult friend Sehei, who owned a shop specializing in Chinese goods, to take him along on a trip to "New Pillow." He was still feeling the pleasant, reckless urge induced by yesterday's chrysanthemum festival—with immoderate helpings of sweet rice wine—and this was to be an adventure.

Now this "New Pillow" was just a popular euphemism for the town of Fushimi, a few *ri* west of Kyoto. Apparently pseudo-romantic, the name was derived from *makura kotoba* ("pillow" phrases), or clichés used by the poets of old. There must have been some amorous association here, an unblushing parody on the venerated versifier's "pillow." Well, anyhow, the thing that piqued Yonosuke's curiosity was the town's gay life in Shumoku-machi.

The evening temple bell of the Tofuku-ji was tolling away when the two visitors reached Shumoku-machi. Stepping out of their palanquins near the tearoom of Yariya-no-Magozaemon, they found the eastern gate closed.

"Why has this entrance been barred?" Yonosuke mumbled. "Irksome love lane, isn't it?"

They hurried toward the south entrance. It was open. Walking along leisurely, Yonosuke peered into the interior of the gay houses. In one of them he observed some pleasure-bent guests wearing white turbans that looked like ghostly crowns. Possibly some noblemen from Kyoto plucking forbidden flowers here among the plebeians in poorly managed disguise. There was a distinguished-looking man in another house who, no doubt, was the agent of the famous tea master of Uji.

A pack-horse leader and a number of travelers were passing the time on this street while waiting for the ferryboat that would take them downstream on the River Yodo. It was a comical sight, these transients with *furoshiki* bundles of carrots and rice dumplings slung over their shoulders. They were inspecting the prostitutes closely, evidently before making up their minds. At the same time they were lugubriously counting what remained of their silver and copper coins. Others tramped across the lane in search of cheaper amusement.

While he was gazing at this hectic spectacle of single-minded men, Yonosuke's eyes fell upon a humble house on the western side. It had a latticed sliding-door entrance, looking like a proud but tumbledown shack. He could see portions of the interior, hung with a scroll painting of maples reddening on the banks of the River Tatsuta. But the picture had a miserably faded look, covered with what appeared like soot from tobacco smoke, as though there were no further space left that could be soiled. Or it was torn in places as if the maple leaves were being scattered helter-skelter in the river.

A quiet-seeming girl of startling beauty was seated beside the hanging scroll. With writing brush poised in her hand, she appeared to be in the midst of composing a poem. Apparently she found it difficult to complete the opening lines. It was as though that stanza should read:

> The perfume on my sleeve,
> Like fresh-bloomed chrysanthemum . . .

Curiously enough, there was nothing in her appearance that bore even a semblance of indication that she might be waiting for "trade." Yonosuke was mystified. He asked his companion: "Why is this girl staying in such a wretched house?"

Sehei nodded gravely. "Well . . . you see, the *oyakata,* her employer, is noted on this street as a man of poverty. That accounts for her pitiful state. . . . On the whole, the prostitutes here need not be pretty, but they must wear attractive robes. Other girls are bedecking themselves with second-hand finery brought here from the first-class houses of courtesans in Shimabara, or old brocades and figured silk bought for them by their bosses. In that way they can at least put on an alluring front."

The two sat down without ceremony on a bench outside the door of this decrepit-looking house. Yonosuke laid aside his short sword and watched the girl. And the girl, aware of his presence, turned gently in his direction and smiled. Her smile was wistful. She made no move to welcome him or his adult companion. And the more Yonosuke looked at her, the deeper was he impressed with some indefinable quality in her. Finally he addressed the girl in a sympathetic tone: "Why must you stay in an establishment like this? It seems to me this sort of trade is distressing enough as it is."

"I suppose," the girl replied readily, "people see through me because I loathe this profession. The truth is . . . I . . . I was driven to it." She looked away as though to hide the shame on her pretty face.

"Tell me more," Yonosuke urged.

"Well," she continued, "poverty has forced me to beg for favors from visitors. Not to clothe myself, you understand, but to stop the cold winds from coming in through cracks in the walls of this house. I have to provide for my own needs, from Ono charcoal to Yoshino paper handkerchiefs and Hida-in sandals. No one comes here on rainy days or windy nights. There is no one that I can appeal to for something decent to wear when the imperial Go-Ko festival comes around, or the Tango festival, or even the Fujimori Shrine festival. The master is always grumbling. . . . Somehow, under these conditions, I have passed two years here. But when I think of the future I am overwhelmed with fear."

Then, with tears in her eyes, she added: "I often think of my poor parents in the country, wondering how they are managing to eke out a living. I've had practically no news from them since I had to leave them, much less have they come to see me here. I . . . I'm worried."

"Where does your father live?" Yonosuke asked.

"In Yamashina. His name is Gempachi."

Yonosuke thought for a while. Then he said in all youthful sincerity: "I shall visit him there one of these days soon and let him know that at least you are well and somehow getting along."

26

Far from rejoicing over this proffered kindness, the girl protested excitedly. "Please don't. You mustn't. . . . He used to make a living somehow by digging madder roots for the dye market. But now . . . now he is old and weak, unable to work . . . a beggar. Worse than that, by some cruel turn of fate, he has become the victim of a loathsome disease."

Later, Yonosuke's desire to visit the girl's unfortunate father became stronger despite her pleas against it. One day he set out alone for Yamashina.

He found the latticed door of Gempachi's house covered tastefully with morning-glory vines and blossoms. Inside, neatly suspended over the vestibule, was a warrior's halberd. A saddle and other trappings of a warrior's mount were carefully preserved. Mute evidence, this, of a samurai who for some mysterious reason had become detached from his lord, losing his annuity and identity.

When Yonosuke bluntly explained the reason for his visit, Gempachi said tearfully: "This is really mortifying. My daughter has degenerated into a prostitute but . . . but however frivolous she may be, I did not expect her to stoop so low as to humiliate her father even more by revealing where he lived."

There was a great gulf of misunderstanding between father and daughter. Yonosuke saw it and told him so in a kindly manner.

"Your daughter has had no other means of making a living. She did not want to be a burden on you any longer."

"But why . . . why . . . why stoop so low?" Gempachi was in agony. "Of course, a father has responsibilities. . . ."

The girl had never mentioned or boasted about the erstwhile splendor of her family, and Yonosuke admired that spirit. He decided to bring about their reconciliation.

Soon afterwards, with money obtained from his parents, he bought the girl out of bondage and sent her back to her ailing father. Yonosuke was then but eleven years old. He saw to it also that the family was provided for. He visited them often.

DISILLUSIONED

MOON viewing has been associated with the fame of many scenic spots. But nowhere does the thirteenth moon or even the waning moon appear so hauntingly beautiful as on the coast of Suma, along the Inland Sea. Here the sea is so calm that the waves are imperceptible. The bright moonbeams suggest the infinity, yet the illusory nearness too, of the harvest moon. Or so Yonusuke had heard.

One day, impelled by this thought, he hired a small rowboat and set out for that magic spot.

Rounding the Cape of Wada, his boatman rowed beyond Tsuno-no-Matsubara and approached the beach at Shioya. This was a place recorded in song and story. It was here that the illustrious warrior Kumagai cornered and speared Atsumori, the Heike general. Perhaps, thought Yonosuke, that was the penalty for overindulgence in the famous Heike wine. Laughing to himself over this choice bit of private historical invention, he went ashore at a spot that commanded a good view of the sea. There he secured lodgings in a penthouse atop a small inn on the sloping beach.

And here he elected to remain for a spell. Darkness overtook the land. The moon rose over the sea. Yonosuke took out the stoppers from the jugs of Maizuru and Hana-Tachibana wine that he had brought from Kyoto. Other guests at the inn joined him in the merrymaking. And while the night was young, everyone seemed hilarious. But as the night wore on, even the moon seemed ghastly. Then the lonely cry of a sea bird suggested to Yonosuke that perhaps the creature had lost its mate. This provoked the further thought that traveling alone was much too solitary.

"Isn't there a young fisher wench around?" he asked.

The innkeeper fetched a girl to entertain him. She was a common-looking creature. She wore no comb to keep her disheveled hair together. Nor did she seem aware of the art of improving the looks of her face with liquid powder. The sleeves of her robe were much too narrow. The hem was too short. She actually smelt of the fishing hamlet, so much so that Yonosuke felt he might become ill in her presence. He swallowed a few pills of *enreitan* to overcome an impending nausea, at the same time massaging his chest. Then he decided to wriggle out of his predicament by finishing off the meeting with a funny story.

"Once upon a time," he told the girl, by way of a broad hint, "a man called Narihira was banished to a lonely island. There he hired a fisher wench to massage his legs. That, you understand, was by way of banishing his own boredom. When the time came for him to depart, however, he decided to rid himself of his perfume container, his bird cage, his ladle, his earthenware mortar, and all the rest of the household effects that he had assembled for his three-year exile. They smelt too much like fish. 'You can have them,' Narihira told the fisher wench. 'No one deserves them more than you do.' "

The girl refused to take the hint, so Yonosuke cut short his visit the next day and set out for the port of Hyogo. Here, he found, there was a noticeable difference between the harlots who worked as waitresses at popular inns during the day and those who plied their trade at night.

29

There were busy times at this port where many travelers congregated, and there were times that were slack.

A harlot adapted herself whimsically to the urges of the moment. When a familiar boatman's call sounded through the night, she would rise precipitately from the table, abandoning her guests in the midst of a song or even while accepting a drink. Service at the inn was irregular. Favoritism was shown to regular customers. There was an air of noisy excitement, of hurrying to and fro.

All this irritated young Yonosuke. He, too, rose from the table. Why should he waste his time and money with such filthy, capricious women waiting on him? he thought. So he went downstairs to the huge communal bath to cleanse his body.

At the door of the bathroom he was accosted by a woman attendant. She had an attractive-looking face. Curling her lips in a half smile, she said in a language and manner suggestive of worldly wit: "If you were to get mixed up in a scandal, I should be glad to patch it up for you."

Evidently she was referring to his extreme youth. But it was not so much what she had said as the adroit phrasing of her offer that piqued Yonosuke's imagination.

"I like you," he said. "What is your name?"

"Tadanori."

"Well!" he thought. "This I must look into." Nonchalantly he asked her to come up and see him later, and she said: "I shall take good care of you."

He found her attitude refreshingly different. The way she brought him fresh bucketfuls of hot water for the final cleansing, the way she brought him his after-bath tea, the way she tended the charcoal burning in the brazier in his room, the way she helped him with his robe, the way she handed him a mirror—everything was delightfully intimate.

Later, as Yonosuke watched the harlots closely, he saw that they followed a regular pattern of behavior. They wore their robes in the *tsumataka* fashion, lifting the hems and revealing their shins. They used white sashes only, tying them in a rough, careless manner.

"What if I should tear this sash?" one said cynically in the corridor. "It would only mean a loss to the master. He would just have to pay for another, that's all. Here, Kyuzo, bring the lantern. I need some light in the vestibule."

She searched for her footwear with one hand and slipped through the door. Outside in the yard she gossiped with her companions about their friends in a spiteful manner. Then she complained loudly about one thing and another—about the thinness of the morning soup served here, about the pair of scissors she had been promised but never got. Everything she said was jarring to Yonosuke's ears.

On re-entering the inn, she threw her padded cotton headgear against the wall, adjusted the lantern on the mat while still standing, sat among her guests in the center of the poorly lighted room, and puffed away at a thin long-stemmed pipe until the tiny bowl turned crimson with heat.

Standing again when she should have remained seated, she yawned with outstretched arms. Then, as another thought occurred to her, she left her guests without so much as an "excuse me." Slamming the sliding door shut, she went her noisy, shuffling way to perform an urgent task at the end of the corridor.

While lounging in the room, she spoke rudely to the guests now changing their robes beyond a high lacquered screen. If she felt displeased by the questions put to her, she would refuse to answer, hoisting her nose in the air in a haughty manner. Then she used up her guests' paper handkerchiefs without compunction and went soundly off to sleep right there and then with a thunderous snore.

Suddenly, in the middle of the night, she got up to search for fleas annoying her back, waking everyone within earshot to demand: "What time is it?" Then off she went to sleep again, talking shop in her dreams.

"Oh, the cheap wench!" thought Yonosuke. "Where did she learn her manners?"

ETIQUETTE BE DAMNED

DUSK was falling as two youths strolled through the back streets of Kyoto, on Kiyomizu Hill. They moved into Minakami Lane, then into Yasaka. These were questionable haunts of adult pleasure seekers.

"I have heard it said," Yonosuke told his like-minded companion, an apprentice clerk, "that somewhere along these back streets there is a pretty girl who sings well and knows how to drink. Was it at a teahouse called Kikuya? Or was it Mikawaya? Or maybe it was Tsutaya. I don't remember which. We shall have to take a chance."

Yonosuke had tucked silver coins into a sash that he wore strapped around his waist in shop-salesman style to serve as a wallet.

Presently they entered a small lane girded by lespedeza hedges. Toward the end of this lane, beyond the fashionable-looking quarter, they came upon a house whose interior was thrown open to view. There was a tall painted screen depicting a nightingale perched gracefully on a plum tree branch. A samisen with one string broken lay upon the alcove floor, as if it had been left there carelessly by the last player. On the dampish-looking mat was a vermilion tobacco set, and their nostrils were greeted by the odor of steadily burning charcoal.

32

The place had an unkempt, unpleasant look. But the two youths decided to explore it anyhow. No sooner had they seated themselves in the entertainment room than a girl brought in rice wine with cups, lacquered chopsticks, and the usual tidbits on low four-legged trays of Gion workmanship. On each tray, which served as an individual table for a guest sitting on the mat, were dishes of broiled fish on skewers, pieces of choice boiled squid, pickled plums, and red ginger.

Yonosuke glanced up at the girl. She was clad in a wisteria-figured cotton robe, lavender and white, with a wide russet-colored sash tied coquettishly. Very smart, Yonosuke thought, and redolent with lush, hypnotic spring. But a toothpick peeped out of the paper handkerchief in her bosom. Her hair, braided in fours, fell in a slovenly manner down her neck. In her left hand she carried a small pot with a red wooden cover.

"Why are you boys so quiet?" she asked. "Why don't you start drinking?"

She sat down beside her two young guests and began to munch a half-eaten Torreya nut.

She offered to pour a drink. Yonosuke felt something repulsive about her and was loath to accept. But that wasn't etiquette, he decided, once one sat down at table. Reluctantly he lifted his cup.

Next the girl began to stick a pair of chopsticks into the broiled fish, attacking its midribs clumsily to get at the choice meat.

"Have another drink," she urged.

Yonosuke felt vitiated by the unpleasantness of it all. He was about to persuade his companion that they leave at once when the girl stood up and hurried into the kitchen to bring in more hot drinks. They couldn't very well leave now. That wouldn't be etiquette either.

As the girl came back with the drinks, Yonosuke saw something irresistible in the way she swung her hips.

33

"Let's stay and see what happens," he whispered to his companion.

His voice had recently undergone a change, and there was nothing daunted or modest about his urge for adventure, be it ever so crude. After all, it didn't seem so unromantic now.

They sprawled themselves lounging-at-ease fashion on a broad flowered quilt which the girl had meanwhile spread for their comfort and convenience. Their heads rested on hard wooden pillows. The girl went into her room, changed into a faded yellow robe, and came out singing snatches of a song in high nasal tones.

Casually Yonosuke told her about his wealthy parents. Suddenly she stared at him with a shrewd, screwed-up look. Then, easily, the tears crept into her eyes.

"What's the matter?" he asked.

At first she would not answer. Prompted repeatedly, however, she decided to reveal her secret.

"I may look shabby now in this business," she said, as if in a reminiscent mood, "but I once worked in the household of an imperial prince. One of the young princes took to me. I was the lowest-ranking maid there. Yet he came secretly into my room one night and talked to me in a very friendly way. I shall never forget what happened. It was the third day of the eleventh month, and light snow began to fall outside. Opening the side porch shutters, he went out into the ghostly night, grabbed a handful of snow, and threw it into my bosom. He said my skin was as white and soft and lovely as that snow. It was the way he looked as he said it that impressed me most. He looked exactly like you. And your presence here this evening reminds me of him."

Yonosuke was now slightly on his guard. He smiled suspiciously with the corner of his mouth, and asked teasingly: "In what respect do I resemble that young prince?"

"In every respect. You are his exact image. One windy morning he asked me how I felt and presented me with a white robe. When he heard that my mother was living alone in the Nishijin district, he showed great kindness by providing her with rice, bean curd, firewood, and even house-rent money. He was only eleven years old, yet he looked to our every need, and I admired his young, generous spirit. You resemble him most in that sense. You, too, seem so attentive and kind and sympathetic, and I love you for it."

"Ah," thought Yonosuke, now completely on his guard, "that is the line of talk of the greedy, mercenary Kyoto sirens! She is trying to hook me with wiles and lies."

"Let's leave, this very minute," he told his companion.

That wasn't etiquette either, but they fairly leaped out of the siren's den.

STRANGE MATE

THE SPRING of Yonosuke's fourteenth year was over, and on the first day of the fourth month—the day for a complete change of wardrobe signifying the end of childhood —he slipped on a robe with sleeves that had no wide openings under the armpits. Neighbors regretted the change, for they felt that his back view in a child's tight-sleeved robe had been particularly attractive.

One day, with a definite purpose in mind, he went on a pilgrimage to the Hatsuse Shrine with a few of his playmates. Climbing a hill called Kumo-no-Yadori, whose name meant Cloudland Lodging, the group plunged deep into the woods where masses of sweet-scented blossoms had already abdicated to sprouting green leaves—blos-

soms to which the poet Ki-no-Tsurayuki once dedicated
a verse:

> You say you waited faithfully for me.
> Alas, I do not know if it is true.
> But the plum blossoms in the meadow here,
> Unlike you in their faithfulness, give forth
> The same perfume as in the days of old.

As soon as Yonosuke reached the shrine, he stood respectfully before it and mumbled:

> O Lord, I pray thee,
> Tell me with gracious intent,
> When will I be favored
> With the blessed event?

Hearing this, one of his companions thought: "There
he goes again, praying for his first love affair."

Returning by way of Sakurai, which was reminiscent
of the glory of past blossoms, Yonosuke could see the
Toichi and Furu shrines to the north. Toward sunset he
and his party arrived at the foot of Mt. Kurahashi. It was
harvest time for winter wheat, and from every peasant's
house along the way came the sound of farm hands
threshing grain with flails. Children were weaving straw
baskets and cages. There was a long natural hedge extending from a rubbish heap, with sword beans dangling
queerly from vines.

Behind the hedge Yonosuke saw a number of good-
looking youths, just past childhood, who were either
posing or modeling straw figures. Their hair was dressed
in a rather odd way and they wore straw-woven hats
with colorful twisted paper tassels—altogether a singular
custom, Yonosuke thought, for a rural village. When he
called their attention to it, one of the youths said in a
pretentiously knowing manner: "This village is called
Jin-o-do. It's a place where the *tobiko*—you know, those

professional transient boys from Kyoto and Osaka—look for accommodations to ply their secret trade when they make the rounds of the rural districts."

Yonosuke thought: "This is indeed a windfall." He soon made cautious inquiries in the village and chose a small, not too conspicuous lodging house. The innkeeper guessed aright what Yonosuke was seeking and gave some of the names of those youths who were available for the night—queer names such as Somenosuke, Nami-no-Jo, Santaro. When these youths were summoned, Yonosuke found them to be queer-looking too. Each of his party made his choice, and soon the festive board was spread. Wine cups were exchanged, and a wild convivial party followed.

As the night wore on, someone shouted, as it were through astigmatic fumes, that the moon had become distorted, or that the flowers had curved beyond recognition. Meanwhile pairs of eyes looked knowingly at each other and preparations for bed were made.

As to bed things, however, Yonosuke found that the blankets at this inn were of coarse cross-striped cotton and the pillows of bastard cedar chopped into short blocks. Worse, rice bran was smouldering in an earthenware mortar—to drive away mosquitoes, it was said. But the smoke somehow reminded him of aloes-wood incense, arousing his sensual instincts.

Yonosuke moved closer to his chosen mate for the night. His mate began to caress him as an enticement to the sexual act, and his hands still bore scars of a recently-cured skin ailment. So caressed, however, he felt a queer sensation, not exactly glad, nor yet sad. But it was a loving gesture, developed and perfected through years of experience. As Yonosuke concentrated on this thought, he felt much better, even passionate.

He asked his mate: "What provinces have you toured up to now in devotion to your trade?"

"Now that you ask me about it, I might as well confess everything," the youth replied. "First of all, I was a Kabuki actor in Kyoto doing female impersonations, and I stayed with Itoyori Gonzaburo. From there I was sent in turn to live with Kihachi, the flute player, and a theatrical patron in Miyajima. After that I called at the palace of the Lord of Bitchu and the Kompira Shrine in Sanuki Province, without any fixed domicile. Then I moved on to the Anryu gay quarters in the town of Sumiyoshi, also to Kashihara in Kochi Province. Next I came here to dally with the priests of Imaidani and Tabu-no-Mine. Of all the men I met, the worst that remain in my memory were Gakunimbo of Yawata and Shirouemon of Mameyama. They were incomparable homosexuals. When we *tobiko* performed with these men, we were hugged and squeezed and pressed so roughly that it was as though we were crossing a storm-tossed sea. However, after that we experienced no difficulty at all in pursuing our profession, no matter who our mates were. One day I enticed a woodcutter in a forest. At another time, on the seashore, I stripped a fisherman naked. All this, you understand, to earn some spending money. Money, money, money—that's all. There is no longer any such thing as pride of profession, or the spirit of it. I don't remember where I had slipped. It is really regrettable."

Yonosuke thought: "Some lies are no doubt mixed up in his story, but I don't believe he made it all up."

"Then tell me," he said, "about the time you came across a mate you found detestable."

"In this profession," the youth replied, "we cannot refuse any man, no matter if his body is covered with sores or if he has never used a toothpick in his life. We must endure everything he does throughout the long autumn night. More than once I have felt mortified or chagrined and shed many a bitter tear. But time flies quickly, and in the fourth month next year I shall be a free man again. I am already looking forward to it and congratulating myself. Besides, according to the zodiac, we who were born under the sign of the *kanesho* will meet with a turn in our fortune the day after tomorrow, and this good luck will continue for seven years thereafter. So I shall have easy sailing, so to speak."

Kanesho in the zodiac signified twenty-four pieces of gold. "In that event," Yonosuke thought, "he is ten years older than I am. But wait. Why fuss about age differences when you are about to have a night of fun with this handsome youth?"

So he stopped speaking then and there, without asking any more questions about the youth's profession.

YOUNG WIDOW'S PLIGHT

"ILLICIT affairs," said Yonosuke's elderly confidant, "are common enough. Once one yields to the temptation, it is difficult to forego. But young widows," and here he smiled reminiscently, "are perhaps the easiest to seduce.

"Consider the young widow's plight," he continued. At the time of bereavement—if she feels *so* depressed—she probably *can* commit suicide, or she may want to become a nun. But as time goes on, she may want to acquire a new husband. Some do. Usually, out of sheer self-preservation, she decides to carry on the family responsibility and hangs on to her children, if any, and to the property left by the deceased.

"But while holding the keys to the warehouse she neglects the rusting lock, and her sense of insecurity increases. Willy-nilly she depends on others. Dead leaves pile up in her garden, and she forgets to have her house reroofed. On stormy nights the roof leaks, the thunder rolls, and she remembers how, in her fear, she used to nestle close to her husband and cover her head with a blanket. She has bad dreams, and she remembers how she used to awaken her husband to dispel fear and forebodings. And then she realizes that nothing can be more miserable than a widow's life.

"Out of sheer spiritual need she next turns to religion. On her trips to the temple she feels there is no need any more to wear silk robes embroidered with the family crest, and she discards the use of such finery altogether.

"Meanwhile she must keep up her late husband's shop and flatter long-standing customers if she is to survive. In so doing, she sits at his old desk, flicking away at his abacus and counting the profits and losses. But no matter how intelligent she may be, her efficiency is not quite up to what a man can do. She knows it, and inevitably she turns over the responsibility to the chief clerk. That turns the chief clerk's head. He becomes cocky, and he speaks to her without the respect due his employer. She swallows her pride, tries the art of wheedling, but to no avail. She becomes a mere figurehead.

"Then, in this falling state, she degenerates into unseemly familiarity with her servants, male and female. She joins their ribald jokes. Illicit thoughts enter her own mind. And then, in a final crash, she gets involved in a scandal with a young man of her own shop.

"That, at any rate," Yonosuke's confidant concluded, "is the usual road to degeneration. In my own time I have had pleasant relations with many a young widow. This is the technique I have used. Upon hearing that a funeral had taken place, I would first investigate the family situation. Then, wearing formal garments, including a *hakama* and a wing-shouldered jumper, I would present myself to the sorrowing widow. I would gently offer her my condolences, saying that her late husband

and I had been bosom friends. Later I would renew my acquaintance with her, asking after her children. If there was a fire in her neighborhood, I would hasten to her home, easing her fears and assuring her of my protection. In this way I would inspire confidence. Then, as our friendship deepened into intimacy, I would address her in the final alluring phrases. It has never failed."

Yonosuke was only fifteen when he heard this amazing confession.

On the sixth day of the third month he went through the formal rites of adopting the robes that marked the passing from adolescence to youth. He was reaching the most vigorous, the most zestful period of a man's life.

A little over a month later he stood in the front corridor of the Ishiyama Temple, enjoying the view of Lake Biwa, so invigoratingly cool and expansive. He had come to this district with a group of friends, specifically to see the fireflies here at night and, incidentally, to visit this famous temple.

Suddenly, as he turned, he saw a young lady in a light-blue embroidered silk robe coming up the steps. There was an air of subtle distinction about her. She wore a thick woven sash, tied in front. On her head was a lacquered traveling hood, worn deep over the sort of kerchief that was very much in vogue in fashionable circles at the time. Beside her walked a girl companion who evidently was no common household servant—a chambermaid perhaps. The two visitors took in the view from the corridor, talking in low tones. Yonosuke, loitering nonchalantly within earshot, listened intently.

"This," the lady explained to her companion, "is the spot where Lady Murasaki composed her *Tale of Genji*." Soon she was telling her what the story was about.

Then they moved over to where the printed oracles, the sacred lots, were placed. He followed. The lady drew three lots in succession, all foretelling misfortune.

"Of all things! Isn't it exasperating?"

Yonosuke glanced at her profile beneath her hood. Alas, her hair was cut short! She was a widow. "And what a beautiful widow!" he thought. "She looks like the goddess of mercy of this temple come to life."

At that instant she swept past him, giving him a sidelong glance and folding the sleeve of her robe in a swift movement.

Suddenly she stopped and turned upon him.

"The hilt of your sword," she accused him sharply, "tore my robe. See!" And she displayed the torn sleeve. "I demand that you pay for it, you wretched person. I demand that you pay for the mischief by getting me a new robe that is a replica of this one. Immediately, I demand of you!"

Yonosuke was dumfounded, as much by the accident as by her tempestuous voice. "I am really very, very sorry," he said humbly. "You must forgive me, lady."

But she refused to accept his apologies. "Immediately!" she insisted furiously.

There was no alternative. "Very well," Yonosuke agreed. "I shall do as you say. If you will wait for me down there at the village, I shall go at once to Kyoto and get you a new robe, exactly like the one you are wearing."

They proceeded to the village of Matsumoto, and he found an assignation house where she might rest for a while. Then, unexpectedly, the lady held him back by his sleeve.

"I . . . I have a confession to make," she said, softly now. "I am very much ashamed to say so, but I did it on purpose. I mean, I ripped my own robe and blamed you for it. I did it because I wanted to make your acquaintance, to . . . to rely on you. Will you promise to see me constantly?"

Later the lady became big with child. Still later the

child was born. One night, while musing sadly over the lines of Ono-no-Komachi's verse,

> Alas, a mother discarding her new-born babe
> Dreams of the infant crying
> On the empty quilt beside her lying,

she slinked in the darkness toward the Rokkakudo in Kyoto and left her baby on its doorstep.

DEVIL AND SAINT

IT WAS a time when the precious blooms on Mt. Oshio were about to scatter and men's hearts were moved by a delicate sense of regret. But it was an age, too, when dandyism had become a fad. Swordsmanship appealed to the young, with emphasis on style, not skill. The blade was drawn from its scabbard with a dramatic flourish, in the manner of Kembo, master faddist of his line.

Ipso facto, sword-wearing became an integral part of men's attire. Loose-fitting robes that allowed for ample athletic movement, coupled with many-hued sashes, became the vogue. To top it off, men shaved the forepart of their heads, leaving the topknot sloping gracefully backward and the sidelocks showing. The result was a handsome profile, and the long sword slipped obliquely under the colorful sash added a touch of dash and gallantry to their looks. All young men in the social hierarchy of Kyoto took to this new-fangled mode, discarding age-old customs.

If delicacy of feeling had become a thing of the past, dandyism brought in its wake a rough, reckless spirit. Men visited the blossoming plum trees in Kitano or the wisterias in Otani, not to admire the flowers but to crush them in their hands. They saw the smoke erupting majestically from Mt. Toribe and thought no more of it than the smoke issuing from the bowls of their slender tobacco pipes. Most of all they found it egregiously silly to let their servants carry their water gourds. They carried these themselves.

Now, at a place called Okazaki, at the foot of the Higashiyama range near Kyoto, there lived a priestess called Myoju. She resided in a hermitage that served a number of purposes. Mystery lurked in this queer abode, for it was built to avoid the southeast light. The thick sliding doors were covered with scraps of letters in simple syllabaries, so torn as to render the words illegible. One of the rooms was kept in semidarkness. Evidently the priestess was engaged in some devilish activity.

Yonosuke, visiting the place for the first time with a group of friends bent on exploring its interior, was mystified. In the room where the priestess resided, he asked in a whisper: "Say, what sort of place *is* this?"

"A notorious inn, for one thing," one of his companions whispered back. "All sorts of tradespeople from the city come here, from the dealer in silk threads on Ogawa-machi and the midwife on Muro-machi to the lowly shopgirl. They seem to be dependent on the priestess for one thing and another. Strange drugs, for instance, for those who have sinned and secret accommodations for those who wish to avoid scandal. Does that suggest anything to you?"

At this moment a woman entered with a bundle of devil's tongue and a sprig of aronia plant for the priestess. She was of smallish, compact build, no older than four times the number of fingers on one hand. Her eyes were bright and cool, and a few freckles showed on her cheeks. She was altogether the type of female that men desire.

44

But when she became aware of the presence of young men in the room, she appeared embarrassed.

"I just happened to be going on an errand to Kumano for some eye medicine," she told the priestess, "so I brought you these things."

Quickly she left the room, assuming a very busy air.

"Who might she be?" Yonosuke asked.

Priestess Myoju replied: "She used to be a household servant at a place in Karasumaru—you would know the name of the retired merchant who lived there but who is now dead. Well, she is now on good terms with the man who is acting as executor of that estate; so . . . well, she is not to be sought after by other men, if you . . . know what I mean."

"In that case," said Yonosuke, cynicism in his voice, "she must be like a persimmon tree in the forest that bears no fruit. Let us have something to eat."

The priestess was boiling water on the charcoal brazier for some medicinal herbs. She wiped a bowl, then rose to go. "I shall have the maid prepare some tasty things for you."

It was a warm afternoon, and the young men shed their *haori* coats. Even the thick layers of underclothing became a nuisance. Yonosuke alone was wearing, in addition, a *zukin* hood. He felt the heat but kept his hood on.

"Take it off," one of his friends urged him.

"I won't."

"Look here, you are past sixteen and you have a fine head and profile, and I am sure that fashionable topknot and those sidelocks of yours must be very becoming to you. You are the height of the new vogue. Why don't you let us admire you?"

No sooner said than he lunged forward and forcibly removed the hood from Yonosuke's head. Lo and behold, just where Yonosuke's new-fangled left sidelock showed,

45

there was a streak of red about four inches long. It was an unhealed bruise, apparently inflicted by someone who had wielded a club.

Surprised eyes centered on the bruise rather than on his hair arrangement.

"Who punished you in this way?" his friend demanded. "We won't stand for any such attack upon any one of us. The bruise is a mark of defeat. What humiliates you humiliates us. We must get our revenge. Tell us—was it Kimpei, the braggart? Or was it Kiyohachi of the Churokuten? Or Mankichi of the gunpowder shop?"

All heads nodded vigorously in affirmation. "Tell us who did it."

"My friends," Yonosuke protested laughingly, "you are greatly mistaken. I got this bruise when I tried to force my attention upon a woman I had no right to approach."

He realized he owed it to his friends to tell the whole story.

"It was this way. There is a shopkeeper called Gensuke in our street block in Kawara-machi. One day he decided to go to Miyazu in Tango Province to peddle goods. Before he went, he asked me more or less to look after the welfare of his family and shop. And so, from time to time I went over at night to see to it that every precaution was being taken in the shop to prevent an outbreak of fire. His wife, who remained behind, once worked for a family in Sawaragi-machi. I noticed that she was a very gentle woman, very attractive and . . . well, irresistible. So I did what I should not have done: I sent her fervent love letters, worded in a very enticing manner. I received no replies.

"So then, when I met her face to face during the daytime, I renewed my courting with my own lips. She looked me over with fury in her usually gentle eyes and said: 'Even if I were not a married woman, your

46

insinuations are insulting. With two children on my hands, I must say you are insane!'

"That hurt my pride. Having started this sorry thing, I felt now that I had to push it a step further. I said just as furiously: 'If you don't listen to me, I will drive my sword into my own bowels, three times if necessary. Like this.' And I drew my sword and made a feint in a most dramatic manner—the Kembo way.

"Somehow that seemed to soften her anger. 'I . . . I did not know,' she said, 'that you were *that* serious. All right, come secretly to my house late tonight. This being the twenty-seventh of the month, there will be no moon, so no one will see you.' With that, she returned to her work in the interior of her shop.

"That night, when the whole town seemed to be deep in slumber, I stole my way to her front sliding door and stood listening. Presently the door opened and there she stood confronting me. Without even so much as a 'come in, please,' she picked up a piece of wood lying beside her in the vestibule and struck me on the head with it.

" 'That for you!' she said derisively. 'That for insinuating that I should be unfaithful to my husband!' And with that she slammed the door shut on my bleeding face.

"Which goes to show," Yonosuke concluded his confession, "that such virtuous women *do* exist in these free and easy times."

Just then the priestess returned to the room.

"I heard you," she said cynically, taking her seat. "So she is a living saint, eh? You have a lot to learn yet, dear boy. Don't threaten to kill yourself. That shows weakness. No woman will like you for it. Just take her in your arms. Gently. Then squeeze her passionately. Let her feel your masculine power over her, over her mind and body. No woman can resist for long when she

47

feels it in her hot blood. She will hesitate breathlessly. That hesitation is your supreme moment."

"You are a devil!" Yonosuke cried.

"Devil or not, come to see me when you need my help."

FLOTSAM OF LIFE

YONOSUKE was seventeen when he trekked all the way to Nara, the one-time ancient capital, to learn the cotton-cloth trade. Through arrangements made by his parents, a mutual friend got him started at a wholesaler's house on Sanjo-dori. This apprenticeship was to prepare him for a summer venture in the wintry provinces of Echizen and Echigo. Those were rich potential markets.

It was midspring, and nature, ironically enough, offered a pleasing background in the city's environs. Vernal luxuriance covered the slopes of nearby Mt. Wakakusa. At night the fireflies flitted from shrub to shrub, needle points of fire tracing weird curves in impenetrable shadows. To catch these brilliant insects was a diversion not to be missed by the young folk. Yonosuke found more enjoyment in such distractions than in the dry-goods business at hand. Regretfully he counted the ever-lessening days he would be remaining here.

Then came the twelfth day of the fourth month. It was a memorable anniversary in this city of many memories. Yonosuke heard the story of "The Thirteen Bells" retold with many a spasm of fear and trepidation. Even today the stern decree was still enforced, visiting terrible punishment in high bamboo stockades upon anyone who killed the very sacred deer. And as if aware of this lurking fear in the hearts of men, the sacred deer—bucks

48

and does, in twos, in herds—roamed freely or frolicked madly on hills and dales and plains, even in the city itself. Somehow, to Yonosuke, this spectacle seemed ridiculous and shot through with stupid irony. But when autumn came, he thought, the streets would turn into a riot of color, what with lespedezas and miscanthus plants lining the walks in lavish glory.

One day, while entering a street called Hanazono from the west end, he saw a troupe of shrine entertainers, their hair smeared with oil, coming toward him. All seemed adept at piping the flute or thumping the drum. And along with this colorful parade was a mixed crowd of sword-bearing *ronin*, those lordless samurai, making a great commotion. They were transient visitors in this city, apparently from many provinces.

There was an odd character in the crowd who hid his face behind a fan. Just as Yonosuke was wondering what he could be, he became aware, from the things said behind that fan, that the character was a native son. The man was boasting like a barker at a shrine show about the superior attractions that lined the street.

"This," said the voice behind the fan, "is the famous Kitsuji-machi, and that on the north side is the Narukawa. There you will find that our city is hardly behind the vaunted lead of Kyoto in the grand art of entertaining. Now there comes the sound of the samisen, enticing music. You will never forgive yourselves if you were to leave this city without seeing the pretty girls hidden behind those latticed bamboo walls."

"Well," thought Yonosuke, "that *is* an idea!" He, too, was a transient here, and it had never dawned on him until now that he could benefit from the bleatings of a tourist guide.

He turned away from the parading crowd, entered Narukawa, and breezed into an inn operated by one Shichizaemon. It happened that three women—Shiga,

Chitose, and Masa—were available. With these rustic harlots he had a few drinks in lighthearted fashion and then dismissed them all. Next he called for a woman called Omi. As Omi entered, Yonosuke realized after a close look that he had once seen her plying her trade in the city of Osaka, not as a common prostitute but as a courtesan under the professional name of Tamanoi. As much as he knew that these women drifted from place to place, like flotsam on the sea of life, it seemed to him strange indeed, and interesting too, that he should come upon such a beauteous one—and here, of all places.

There were no other guests asking for Omi, and Yonosuke obtained the mistress's permission to engage her as a companion for the evening. With a table of saké and food between them, the two exchanged reminiscences until the small hours. She told him about the hardships, the pitfalls of her profession in a big city and about the quarrels with both patrons and her master that finally drove her out of Osaka and caused her to drift here.

"One must please everybody, but one has pride," she said. "I would rather be a harlot than be forced into the arms of a pervert."

No one waited on them at the table. It was the custom here not to employ young girls. The harlots themselves served as waitresses. "Very odd," thought Yonosuke.

A young male attendant came to fetch Yonosuke. "It is time for you to go to bed," he announced.

Guided to a six-mat room, Yonosuke saw several standing screens that evidently divided the room into sections. The papered portions below were covered with such scrawls of unfinished sentiments as "Your life . . ." and "Thoughts of thee. . . ." What manner of men slept here, Yonosuke wondered, to scribble such words, such desperate attachments for common harlots?

While he was still examining the room, the door slid open, and the same male attendant brought in a teapot.

50

"If you care for some tea before getting into bed . . ." he said and made his exit.

Yonosuke lay down to sleep on his quilt in his cramped space. Alone in this section, he found there was hardly enough room to stretch his legs. But it was all so carefree, like traveling on a ferryboat downstream on the River Yodo. Then he heard a couple speaking in low tones in the section next to his.

Evidently the man was a rice dealer spending his last night here before trekking back to his home in Ueno, in Iga Province, and a woman called Osaki had come to present him with an amulet—a miniature god of horses—from the Nigatsu-do and a temple charm from the Sai-dai-ji as parting gifts.

"If you should incur the displeasure of the mountain god in your province," she was telling him with laughter in her voice, "you might get fits of ague. Shake them off with these charms."

"An odd sense of humor," thought Yonosuke.

As the time came for the man to depart, he called the proprietor into his section. "Thanks to you all," the man boasted, "I have had a good time here and I have not paid much for it and I have therefore saved a good deal of money that I might have had to spend. Considering the times," and he laughed, "I think I have become a very shrewd man."

But Shichizaemon, the proprietor of the inn, was no dullard himself.

"Well, well, that is fine—fine indeed. But let me tell you this," and he laughed with good-natured cynicism, "if you were such a shrewd man, you would not have come to a place like this. You would have stayed home like a decent man, counting the copper coins in your shop."

The next morning Yonosuke left the inn, but he soon returned, drawn by a feeling of attachment for the lovely

51

Omi. He asked for her again, and they met again in intimate discourse. She embroidered her name on his garment, and they sealed their friendship like the prints on a piece of Nara cotton cloth.

ROAD TO DEGRADATION

LEAVING the gray mist-shrouded Kyoto mountain range behind him, Yonosuke hit the main trail where the feudatory barrier lay athwart his path. It was the ninth of the twelfth month, and he was on his way to Edo, the thriving shogunal capital in the east. He was eighteen. His fresh sandals became soaked with melting snow that dripped down from the trees lining the trail. Messy, uncomfortable, and cold—that was how he felt.

Well, but he was going on a mission for his father to examine the financial condition of the family's cotton-gauze establishment in Edo. Hardships on the way were but life's lesson. At least his intentions were good. He set his foot firmly on the soggy ground, unmindful too of the sharp craggy rocks over which he had to pick his way here and there.

Stopping at wayside inns when dusk overtook him, Yonosuke finally arrived after many days of traveling at a seaside town called Ejiri, in Suruga Province. Tomorrow he would resume his journey by boat along the coast, and there was no telling what misfortunes the sea might hold for him. "Tomorrow will be tomorrow, so why not spend the evening here as if this were my last night upon earth?" he told himself.

The view from the Funakiya Inn was restful and beautiful to see. There, spread out before his very eyes, was the storied Miho Bay with its pine-lined beach where an angel once bathed and danced in a feather robe for a mortal fisherman. The proprietor of the inn, Jinsuke by name, had a way of giving sumptuous satisfaction to his guests. He spread out a table of fine sea food for them. There were choice edible seaweeds garnered from the bay, and saké was plentiful.

After a full meal Yonosuke was counting his money for the rest of the journey, preparatory to going to bed, when he heard a strange melody. Someone on the road was chanting a popular air, sutra fashion. It sounded very mournful.

"Who is that singing?" Yonosuke asked the woman cook who happened to be boiling the next morning's rice.

"That," replied the cook, "is someone imitating the song of Wakasa and Wakamatsu, two sisters employed here as entertainers. You should see them at close range during the daytime. They are so beautiful!"

"Well! And how may one meet the girls?"

"You cannot see them now. It's out of the question. Some guests wait patiently for as long as seven days before they are given a chance. Others extend their stay here indefinitely, pretending to be ill, just to wait for their turn."

That, to Yonosuke, made all the difference in the world. The prospect of continuing his journey to Edo palled on him. If the singing sisters were so beautiful, so sought after, so hard to meet, then he would remain right here! Their very inaccessibility challenged his ego.

But with his winning, cajoling ways he encountered little difficulty in making the girls' acquaintance. And for the next few days he enjoyed their amorous company, earning for himself the enviable title of lady-killer once attributed to an ancient courtier named Narihira. He finally decided to take the girls back with him to Kyoto. They were willing enough, and he prevailed upon the

53

proprietor of the inn to accept his promissory note as the price for their release.

On the long road back, however, Yonosuke's travel money, with expenses trebling at the inns where they tarried fondly, became exhausted. Willy-nilly they went their separate ways. The girls, Wakasa and Wakamatsu, started a wayside noodle shop at a place called Imokawa, hoping to attract passers-by with their charming songs. Later it was said that the sisters, failing in business, entered a temple at the foot of Mt. Hanazono, where they shaved their heads—the fate of all misplaced confidences.

Yonosuke meanwhile resumed his journey to Edo. But hot blood now surged in his veins. He tarried at every inn on the way, writing more promissory notes, making new conquests, discarding old flames. Months later, in a pitiful state of dissipation, he reached the family branch shop in Edo.

Letters had meanwhile been exchanged between Kyoto and Edo, and promissory notes too, and his wayward travels had worried and angered his mother. But instead of getting down to serious business, Yonosuke continued his dissipations in Edo with the money made available to him at the branch shop. Without ceasing he spent his nights and days in one fashionable teahouse after another —in Honjo, Meguro, Shinagawa, Koishikawa, Shitaya, and Itabashi—finally becoming a regular frequenter of the Yoshiwara gay quarters. Profligate and intractable, he became an unregenerate playboy.

One day a sharp letter arrived from his mother in Kyoto. His father had disowned him.

Stripped of ready cash and physically worn out, Yonosuke found himself literally left out in the cold, with nowhere to turn.

The keeper of the family's branch shop, being wise in his way and fearing for Yonosuke's health, asked an aged priest to take him in hand and initiate him into the

54

ascetic life of monks. Yonosuke accepted his fate with tardy humility. He shaved his head on the seventh of the fourth month. He was nineteen now.

TORMENT

PROCEEDING far into the bamboo forests of the Musashi region west of Edo, Yonosuke built a reed hut in a lonely valley, with a footpath cut across honeysuckles and bindweeds. This was to be his hermitage, with no companions whatsoever save the Musashi moon on cloudless nights. Water was scarce hereabouts, so scarce indeed that he had to build a long conduit that brought precious trickles into his cupped hands from up the valley.

For a few days, cut off from the mundane world, Yonosuke read the sacred Buddhist sutras with commendable zeal. But alone with his prayers and meditations, he soon tired of his hermit's life. Doubts entered his mind. "No one has ever actually seen the promised hereafter," he argued with himself. "Nor has anyone ever actually grappled with the demons of flaming hell." And his past life of sin, from which the stern spirit of the Buddha seemed to have conspicuously kept away, now appeared in retrospect to be more desirable than ever.

So in a fit of impious disgust he sold the coral beads of his rosary, all of them. Silver coins jingled on his palm. And now again he thought of the life of the flesh.

While wondering how he should make a new start, he saw a lad of some sixteen years of age going past him in the lonely valley. The youth wore a brown crested robe with a satin sash tied behind his back, a pair of neat Takasaki socks, and leather-soled sandals. His hair was tied rather loosely in a knot, giving it a feminine appearance. Inserted in his sash was a medium-length sword. The little medicine case dangling beside it was very charming indeed. Altogether he seemed like an attractive youth. And trailing him was a business-like man holding a sewing box, a record book, and an abacus. They made a stylish, good-looking pair—the conventional type of attraction, however, that attracts without arousing the suspicion of the onlooker.

Recognizing their profession, Yonosuke felt oddly moved in this desolate region. Matter-of-factly he called them back: "I should like to buy some aloeswood."

After he had made his purchase, Yonosuke said: "Where do you live?"

"In Shiba, in front of the Shimmei Shrine, at Goro-kichi's flower shop called Tsuruya," the lad replied. "My master is called Juzaemon."

That conveyed nothing significant to Yonosuke. But later, upon making inquiries at the nearest village, he was to learn that there is nothing so awkward as being ignorant of open secrets.

Itinerant perfume sellers, he was told, were masquerad-ers: womanish youths who called at rich widowers' estates or made the rounds of poor sections where country sa-murai lived. They might peddle other dainty goods be-sides perfume, but they were like gadflies and their trade was a screen to hide their true identities from the un-knowing. They followed a set pattern of conduct and a line of talk easily recognizable to men acquainted with their secrets: men who felt no attractions in real women.

In his present desperate state of mind, it struck Yono-suke that here, as business master of such a group, was a convenient means of eking out a living. Whatever he thought of the business itself, it would at least bring in money. And he needed money in a hurry. Plenty of it.

His hermitage became an itinerant perfume sellers' hideout. There came Nagahachi and Mankichi and

Kiyozo, three good-looking womanish lads. Yonosuke felt no qualms of conscience about exploiting them for money. His sacred robe was ripped up for dishrags. The kitchen became littered with leftovers and the bones of white geese. He was back again at his old sinful life, now complete with degradation.

MUDDY RIVER

"NEVER," a beautiful woman once wrote, "has the moon shone upon an exile who is without sin." Himself an exile now, Yonosuke pondered over that line and nodded forlornly in affirmation.

The night wind howled under the eaves of his hut, and the reeds quivered in the shadows. In the morning the peddlers of bean curd avoided this valley. Forced abstinence gave him a vague sense of loneliness. Men might think he was a true ascetic. But he knew that the devotionless fire of the incense of his life would soon be smothered by the ashes piling up. "I cannot be wasting my life here," he decided.

All he had needed was money. The lads would have to shift for themselves. He was through.

Late one afternoon, while there was still enough light for him to see his way, Yonosuke left his hermitage forever. He walked up the hill, where the sunset glow still lingered. As he reached the heights, he encountered a group of monks from Mogami going on a devotional journey. The leader of the monks seemed like a kindly man. Seizing his sacred robe, Yonosuke pleaded: .

"I beg of you, Dairakuin-sama, let me go with you to Yoshino."

The eminent monk, recognizing Yonosuke's plight from

the ragged robe he wore, took pity upon him. He quoted
a famous verse:

> O mountain cherry,
> With compassion look at him;
> For autumn friends he has not
> Save for flowers wild.

Then with a smile of benediction he accepted Yonosuke as a disciple.

Incited by an inward need to move on, Yonosuke
hurried with the monks across the long footbridge near
Okazaki. At sight of the villagers he turned his face away.
He shifted his *hinoki* traveling hat, the better to hide his
identity. The memory of the ignoble trade he had just
abandoned began to torment him. Other sins crowded
his mind: the cowardly way he had set adrift the two
singing sisters Wakasa and Wakamatsu and many more,
the dissipations that had lost for him forever the blessings
of his parents.

Days later the group approached the steep and craggy
Mt. Omine. This was an awe-inspiring volcanic region
where tradition told of the terrible demons of hell who
crushed the bones of wrongdoers. It was a fitting place for
Yonosuke to repent his sins. He saw a glimpse of the
future life that awaited his kind. Fear crept into his heart.
He prayed. Indeed this was the way taught by the haloed
Bodhisattva, he reflected with grim humility. He hurried
along the dangerously hewn paths down the rocky
mountain.

But when the group reached as far as Yome-ga-Chaya,
on the trail approaching Kyoto, Yonosuke's penitent
mood vanished with the waters flowing down the river.
"It's no use," he argued with himself. "My life is just as
muddy as this river. It can never be purified."

Deserting the ranks of the monks, he took a side road
that led toward the city of Osaka.

58

At a place called Fuji-no-Tana, southeast of Osaka, he rented a small house and settled down to an empty, precarious existence. Here he opened a handicraft shop, selling nothing more useful than whalebone ear scratchers made by his unschooled hands. But in spite of poverty and misery the lure of amorous women never failed to attract him. The lessons of his recent past were as nothing before this ever-beckoning enchantment.

Within a short time he turned adventurer again in search of women of easy virtue. The harlots of Kodani and Fuda-no-Tsuji, the concubines who served different masters on a monthly basis, the casual women who turned out to be easily accessible—with all of them he came to strike up more than a passing acquaintance. His reputation as a libertine grew, but he was indifferent now to the stigmas or the penalties of notoriety. "They are but the consequences of my natural bent," he told himself with an inward shrug.

The harlots, he found, feared the law but managed to evade it ingeniously. Some of them set up a domestic maid disguised as a male to masquerade as master of the household. In this way they turned away officers of the law whose duty it was to expose houses of corruption.

They were sycophants, too, who traded their wiles and charms for gold. They could not very well roam the streets of Nakadera and Obashi. For one thing, they were no longer young and attractive. For another, such streets had become perilous at night since the murder of a priest. But they found easy prey among retired old men, wheedling and squeezing them out of their lifetime's carefully hoarded savings.

Some houses still bore a faint sign, "Laundry Shop," on their rattan blinds. But the sliding doors were always closed. Inside these "shops" you found fresh and gleaming mats—proof of altogether incommensurable elegance. They were homes of mistresses where men of wealth were snugly, secretly accommodated. One could per-haps overlook these practices among men whose wives were incurable invalids or could bear no heirs. But such was not the case. There was something shocking and re-pugnant in the goings-on in these houses behind false fronts.

And the women were fickle. A young man from Kita-hama today, a silk-yarn buyer tomorrow, a samurai by night—such was the shameful routine. Yet they went about looking innocent and unconcerned.

But Yonosuke saw another phase of life here. There was a long narrow lane which began from a rice-wine shop that bore the sign of a cryptomeria leaf. On both sides were rows of tenement houses, all admitting the north light. As he peeped into each of the houses, he found men and women plying all sorts of trades, from makers of millstones to dealers in sieves. Hardly any smoke rose from the kitchens in the morning and evening: mute testimony of extreme but honest and upright pov-erty. If Yonosuke had had any conscience left in him, their life might have awakened him, be it ever so little, to the folly of his ways.

At the end of the lane there was a large ditch beyond which stood a house with bamboo poles on which loin-cloths and small rice-bran bags were being dried. These drying things indicated this was a house of questionable pursuits. Yonosuke peeped through the door and saw an old sorceress type of woman whom Priest Kenko might aptly have described as a "robber of men's lives." Beside her stood a young gentle-seeming girl.

Evidently the girl could read and write. Lying on the mat was a familiar-looking box that contained an ink slab and writing brushes. There were other things: a huge cutting board, partly smashed wine containers made of brass. They were much too pretentious for an ordinary abode.

Observing these things, Yonosuke sensed—and it was instinct with him—that here was a household whose past had not always been thus: an old family, perhaps, that had degenerated into making money in the most ignoble but easiest way.

He went in. "Please accept me as a member of this family," he said to the sorceress-like woman.

She looked him over with a knowing eye. She made a wrinkled grin.

"You may stay here," she said.

JEWEL IN THE MUD

BUT NOT for long. Within a year Yonosuke was on the road again, a disowned unregenerate youth with no means to fall back upon, nor, for that matter, to provide him with the wherewithal for profligate living. Except for one thing: an early musical talent that now served him in good stead.

He became a wandering minstrel, roving up and down the River Yodo on thriving ferryboats. Blending his dramatic Noh chants with the music of splashing waters, he accepted coins flung at him that amounted to hardly more than alms. These gratuities came from rustic passengers or, at intervals, from loiterers at such river ports as Katano, Hirakata, and Kuzuha.

Whimsical and aimless, he went ashore at Hashimoto. There he registered at a shabby inn where he found a good many people in no more exalted circumstances than himself.

This was a regular haunt of cheap itinerant entertainers. The showman from Nara with a monkey on a leash, the frightful freak from Nishinomiya who exhibited himself as a "barbarian," the romantic hand-to-mouth idler who posed as a mendicant priest and chanted Buddhist sutras for a few coppers, the wayward monk with an eye for sensual pleasure, the ubiquitous peddler of gewgaws —all were there. And all were fly-by-night actors on the seamy stage of life, existing precariously from day to day and spending their day's earnings in one night of unrestrained fun. All that remained in their possession the next morning were their shabby stocks in trade, their battered fans, and their straw traveling hats.

Inevitably Yonosuke saw an image of himself in their faces, in their cheap parasitical way of living just this side of the beggar's lot, in the few tricks they performed for one night's pleasure in a harlot's arms.

His heart filled with repugnance and shame, he sneaked away from the inn, hiding his face behind his wide-brimmed straw hat. Crossing the Hosho stream and taking a roundabout way, he entered a village called Tokiwa. Here in the suburb, among a grove of bamboos, he came upon a huge estate, a splendid dwelling. There was no one about except for a young person in the robes of a temple page.

He asked a passing villager: "What sort of place is this?"

"A house where rich men come to play."

Actually it was an enormous private abode, the home of a retired tradesman who had assumed the name of Rakuami. Once a handsome man about town, Rakuami had always regarded the wearing of stiff formal attire— the *kamishimo,* with its skirtlike *hakama* trousers, its wing-shouldered jumper, and all—a boring nuisance. Nor could he endure with equanimity the daily morning ritual, as a fastidious man should, of having his hair dressed for the modish topknot. So he had shaved his head to live a free-and-easy life here, surrounded by entertainers twanging music.

The left wing of his mansion contained an iron depository filled with some 300,000 *ryo* of gold coins. But he had a taste for art too. The right wing he called the "silver room." Here the lower portions of the panels and sliding doors, which, when drawn, turned the whole wing into one huge room, were decorated with beautiful paintings. And in this wing he assembled pretty women entertainers from Kyoto. Sometimes he went to the extreme, without any qualms whatsoever, of letting them wrestle on the padded mat floor with nothing on save a thin loincloth, revealing their gleaming white skins. For he was rich in experience too, having observed all the tricks among harlots in the northern ports.

Yonosuke felt drawn to the obvious splendor of the mansion. But if this were just a house of recreation, he thought, then his dramatic Noh lyrics would never do. That would be much too profound for light-minded souls. So he approached the latticed door and sang a popular air at the top of his voice, in the manner of the celebrated Chubei:

> O, fickle cuckoo,
> Tell me truly
> Whither fliest thou,
> Forsaking me rudely?

Someone inside the mansion with an ear for music heard the song and tipped his head. "He sings too well for a mendicant," he told the master.

"Go and see what he looks like," Rakuami ordered.

Tiptoeing to the vestibule, the man so ordered peeped through the latticework. He gave Yonosuke a sweeping appraisal. "For all his shabbiness, this strolling minstrel does not look to me like a man of humble origin," the man told himself. "He may be a court noble's illegitimate son. Chances are he is a confirmed spendthrift, wasting his neglected mother's hard-earned money on frivolous women. He may have been forced to shift for himself as a lesson to be learned the hard way."

"Ask him," the master, his curiosity aroused, ordered the man when he tiptoed back to report his findings.

The door slid open, and Yonosuke, questioned point-blank, replied: "Yes, I am ashamed to say so, but I have been sent out of my home to earn my own living. That much is true."

"Then come in," the man invited.

Rakuami, the master, made him welcome. "My friends are having an archery tournament in the rear court. Why don't you join them?"

Yonosuke saw at once that the archers were novices, dilettantes who boasted love of the sport but hit wide of the mark.

"Let *me* try, if I may," he asked. He borrowed a bow from one of the contestants.

He shot four arrows in succession, all hitting within the periphery of the target, the last one flying straight for the bull's eye. There was a great shout of applause, and the crowd asked for more of his exhibition shots.

In one of the rooms a koto musician pulled out her instrument before a small sedate audience. But search as she would in the accustomed place, there was no plectrum to pluck the strings with. It had evidently been misplaced or lost.

Noticing her embarrassment, Yonosuke walked up to her and produced a small lavender crepe parcel from his shabby sleeve pocket. "If this would serve your purposes, I should be pleased . . ." he said gallantly, presenting her with a shiny plectrum with an inscribed carnation crest.

"Thank you." The woman beamed appreciatively.

Rakuami, too, was pleased.

"Your robe," he told Yonosuke laughingly, pointing at the dirty rag of a garment, "seems to belie the elegance

of your mind. And you speak like a man of breeding. If you will pardon my saying so, you are like a jewel in the mud. Why don't you stay here with us for a while?"

"The jewel," Yonosuke replied with a bow, "accepts with pleasure the honor of being provided with a cleaner mounting."

The two laughed together over that, instantly becoming pat-on-the-back friends.

Days later the master told Yonosuke: "Tomorrow I shall go up to Kyoto to select a young girl. Why don't you come along with me?"

Kyoto, the seat of the imperial court, was Yonosuke's home town, where his parents lived. And they had disinherited him. His head dropped in embarrassment. But the opportunity was too good to be missed.

He said: "I happen to know something about the girls in Kyoto, but I . . ."

"Tell me about them."

"Well, the water in Kyoto is so clear that there are many girls with beautiful skins. Besides, their faces are steamed from early childhood. They are made to wear rings on their fingers and sent to bed with their *tabi* socks on. Their hair is dressed with the juice of a wild vine, while their bodies are always smeared with *araiko* cosmetics. They are given only two meals a day, along with lessons in womanly refinement. And they are not allowed to wear cotton undergarments. To be sure, this ritual is intended to improve their looks. But it is not natural beauty. Seldom will you find a girl there who is naturally lovely. The conventional girl of Kyoto has an oval face with a skin the color of cherry blossoms. One must examine the girls very closely to make a good selection."

That was quite agreeable to Rakuami. On the morrow the two departed for Kyoto, where they relied on the good offices of an agent named Jinshichi on Miyuki-machi to summon prospective applicants.

"Spread the word that we are commissioners of a great western lord," Yonosuke told the agent. "Girls from twenty to twenty-four years of age may apply. We shall make our selection after comparing faces with a picture of the type we are looking for."

Jinshichi spread the word. Before sunset some seventy-three women had applied for the privilege of becoming a concubine of a supposedly great western lord but actually of a rich bald-headed old retired merchant. Some came in stately palanquins with their chambermaids or servants. All were arrayed in their loveliest silken finery, and the scramble for the dubious glory resembled the fabled "battle of flowers" of ancient China.

The glory fell on a girl named Osatsu, daughter of an embroidery dealer on Yanagi-no-Baba. A grant of a hundred and fifty *ryo* to prepare for her journey to Raku-ami's gilded mansion was duly made.

"Why don't you choose one for yourself?" the master told Yonosuke.

"Well . . . if you insist! My choice is Okitsu."

Okitsu was the daughter of a parasol dealer on Shichi-jo-dori.

The agent Jinshichi was duly rewarded for his assiduous labors. Simple rites were held in his house to toast the happy event. Immediately afterwards the master and Yonosuke journeyed back to the gilded mansion with the two girls. Such unmitigated license could have happened nowhere but in Kyoto.

Down south on the island of Kyushu, in the seaport town of Kokura, there lived a man of some means, one of those traveling tradesmen who appeared off and on at Rakuami's gilded mansion. Yonosuke knew him slightly more than casually. He came up to Kyoto to attend the annual Hi-no-To Shrine festival just as Yonosuke became footloose again. The two met at the festival and renewed their friendship.

As the celebration came to an end, the man from Kokura said: "Now show me the vaunted entertainment houses of Kyoto."

Yonosuke guided him through the cheap houses, for he had to foot the bills. His friend saw or felt nothing of sustaining interest. Even Yonosuke himself was already feeling more than a trifle bored.

"Come with me to Kokura," the man invited.

"I'd like that. It may mean a new adventure for me."

They sailed down the River Yodo, passing Udono in Settsu Province, where rushes thrived in shining abundance. Here Yonosuke's love of natural beauty reasserted itself: he took due note in his diary of the silvery stretch of lush primeval pomp. Then, as the ferryboat followed the winding river, the River Amano loomed to the left. Along its left bank nestled a town called Isoshima, where "secret girls" were wont to answer the boatmen's calls. On the right bank stood a lonely hut, in the shade of a huckleberry bush. Ironically enough, it was here that the saintly Priest Saigyo once tarried for lofty meditation and dedicated a verse to it.

Further down the river was the village of Mishimae,

68

then Kanzaki, then Nakamachi, the birthplace of such noted courtesans in ages past as Shirodo and Shirome. Their oft-repeated charms were but memories now, but the fluttering ghosts of their past evoked a responsive echo in Yonosuke's heart.

From there on, the river turned shallow, beset with huge rocks, almost a swirling cataract. At Shiosakai they transferred to a rowboat capable of twisting nimbly between rock and wave. But at Tomo-no-Tsu in Bingo Province the two went ashore, for it was said that three well-known courtesans, Kacho, Yashima, and Hanakawa, were plying their trade here.

But there happened to be not enough time for elaborate dillydallying in their company. All Yonosuke could do was to spend a few all too swiftly passing hours with Hanakawa before the boatmen's summons came for them to resume the journey. Their meeting, conducted without proper ceremony or introductions and in a most commonplace fashion, left no lasting impression on Yonosuke's mind. He could not even remember how she looked. But he did succeed in getting the courtesan to compose a friendship pledge. To this she affixed her name and sealed it with a smear of blood from her little finger. Even this memento, however, was left behind as Yonosuke hurried down to the boat at the river bank and the planks were lifted.

Some three *ri* down the river he suddenly realized he had forgotten to retrieve his paper handkerchief case, into which the pledge had been hastily shoved. He spoke of it regretfully to the man from Kokura. The helmsmen heard this, and they broke out hilariously in a belly laugh. They slapped the gunwales from sheer amusement. "A sealed pledge! What a sentimental womanchaser you are!"

When finally the two men arrived at the port of Kokura, Yonosuke's eyes fell upon a picturesque scene. A long line of women with shallow wooden tubs balanced on their heads was coursing along the waterfront. They were wearing cotton robes with splashed designs the color of young fawns. The hems of their robes fluttered in the wind, revealing madder-red undergarments. Their sashes were tied in front, their sleeves rolled up to the elbows. The dripping tubs on their heads contained flatfish, mollusks, clams, and edible seaweed. Presently they crossed a huge wooden bridge and went their separate ways.

"Who are they?" Yonosuke inquired of his friend.

"They are known as *tata* or *jo* hereabouts: fish peddlers from such neighboring towns and villages as Dairi and Kojima who come here daily for fresh supplies."

They were a conspicuous group in every seaport town, Yonosuke was further told, with different group names in each province. In Isé, for instance, they were known as *yaya*.

"Competition is strong," his friend added, "so they are generous to their customers. Favor them with your patronage, and they will as likely as not come right into your house and offer themselves as bedmates."

"Very interesting," mused Yonosuke. "But when you think of the odor of seaweed on their garments . . . well!" He added: "If that is all you can offer here, I shall be off to Shimonoseki."

Alone and with a light heart, Yonosuke journeyed by sea to another thriving seaport town, further north and on the mainland, to see the courtesans of Inari-machi.

He found them to be the quiet and ingenuous sort reminiscent of Kyoto belles. Their provincial speech had an accent, and it was rather charming. Most of them wore long overkimono and fixed their hair in loose, rippling fashion. Most popular, Yonosuke heard at one establishment, were Minakawa of the Nagasakiya, Etchu of the Chaya, and Fujinami of the Tabakoya. They had poise and were easy to converse with.

70

"What do they charge?"

"Just 38 *me*. So they are popularly known as 'the 38.' "

Even at the regular teahouses Yonosuke found a large-hearted welcome. It seemed they were patronized by many provincial men of means who spent money liberally, and the service was good. At one place he was ushered into an enormous room where the master and mistress took turns in paying their respects to him in a most flattering manner.

"Since you are from Kyoto," the master said, "we should like to serve you nice delicacies and show you some real local beauties that you will remember us by."

Then the drinks arrived—and the courtesans. These "local beauties" began to pour the drinks, pressing Yonosuke with cup after cup of the amber-colored saké. They were so insistent that the pleasure of leisured drinking turned to the discomforts of sudden surfeiting. Worse, the food began to arrive on tray after tray in appalling quantities. Evidently the establishment was continuing an age-old custom, but the final reckoning would be enormous. And he was almost as poor as a beggar.

To top it all, the courtesans began to sing and strum samisen music. They forced him to sing too. There was no subtlety, no graciousness, no feeling of ease and well-being. All was one confusing bedlam.

When they put him to bed at last, Yonosuke was thoroughly drunk, uncomfortable, and ill. Only dimly was he aware of the women around him, now throwing aside their professional masks and gossiping unkindly about "the behavior of unwelcome guests."

The next morning he felt he had been cheated in more ways than one. Well, he decided, if the custom here was merely to surfeit guests with drinks, food, and noise, and to gouge them besides, then he must devise a way of evening up the score. He remained for almost a week, dallying clandestinely with the courtesans. The master

71

and the mistress accused him of seducing the women in
their employ. They felt they had been mulcted of profits
that should have come their way from these acts. There
was a great hullabaloo. Again Yonosuke had to leave
without parting salutations—secretly through the back
door.

THE LOTUS LEAF

Asking his way through unfamiliar territory in the
general direction of Osaka, Yonosuke finally arrived at
a place called Nakatsu, with the dust of weary travel on
his robe. There was no one here to whom he could possibly turn for food or shelter. So he trudged on. That
evening he entered the town of Tsujido. He was wondering what he should do next when he heard the muffled
beats of a turret drum in the suburb.

Drawn by the rhythmic pounding, he went to investigate and found an itinerant show making a jolly racket
to attract customers. A barker stationed beside the entrance was shouting in glib, professionally persuasive
tones: "Listen, everybody! This is the famous Fujimura
troupe, here to entertain you on its tour of the whole
country. Come one, come all!"

Yonosuke glanced up at the roster of actors. To his
pleasant surprise, he found the name of Shoshichi, the
musician. Shoshichi was a veteran showman whom he
had once befriended in Kyoto when times were brighter.
To him, as an admirer, he had presented gifts in the form
of costly outer robes.

"This is indeed fortunate for me," Yonosuke thought,
and he went around to the greenroom to see the musician.
Not as a bearer of gifts this time, of course, but as an old

friend in dire straits and in need of immediate material aid.

Shoshichi greeted him warmly.

"Do not feel discouraged," he said sympathetically when Yonosuke told him about his shiftless past and penurious present. "Human life is forever a mystery and we are but victims of the whims of fate. But you . . . you have an agreeable talent for music. Why not join this troupe as a stage singer?"

Hired on the spot, Yonosuke was provided with an old stage costume, a trailing *naga-hakama*. His first part was the dramatic entrance of a character called Shina-no-Jo. This called for a good chanting voice and mimetic ability, not the least of which was a vigorous, stylistic shaking of the head. Somehow, though his feet in the *naga-hakama* were uncommonly unsteady, Yonosuke acted the part with tolerable verisimilitude. What he could not put over with the grace and precision of a trained actor he managed to gloss over with improvisations which proved—to the ingenuous country audience at any rate—comical rather than clumsy.

Had he continued this role with serious determination, he might have been assured of a longer lease on luck. Being an inveterate amorist, however, he soon became involved in affairs with promiscuous women of the town whom other members of the troupe had pre-empted as their exclusive conquests.

"I don't care how deeply you are indebted to that rascal Yonosuke," Shoshichi was told. "Out he must go. Let us not pick up any more of these ungrateful vagrants. He is a ham anyhow."

Thus, for his superior ways with women, Yonosuke was promptly driven out of the troupe, and Shoshichi wept as they parted.

Yonosuke laughed. "I have had a few square meals anyhow, thanks to you. Remember what you said about life's being a mystery. We are but victims of the whims of fate—in my case the whims of a bad loser in love-making. Ha ha ha."

For some time after that he roamed aimlessly down the road back toward Osaka. Then, from a chance remark dropped by a passing stranger while they were sipping tea together on the bench outside a wayside tearoom, he learned that in a small lane in Osaka's market section there lived a woman who often spoke very kindly of him.

"This *is* a windfall," thought Yonosuke. "Whoever she is, whatever her situation, she might be prevailed upon to offer me shelter and at least a meal or two."

So thence he plodded his way, desperate and curious and hopeful.

The house he sought stood next door to those of a tobacco cutter and a palanquin bearer. A persimmon-colored shop curtain hung over the doorway. He went in and found a middle-aged woman living alone, without any apparent means of livelihood.

Failing to recognize her, he said: "I am Yonosuke."

The woman welcomed him with all but open arms. "Perhaps you don't remember me," she said, beaming, "but I am the younger sister of the woman who served as wet nurse to you when you were a baby. I used to carry you myself."

"Ah, yes . . . I remember now." Obviously he did not. "And how is the wet nurse of my infant days?"

"She passed away about three years ago." Then the woman smiled as if to say: "Never mind about the past. You must be tired and hungry." Aloud she said: "Make this your home. I shall prepare a nice meal for you."

That evening a garishly powdered woman in a gaudy, saffron-colored robe clattered into the vestibule in her paulownia clogs. She was wearing a red apron, and her sash was tied rakishly under her left arm. In her hands was a bunch of burdock and citron flowers. "Evidently," thought Yonosuke, "she is a frequent visitor here." She addressed the mistress of the house in a voice hardly above a whisper:

"Some time ago I left a pawnbroker's ticket with you. It was for a striped kimono. Have you got it with you still?"

After she had duly retrieved her ticket and left in a flurry, Yonosuke said: "Very amusing. What sort of woman is she?"

"She is a maidservant in a business establishment farther up the street."

Yonosuke laughed. "But the robe she wore, the powder on her face, the clogs—they are incongruous in a woman of her lowly position. Even a hired weaving woman cannot afford such luxuries. How does she earn so much money?"

The sister of his former wet nurse gave him a sidelong smile. "You are getting so you notice such small secret details, aren't you?"

After a while she explained confidentially: "She is what is known as a *hasuha*—a lotus leaf. In other words, a promiscuous woman. Many big wholesale houses here maintain extra rooms to accommodate buyers from all over the country. These establishments usually hire good-looking women to look after the buyers' needs. She is one of them."

"Chambermaid?"

"More than that."

"How so?"

"They are wantons. Between busy hours, whether night or day, these women chase after men in one small inn after another in the neighborhood. They are utterly without shame. Whenever they become big with child they commit abortions and think nothing of it. All their clothes are bought for them by the men they lure, but they sell them—holiday and seasonal robes and all—before they even have a chance to wear them. They spend money freely on rice wine and noodles. When they visit shrines and temples, they ignore etiquette or respect for the holy, refusing to take off their cotton hoods. They are full of trivial talk—about the price of tortoise-shell combs, about falling asleep while writing letters at night. If three of them should get together on the street, they would gossip and laugh out loud, forgetting their errands. They visit small inns, wheedling male guests out of their money. Most of them lead this corrupt, happy-go-lucky life."

"Where do they end up?" Yonosuke asked. "Isn't there some kind of retribution for them?"

"Eventually they end up by marrying some menial laborers. Suddenly there is a marked change in their way of life, in their looks, in their habits. You see them carrying babies in their arms or on their backs or leading their eldest by the hand, visiting rice shops, watching the scales closely, grumbling, arguing with the shopkeepers, fighting for every *mon's* worth."

Yonosuke beamed accusingly. "You forgot to mention one other thing."

The sister of his one-time wet nurse guessed the allusion correctly. "Yes . . . I might as well admit it. You will find it out anyhow. This house here, my sole means of earning a living, is just such an inn where those wantons come to seduce their men."

Yonosuke was highly elated. "This promises new adventures!"

"You . . . without money?"

"Yes, for free. Someone must turn the tables on them. It wouldn't be justice to let them get away with such plunder. You'll see!"

And in that way Yonosuke spent the twenty-third year of his life. Where would it lead him?

76

ALL DEBTS must be paid on the last day of the year, and there is nothing so excruciatingly damaging to one's dignity and peace of mind as one's inability to pay them. Or so Yonosuke ruefully admitted to himself. He shut himself up in his upstairs room.

In this way—by making it appear as though he had gone on a long trip—Yonosuke contrived to avoid or to deceive bill collectors bent on paying him annoying visits. He even feared the bright accusing finger of day. And even the slightest rattling of the door downstairs brought a stab of pain to his heart. He would press his hands to his ears.

All very sad and humiliating, he mused, for he would pay if he could.

But however painful his present situation, the thought came to him, rather like a streak of inveterate optimism, that if in the future fortune should ever smile upon him, then he would be able to look back upon this day's embarrassment as something monstrously trivial to laugh over. Yes, to laugh over.

Then the New Year dawned, quietly and brilliantly.

Soon on the street below, hawkers were crying their wares: "Fans for sale! Fans for the New Year!" "Ebisu pictures! Get your pictures of the god of wealth for the New Year!"

Now that the day of reckoning was over, Yonosuke went downstairs and stepped out into the bright sun. No bill collectors would try to annoy him until the *next* year end. The air was springlike in more ways than one, and he felt somewhat better—in fact, serene.

77

The gates of wealthy homes were decorated with sprigs of good-luck pines, resplendently green in the flashing light. Voices of men and women extending New Year greetings filled the air. The sound of little girls in bright robes hitting shuttlecocks with battledores could be heard everywhere. Young people were buying and reading printed oracles that foretold happiness or despair in love affairs. And this, so typical of the New Year spirit, gave Yonosuke a renewed sense of well-being—an old custom that always exuded freshness and hope.

But New Year's Day was soon over, and another day dawned. On this day Yonosuke, invited by friends, set out on a visit to the temple on Mt. Kurama. Passing through a place called Ichiharano, he saw exorcists noisily performing the usual rites to ward off evil, either with a talisman or by flinging dry beans. Peddlers were selling *takarabune,* miniature good-luck ships. Sprigs of the holly tree and dried sardines, wishful symbols of coming prosperity, hung from the eaves of almost every home. But front doors were tightly closed from early morning so as to prevent the entry—or so it was believed—of the spirits of evil.

One more hill to traverse, and there stood the Kurama Temple. This was a place where many travelers met, an object of pilgrimages of young people and old. Many a story had been related of how young strangers, meeting here for the first time, fell in love at first touch. Now this "touch" usually eventuated when two worshippers at the crowded altar, one male and the other female, reached almost simultaneously for the cord with which to sound the ceremonial gong. A rough masculine hand came in contact with a soft feminine hand; eyes met, held for a moment or two; and mutual admiration was born.

Other stories told of how young men from the hinterland, seeing beautiful pictures of women on the fans at the temple, felt burning passion for the first time. A

high-born lady from the imperial court once tarried here
and composed a verse:

> Fireflies glint in the marshy darkness
> Searchingly, and I think of
> My own soul hungry for love.

The night was late, and someone imitating the crow
of the rooster became the signal for all worshippers to
depart.

Suddenly Yonosuke remembered something. "By the
way," he whispered to his companions, "this is the night
of the *zakone* in nearby Ohara when all the villagers,
young and old of both sexes, masters and servants, are
allowed to lie down together and sleep at the portals of
the Shinto shrine. It is a kind of vigil, a religious custom,
and for once no restrictions whatsoever are placed on
what the sleepers may venture to do. Aren't you curious?
Let's go and see."

And so they went, skirting dark streams, groping in
the shadows of huge boulders, following the trail among
small pines. When they finally approached the Ohara
shrine it was so dark that one could almost bump into a
stray cow without being aware of the cow's presence.

Presently they heard a frightened young girl protesting
in innocently aggrieved tones and fleeing from the shrine.
On approaching closer they saw a woman, held in the
grip of tough male hands, calmly and resolutely refusing
to mount the shrine portals together with the man. Another woman, on the other hand, was boldly and coquettishly persuading an unwilling man to lie down beside
her. In one corner two young people were whispering
tenderly to each other. In another, two men were arguing
over a woman, and to her it seemed a matter of utter
indifference who lay down beside her. A grandmother
nearing seventy years of age was being teased and frightened by a young prankster. A servant was nagging his

79

master's wife, seizing this opportunity that came but once a year to exercise the freedom and liberties of a socially equal male adventurer. In the end, as Yonosuke watched, the whole scene became one of wild disorder, filled with cries of laughter and lament, of defiance and glad acquiescence.

As the first streak of dawn lighted up the eastern horizon, the revelers began to leave the shrine. They now seemed to be in all shapes and states of dishabille. But there was one woman, very old it seemed, with bent back but very neat and with a cotton hood covering her face, as though she were afraid of having her identity detected. She leaned heavily on her bamboo staff as she shuffled away, seeking a lonely bypath.

Yonosuke, his curiosity and suspicion aroused, tore away from his companions and followed the woman stealthily along the dark trail. As she reached a stone lantern that lighted the way, the aged woman paused in her walk and looked behind. Then, as if satisfied that no one was following her, she stretched herself to her full height, threw away her staff, and took off her hood.

In the pale light of the lantern, her face was revealed in full view: a young girl, no more than twenty-two years of age, very beautiful to behold, very white of skin, and with jet black hair.

"Well!" thought Yonosuke. "I knew she couldn't be an old woman fleeing. Not after joining the *zakone*. She is daring and shrewd. And she has a very shapely figure, slender and with just the right amount of bulge at the hips to be an attractive courtesan in Kyoto."

"What are you afraid of?" he asked, coming out of hiding and smiling in friendly fashion.

"Oh!" she exclaimed, not so much frightened as annoyed. "Please leave me alone. I beg of you. You seem like a well-bred man from the city. The young men of the village are after me, have always been after me, and

I detest it. They are disgusting fellows. That is why I went there in disguise and came away in disguise. Now please go."

"Here," thought Yonosuke, "is a fine upstanding girl. I could love her forever."

"Come with me," he invited, "and you will never be bothered again by those village crows. I'll take you to the city."

She looked at him long and appraisingly, and a smile lit up her eyes.

"All right," she replied, "I'll go with you. That is, if you . . . if you promise never to leave me, ever."

Suddenly mixed voices came from the darkness along the trail. Quickly Yonosuke seized the girl and pushed her behind thick nearby bushes. Hiding there together, they held their breath.

Groups of young village scalawags in sixes, fours, and twos came running up, mumbling or yelling. As they reached the stone lantern, Yonosuke and the girl could hear them cursing and arguing.

"Where could that sneaking wench have gone to?"

"She's the prettiest one in the village, remember that. I'd like to . . ."

"I guessed she was at the shrine all the time, but I couldn't find her in the dark. That made me angrier than ever. She's always giving us the slip. Wait till I get my hands on her!"

"She must have been mocking us all the time. *Chikusho!*"

"We'll all share her if we ever find her now. Tonight it's free for all. Damn her!"

"No, you don't! She's not for the likes of you young evil-minded roosters."

"Who said that?"

"I saw a shadow slinking this way. It *must* have been her."

"You must have been *seeing* things. There's no one around here. Oh, *ahorashii,* let's go home. We're making fools of ourselves."

"She'd better not come back to the village, or we'll . . ."

"Oh, be quiet. It's fellows like you that are driving her out of the village. Go home to your mother, crybaby!"

"Who said that?"

One by one the small groups, still quarreling and cursing, retreated along the trail and were swallowed up by the darkness.

Yonosuke led the girl by the hand out of the protecting bushes and up the trail toward Shimokamo way. They sought temporary shelter at a wayside inn, then proceeded along the way in the glaring light of day. Soon came the procession of *Ohara-me,* girls of the village of Ohara entering Kyoto to sell the bundles of firewood that they carried on their kerchiefed heads. The sought-after girl feared she might be recognized by these quaint peddlers.

Yonosuke patted her gently on the shoulder.

"Cover up your face with your sleeve when they look this way. There is always fun in running away, fun in fighting off detection, fun in leading a free, daring, adventurous life."

NIGHT FLOWERS BY THE SEA

FOR SOME six months Yonosuke shared a dingy old thatch-roofed house in Kyoto with the runaway girl from Ohara. But no further scraping of the food box would yield another meal together. No one would risk advancing them any more credit. Nor could they live on promiscuous love alone. Suitable employment was not to be had. And so, in this state of impending disaster, they decided that one person could somehow live cheaper alone, and they parted.

It was Yonosuke who left the house. He was now twenty-eight. Thinking desperately in terms of quickly and plentifully acquired wealth, he beheld visions of gold beckoning to him from the rich mines of Sado Island. That was far, far to the northwest. Reaching there would require months of tedious, dangerous trekking over high mountain trails, across valleys and coastal plains. Nevertheless he must risk the pitfalls in order to follow that imperative urge. Anyhow, it seemed to him to be the most promising way out of his predicament.

It was long after summer when Yonosuke arrived at a seacoast town called Izumosaki. The golden island of Sado lay eighteen *ri* across the sea from there. He took a scheduled vessel, but winter comes quickly in that northern region, and it was impossible to hunt for alluvial gold in the deep snow. He returned crestfallen to Izumosaki.

But Yonosuke's wits, as always in a tight situation, were far from dull. He remembered the old saying that salted salmon had great medicinal value in curing frostbite. And frostbite was a common winter ailment hereabouts. Through the help of the generous innkeeper at whose place he secured lodgings, he was able to start a one-man business: the peddling of that precious fish.

Stringing the two- to three-foot salmon by their mouths in batches of threes on both ends of a long flexible pole, he carried them coolie-fashion across his shoulder from door to door. His principal customers were the inhabitants of snow-bound mountain villages where frostbite was frequent and salmon otherwise unavailable. In this way, as a lonely peddler—half medicine man, half salesman— he pushed his way with invincible determination across slippery ice packs on hinterland trails. He earned a tolerable livelihood, and the winter passed and spring came.

83

And then Yonosuke descended upon another port town called Sakata. Here the cherries bloomed magnificently along the banks of streams, their outspread beauty reflected in the clear running water. Yonosuke, the poet within himself responding quickly to this vista of natural charm, was reminded keenly that it was here the Priest Saigyo composed the memorable verse:

> The rising tide bears along
> Scattered cherry blossoms wave on wave.
> Behold, in heaven's fishing boat
> I row across a bed of flowers!

Then, as he stood before a temple gate, gazing out at the sea toward golden Sado Island, he heard singing voices, reminiscent and melodious. Turning, he saw two Buddhist nuns approaching. They were mendicants soliciting alms for their temple, with subscription books in their hands. There was nothing extraordinary about their appearance, for they wore the usual black hood and black sash tied in front.

But the profession of these nuns had long since degenerated into a state of semiprostitution. It all started when they began living together in the boarding houses called *goryo*. Nowadays, along with their calling, they were known to offer themselves to any almsgiver at the price of a hundred *mon*, a most shameful norm that drew the scorn of virtuous people.

Suddenly Yonosuke was struck by the resemblance one of the nuns bore to a girl he had once known.

"Weren't you the little girl that used to live with the nun Seirin on Metta-machi in the Kanda section of Edo?" he asked.

"Why . . . yes," he nun replied, surprised, and she stopped to engage him in a wayside chat.

"I knew Seirin well," Yonosuke said. "She was not a virtuous nun. You **were** then a little girl who used to walk around like a sedge hat on parade. Well, well, you certainly have grown. And you have taken after Seirin."

The nun laughed derisively. "What about yourself? You were a fine-looking youth then, with money to spend on women. Now you . . . you are a smelly fish peddler. How you have fallen!"

Yonosuke laughed good-naturedly. "To tell you the truth, I have played with women so much that I am surfeited with them. For the time being, I am trying to rid myself of that habit. This here . . . this trade of mine is not a serious occupation. It is just to tide over present difficulties—shall we say to earn some saké money?"

The nuns resumed their dubious calling, and Yonosuke went in search of a certain wholesale establishment. The proprietor there was a family acquaintance.

This port town was a prosperous one, carrying on a brisk trade with many provinces, both far and near. Those stopping at the wholesale house were rich tradesmen come to buy or sell. The proprietor and his wife were profuse in their lip service, for the guests were laden with gold that really glittered.

The shop, Yonosuke observed, had a huge innlike wing where the guest merchants were made comfortable. In the large living room he saw some fifteen young women dressed very smartly, with hair wound prettily and piled up on their heads at a smart angle. Their lips were painted garishly. All seemed to exude the invitation: Come and take your pick.

"Don't misunderstand," the proprietor told Yonosuke. "These women are not in my employ. They have homes of their own and come to work here of their own accord. Each looks after a single guest merchant, waiting at table, taking care of bed things, massaging, trimming beards, and doing all the little chores usually done by a personal maid. The traveling merchants tarry from ten to thirty days and leave small gratuities that gladden their hearts.

For money is a rare possession among these women. But their main object is *iro-kasegi*—sharing beds with guests. They are known here as *shaku*—ladles, that is."

"Is it because," Yonosuke asked laughingly, "these women 'ladle out' men's passion or their . . . their money?"

"No one knows why. Some anonymous person for reasons of his own must have started calling them that, and the name just stuck. That is the way most things happen."

Late that evening Yonosuke went out to the beach to see for himself if some of the stories he had heard about this town were true. Sure enough, he saw a woman, to all appearances the wife of a townsman, yielding coquettishly, willingly in the dark to the embrace of a rough seaman as if she herself had ensnared him. Presently they got into the seaman's boat.

"She is a *kampyo*," the wholesaler told Yonosuke later at the lodging.

" Dried squash shaving? What do you mean?"

"Women like her make themselves up like the flowers of the squash plant and bend to the gifts of men. You may interpret the word 'gifts' any way you wish. They will take money if offered. If none is offered, they go home satisfied anyway."

The wholesaler continued: "They sleep by day and at night make up their faces and wear their most alluring robes, usually open at the armpits. In the dim light they look young and attractive, and many an unwary man is known to have been deceived.

"When these women set out on their nightly profession, they usually try to hide their identities from their neighbors by covering their faces with towel kerchiefs. More often than not they are followed by a male companion. Together they loiter at lonely street corners or by the sea. As the night wears on, they sing bawdy songs, and that awakens the Sanzos and Jinsukes. As dawn approaches, the women entice the early pack-horse leaders or call out to the boats waking in the cove.

"The male companion carries a long bamboo staff to chase away hostile dogs. As early light creeps out of the sea, street doors open one by one, and these nocturnal women hasten their steps homeward, often running off into dark side lanes to escape detection.

"Some of them earn money in this way to help out aged parents. Others, with no other means of family livelihood, are forced into the clandestine trade. Mothers leave their babies with grandma. Older sisters sacrifice younger sisters. Uncles, aunts, nieces—all exploit one another just to keep body and soul together.

"They are so poor that on rainy nights they have to borrow high wooden clogs and parasols. They cannot afford to buy any. Never staying more than a month at one back-street shelter, they move from place to place or seek new hiding nooks. They wheedle new landlords. They insinuate themselves into the good graces of new neighbors with gifts of cheap wine. They buy their firewood with what little cash they own. Soon the smoke will vanish from their kitchen. They know nothing of the pleasures of moon viewing, nothing of the beauty of snow, nothing of the happiness of the new year. Oh, the ignominy, the misery, the pity of it all!"

FAKE ORACLE

A HANDSOME neatly attired girl came passing by on the main street of Sakata, ringing a cluster of small brass bells. This was a Shinto summons to the townspeople to purify their homes.

87

"Plant a pine tree beside the kitchen," the girl chanted, "and please the god of the stove."

She was a young *miko* attached to an imperial shrine. From beneath her gleaming white robe the folds of a pale green undergarment peeped out at the neckline, and a thin red silk sash of sun-and-moon design was tied at her waist. Her face was only slightly powdered, but her eyebrows were painted jet black. Her long hair rolled down her back and was tied together in midsection with a simple knot.

Yonosuke marveled at her fastidious attire.

"That is rather unusual for a shrine girl," he pointed out to the Sakata inn proprietor. "Truly she must have had quite a bit of experience in some other work. I mean . . . work that calls for an attractive appearance."

"Yes. You have a very discerning eye for such things," the innkeeper said. "She may be a shrine girl, but she can also be an entertainer for the night—that is, if you so desire."

"That I wish!" exclaimed Yonosuke. It rekindled the fire of long-repressed urges. He hurried forward to speak to the girl.

Sure enough, she allowed herself to be invited to a rooming house. There, as Yonosuke tactfully suggested, the girl disrobed herself, revealing to him new feminine beauty in form and lines. He took her to bed and slept with her. When they awoke he presented her with the usual alms people gave to Shinto *miko*.

From the kitchen Yonosuke brought in a flask of sacramental *o-miki* rice wine. They drank it, and the wine made them drunk and the girl began to quote from the Shinto oracle in maudlin fashion.

"Let us forget the divine revelations for today," Yonosuke said.

As he drank in her beauty with his eyes, the suspicion rose strongly in his mind that she might be the sister of the high priest of the Myojin Shrine on Awaji Island—a girl noted far and wide for her loveliness.

"How old are you?" he asked.

"Twenty-one."

Yonosuke's suspicion mounted. As though reading his thoughts, the girl became visibly disturbed.

"You need not be afraid," he said. "This being the tenth month, your eminent brother is no doubt visiting the Izumo Shrine. No one back home will hear about this affair."

Together they set out for the town of Kashima, her destination, in Hitachi Province.

Meanwhile it occurred to Yonosuke that this holy function of spreading Shinto revelations held unique possibilities. It could be made to serve his own purposes, which were anything but divine. He decided to become a shrine oracle himself.

By clever persuasion, for he was gifted with a many-faceted mind and a glib tongue, he got himself ordained at the Kashima Shrine. Thereafter he toured the surrounding districts alone, inspiring hopes and fears in the hearts of the people with bogus predictions. Upon entering the big town of Mito, on the main street he chanted the most ridiculous "revelation" of all:

"Listen, one and all, and you shall hear the Shinto oracle handed down on the twenty-fifth day. The enshrined god of Kashima, defeated in the heavenly ritual by the god Tenjin, has with bristling anger ordered that a divine wind shall blow and that it shall kill all chaste girls between the ages of seventeen and twenty under Tenjin's protection and all wives who, in conformity with Tenjin's decree, remain faithful to their husbands. Truly it is fearful, for the wrath of the frustrated god of Kashima is merciless. For those of you who have cause to fear this divine fury there is but one way of escape. Answer all love letters, and if any man approaches you, be sure to accede to his wishes." After he had thus set the town's wives and girls trembling with fear, he entered an inn with a majestic air.

"Tell me," he said, "where will I find those women who are most likely to abide by the Kashima oracle to save their lives? I propose to help them."

The suspicious innkeeper replied shrewdly: "The lord's edicts here against harlots are very strict. We have no loose women to speak of. However," and he looked askance at Yonosuke, "when one is lonely, there are women called *momi-hiki* at the government granary."

Momi-hiki were women of the servant class who were employed at the granary to hull rice during the busy season. Many of them could be seen in the morning on their way to the rice-hulling establishment.

"The usual way," the innkeeper continued, "is to go up to one of them with a friendly smile and tug at her sleeve. If she responds, well and good. But a woman with a pretty face is more likely than not to snub the libertine. She who yields is bound to be an ugly wench, desired by none. She who looks fairly well attired is sure to have a lover, and it may be indiscreet, if not dangerous, to flirt with her."

At sunset these women were seen walking homeward from the granary with their aprons on, shaking off the bran dust from the lower part of their robes, cracking their knuckles, massaging their stiff arms.

Yonosuke boldly attempted the "sleeve-tugging" trick, but one of them complained about feeling queer in the belly, and he left the town abruptly.

He followed the trail into Iwashiro Province, spreading the same "revelation." Then he headed for the fortress city of Sendai. Here he found the decrees against loose morals even stricter. The famed gay quarters in the shadow of the castle had been destroyed by the hands of the law.

But on the isles of Matsushima and Ojima, where he next tarried, the naive women on wave-swept rocks were all too willing to believe and conform.

Thence Yonosuke proceeded to the Myojin Shrine in the town of Shiogama. At this big shrine he observed a woman in sacred robes performing tea rites with bamboo leaves. She was beautiful and young. He decided to stay. Suavely he approached the chief priest:

"I have come from the Kashima Shrine under instructions to conduct seven days of prayer here and seek divine inspiration."

"Splendid!" the chief priest welcomed him with the utmost warmth.

That gave Yonosuke the desired opportunity to be close to the woman attendant. But she was difficult to approach. While ostensibly performing devotional prayers he paused often, showering her with flattering remarks to insinuate himself into her good graces. She avoided him. He pursued her.

"I must tell you," she said firmly, "that I am a married woman. Please leave me alone."

But that did not deter him.

One evening, upon learning that her husband was a night watchman tied down to his work at the shrine, Yonosuke visited her at her home. He took some gifts dear to the hearts of women, believing they would soften her rigid, impeccable front.

To his amazement, she spurned them. But it was now or never. Stiffly she tried to fight off his sudden, tight embrace. The more she resisted, however, the tighter he clung to her. She felt outraged. Tears of helplessness filled her eyes. Yet she could not summon enough courage to scream for help. Angrily but in a low firm tone she cried:

"Set me free! You are a man utterly without morals— a beast!"

91

That maddened Yonosuke. He pressed closer.

"I don't want you!" he said in a tone rusty with contempt. "I merely gave you a chance to give absolute freedom to your instincts. Many another woman has thanked me for it. . . ."

"Well, I do not. Now let me go."

"Do you think a man would stoop so low as to humble himself before a woman just because she chooses to make a fool of herself? No woman is going to make a fool out of me!"

"Let us not argue," she cried and bit into his flesh. And he yelled with pain.

At this moment her husband, returning from the shrine earlier than usual, heard the commotion in the vestibule. "A burglar!" he thought.

Rushing into the room, he seized the wounded "burglar" from behind and tore him away from his weeping wife. But he found the intruder to be young and defiant, in no mood to make his escape. Desperately he ran into the adjoining kitchen, fetched a thick chopping knife, and took a wide swing at the crouching Yonosuke. The knife sliced off a chunk of flesh and hair from Yonosuke's temple.

Stunned by the attack, Yonosuke felt he was being roped into submission. Horror showed in his eyes as he regained his full senses. Blood was trickling down his face. With a terrific effort, kicking and wriggling, he managed to struggle free. Then with a final blow that sent the outraged woman's husband sprawling to the floor, he staggered to the door and fled into the night.

RETRIBUTION

"THAT is utter nonsense; you must be a fake!" Yonosuke
had exclaimed, half incredulously, half in derision. But
that had happened last year, in the twelfth month. That
had been his answer to the warning of a soothsayer named
Abe-no-Geki. The soothsayer had said:

"You had better mend your ways, Yonosuke. This
being the twenty-eighth year of your life, you will meet
with dire misfortune. Acting on a sudden impulse, you
will make love to another man's wife, and your life will
be endangered. You may escape alive, but you will wear
a scar forever."

And now, as Yonosuke felt the wound on his temple
where a chunk of hair had been uprooted, marring his
looks, he could only marvel at the fearful fulfillment of
the soothsayer's prophecy. Upon further introspection,
he became vaguely aware that this might be *retribution*.

As he trudged hastily along a hilly trail in Shinano
Province, Yonosuke hid the wound with a kerchief hood,
turning his face away when he met travelers on the way,
ashamed of that telltale brand on his head.

Now the famous Usui peak was far behind, and there
stood before him the mountain town of Oiwake. Here
Yonosuke spent the night at an inn. He had tried once
more to put all thoughts of women out of his mind, but
the entertainers of this rustic community intrigued him
anew. Not that they were charming or attractive. He
could see that these peasant-born wenches had been
brought up as tillers of valley soil and reapers of swamp
reeds. Their dark chapped hands and faces had been
sedulously polished, nursed, and powdered up. Common

cotton robes had been discarded for colorful silks and thin translucent linens. They must have waited on travelers schooled in their trade, for they seemed to have acquired the rudiments of entertaining at table and of filling delicate wine cups with a certain measure of grace. "Tolerable," thought Yonosuke, but they didn't suit his fastidious taste.

At dawn the next day Yonosuke resumed his travel along the hill-country trail. Suddenly, while rounding a corner at a lonely spot among forested ridges, he found the trail blocked by a police barrier. Grim-looking officers of the law were halting all travelers, both ways, and subjecting them to a grueling inspection.

"Stop," an officer addressed Yonosuke, "and submit to inspection. We are searching for a wounded man."

Consternation seized Yonosuke. *He* was a wounded man, hurt in a disgraceful affair.

"Why," he asked, "if I may be so bold as to inquire, are you looking for a wounded man?"

"Because," the officer replied, "there has been a night robbery in a village called Kayahara up in the hills west of here. The robber not only stole goods from a shop but he also killed a hired man while trying to escape. The tussle awakened the shop proprietor, and he quickly grabbed a knife and attacked the killer. He wounded him in several places, perhaps on the head. But the killer ran off into the night, and the shop proprietor couldn't say what he looked like or where on his body he had inflicted the wounds. Barriers have been set up throughout this district to round up all suspicious-looking men."

"I see."

"Take off your hood." Reluctantly Yonosuke obeyed.

The officer looked at Yonosuke's temple, said harshly: "Explain that wound on your head. If you can offer a decent excuse for it, well and good. If not, we cannot let you go until this investigation is over."

94

There was no getting out of it for Yonosuke. Explain the truth he must, if he was to avoid suspicion for a crime that he had not committed. He made a clean breast of the affair with the shrine woman and her watchman husband in the town of Shiogama, in another province.

The officer glared at him. "Why you . . . you are a scoundel! *Your* crime calls for a separate investigation. In you go to the village jail!"

And into the village jail Yonosuke was pushed, unceremoniously.

Horrified but submitting helplessly to the strange workings of justice, he felt at last the humiliating lash of retribution on mind and body, cumulative and inexorable. Remembering his past misdeeds, he realized with misery and fear in his heart that this was not vicarious punishment but real and just.

When prison fare was brought to him in his cell, Yonosuke contemplated it with utter loathing. It was food fit only for dogs. The wretchedness of it all filled his eyes with tears until his eyelids became bloated flesh. But eat the food he must, if he was to keep himself alive. He felt so nauseated that he was not even aware of his cellmates leering at him from a corner.

Then a raucous chorus, sounding like a mean threat, came from that corner: "Hey there, newcomer. We are going to toss you around in this cell. Initiation into prison manners, you know."

A huge rough-looking man with long grizzly hair and eyes glinting like those of a beast of prey came forward and seized him by the shoulders. The next instant Yonosuke felt himself being tossed up and down, hurled here and there unmercifully, his breath stopping and coming out in painful gasps. He thought he would die, but he fought against the temptation to desire such a merciful end. Finally he found himself free, panting on the floor.

"Now," came the threatening chorus again, "seek our

friendship by singing a song or doing a little dance for us."

Blindly obeying that command, Yonosuke staggered to his feet and sang the first few lines of a bawdy *numeri-bushi,* then popular among the teahouses in Kyoto. But his rough audience only looked on glumly. Thereupon Yonosuke switched to a song-and-dance act, a lively piece that had originated in the province of Ise. This they liked. They applauded noisily. He became their friend.

Thereafter Yonosuke became accustomed to this hell in a prison cell. He no longer minded the hard floor matting on which he sat. He slept together with his cellmates and talked freely with them.

One day, in frank camaraderie, they confessed to him: "We made a living in the Fuseya forest by robbing travelers, sometimes killing those we robbed. But none of us committed the crime which the officers of the law are now investigating. We got thrown in here anyhow when they found out what we had been doing in the forest."

Sunset brought melancholy to the cell; and daylight, loneliness. So they made a *sugoroku* board on which to roll the dice, playing the game with zestful determination as a way to forgetfulness. Ironically enough, there were certain expressive phrases used when moving the pieces strategically from square to square. "Kill it!" was one. "Lock it up!" was another. All too suggestively, these pithy phrases reminded them of their own unpleasant fate. There was no escape.

Yonosuke said with laughing irony: "In ancient China, it is said that the Princess Yang Kuei-fei and her lover prince also played this game of *sugoroku* in a prison cell. Think of it!"

But the poetic humor of it was lost on his audience.

While gazing at the small window-like opening in the wall that afforded a glimpse into the adjoining cell, he observed a gentle-seeming woman.

"Who is she?" Yonosuke asked.

"That," replied one of his cellmates, "is a woman who left her husband, whom she detested. She got thrown into the cell next to ours for desertion. Something very unpleasant must have happened to her."

Instantly Yonosuke's sympathy was aroused. He made light ink with the cobwebs gathered from the ceiling corners and composed a tender letter for that anonymous woman. This he passed to her through the opening and received a reply:

"Yes, let us meet again in more pleasant circumstances. That is, if good fortune should ever favor us with life beyond our jail terms."

Late at night, while the others were snoring, the two crept to the opening and there, bitten by lice and fleas, they whispered confidences to each other, regretting at the same time the futility of it all.

ATONEMENT

SOME months later the central feudal government in Edo held grand memorial rites at court for one of the late and lamented shogunal rulers. Temple bells tolled throughout the city. Incense was burned at the altar, and sutras were chanted by purple-robed priests.

It was a time when even the tyrannous rulers felt a little softening of the heart. For life upon earth is short, and the rewards of the hereafter are at best uncertain. Charitableness was in order. Thus, by way of propitiating the Great Arbiter enthroned in paradise, the Edo cabinet issued an edict of general amnesty, emptying the nation's jails.

Thanks to this token of forgiveness, Yonosuke, who

might have been beheaded or left to rot in his cell, tasted freedom again, out in the cold autumnal fields. He crossed the wide but shallow Chikuma River, carrying on his back the woman he had befriended in the cell adjoining his.

As the shadows of night fell, a hailstorm struck the district. While seeking shelter with his precious burden beneath the eaves of an abandoned thatched-roof hut, Yonosuke saw the melting hailstones, now muddy-looking from the immemorial dirt absorbed by the roof, dripping to the ground like brown bean curd. The thought of bean curd reminded him of food, or rather the lack of it. Poignantly he remembered a bit of dialogue in *The Tale of Ise* which said: "When a man is hungry, anything looks delicious: bean-curd balls or what have you."

"You must be hungry too," he said sympathetically to the woman on his back.

"Yes, and I am wet and cold and miserable."

There was an old handcart filled with cut grass at Yonosuke's feet.

"It is dry here," he said, lowering the woman into this sheltered soft-cushioned receptacle. "Rest here for a while. I'll go down to the village and fetch some food."

Kind villagers obliged him with boiled millet and eggplant pickles wrapped in green leaves. Thankful for this gift, Yonosuke started to hurry back to the woman. Now he felt misgivings for her safety; he should not have left her alone in the dark. His worries were justified, for some two *cho* from the hut he heard her scream and call his name. Running back the rest of the way, he saw a group of four or five rough men attacking the woman with bamboo spears and deer-threatening bows.

"You shameless, sulky wench!" one of them, apparently her husband, was reviling her. "Why didn't you come straight home when you were freed from jail? Who did you tie up with and where is he taking you? Answer me! Don't you know you have disgraced your parents, your brothers and sisters? You . . . you hateful, ungrateful wretch! We might as well kill you, here and now."

Yonosuke sprang into their midst. "Stop! She's not to blame."

The men glared at him with instant suspicion. "You must be the man who seduced her!"

No sooner said than they crowded around him and pushed and knocked him into a jasmine thicket. The impact stunned Yonosuke. Gasping for breath, he felt his consciousness leaving him. But the wet branches in the thicket showered him with raindrops and his senses returned.

After a while he rose painfully to his feet and said apologetically: "I was wrong. I won't take her with me."

But there was no one there. While he himself lay in the thicket in a state of semicoma, the men had left with the woman. Only the handcart remained. Perhaps, believing they had killed the seducer, the woman had been urged to return home for reconciliation.

The empty cart reminded him poignantly of the wistful figure that had lain on the pile of grass. He mused, mixing poetry with his habitual mood: "Tonight would have been ours together, for the very first time. On a bed of jewels, like the moon against the star-studded sky, or the white crystals against the soft green earth. Gently I would have covered her with my robe. And her thoughts were gentle too, I know. And she knew mine also. And now . . . now she is gone. Gone, without my even knowing how she looked beneath her clothes. Oh, the sadness of it!"

As he stumbled away, he found a boxwood comb she had left behind.

"A keepsake for me," he thought. The odor of hair oil on it, evidence of long and constant use, seemed to him to call up an acute memory of the woman. "With this, perhaps, I could have our fortunes told."

Further down the field, as Yonosuke groped in the shadows of a rocky ridge, he saw a hunter passing by with a pheasant hen dangling from a gun on his shoulder. The hunter was talking aloud to himself: "How frail indeed is life. . . . I can well imagine the mate of this pheasant crying over his loss."

That reminded Yonosuke of his own loss, and he felt rather distraught.

For a whole week thereafter he roamed the wild district, searching for the woman by day and sleeping in the fields by night. On the evening of the twenty-ninth of the tenth month, while wandering about with a weary heart, he came upon a field of pampas grass, far from any human habitation. Presently he saw a tiny bonfire and, in the dim light, a number of gravestones in a row. Pausing in the shadow of a bead tree, he wondered: "What kind of people lie buried here? Surely there must be some whose death is being deeply mourned."

Then he saw a fresh grave marker made of bamboo, and his sympathy grew. He thought: "Whoever has been laid to rest there must have died suddenly of some awful disease—smallpox, maybe."

Suddenly, rising beside the fresh marker were two crouching figures, peasants evidently, digging up a coffin! Horrified, Yonosuke rushed forward and demanded reproachfully: "What are you two trying to do?"

The grave robbers, caught unawares and visibly embarrassed, refused to commit themselves.

"Answer me!" Yonosuke demanded, unsheathing his sword. "If you don't come out with the whole truth, I'll drive this sword into both of you and bury you in there."

Trembling, with hands in the attitude of prayer, the elder of the two men begged: "Forgive us . . . please. We are poor and desperate. We did not know which way to turn. Then we found out that a beautiful young woman had just been buried here. We . . . we dug her up to get her hair and fingernails."

"You beasts! What profit do you make by mutilating the dead like that?"

"We . . . we can sell the hair and fingernails in the gay quarters of the city."

Astonished at so base a motive, yet somehow curious, Yonosuke said: "What possible use can the buyers put them to?"

"It is this way. When courtesans pledge their fidelity to a favorite patron, they usually clip off strands of their hair and fingernails too and let the favorite keep them as a kind of memento. . . ."

"Yes, I know, but what has that got to do with dead women's hair?"

"Well, there are usually many other patrons whom the courtesans must please in order to keep up their popularity. So they buy clipped hair and fingernails from traders and pass them off as their own. The poor men don't know the difference. After all, it's a very secret affair. Those men, not knowing they have been fooled, slip the stuff into their charm holders. It is all so foolish, but then . . . it means money, so we . . . we planned to cater to that trade."

"Such deception," Yonosuke said dryly, "is the first I have heard. Anyhow," he added sternly, "you cannot rob graves, even to stave off starvation. It is an unforgivable sin. Cover up that coffin intact and bury it again . . . reverently now. And while you are at it, ask the forgiveness of the dead."

He leaned over and peered into the coffin. To his utter amazement and horror, he saw that the beautiful young woman lying in it was the one he had been searching for.

So they had killed her after all! And they had buried her in the wasteland here. The sadness, the pity of it brought tears to Yonosuke's eyes. Contrite now, he bent down and cried to the corpse: "This . . . this must be heaven's retribution—to meet again in this terrible way. It was all my fault. If I had not taken you with me from the jail, this would never have happened to you. Oh, forgive me, forgive me."

And in the fullness of his grief he flung himself down on the open coffin and wept. Strangely enough, he thought he saw the body open its eyes for a moment, smile, and return to the stillness of death.

Overcome by emotions brought on by self-reproach, he sobbed: "I . . . I have lived to be twenty-nine. I have nothing else to live for."

Deathly pale, he turned his drawn sword upon himself. Quick as a flash, however, the two grave robbers snatched it away from him. He was too overwrought to offer any resistance. They returned the coffin to its grave and covered it up reverently. Then they took the grief-stricken Yonosuke home to their hut.

TORTURED SOUL

THE HUMAN body is a borrowed article composed of elements drawn from five basic things: earth, water, fire, wind, and air. We simply return it to Emma-dai-o when that Prince of Hell comes to fetch it back. That is all there is to life. Or so, at least, Yonosuke mused. "For thirty years," he thought, "I have inhabited this borrowed thing, and it has all been hardly more than a dream. Let the future be what it may."

But this made Yonosuke more restless than ever, without roots, without a serious aim. Then, casually enough, he thought of his old-time schoolmate who, he now remembered, was reported to be living at a place called Sagae, in Mogami Province. Weary of heart, he felt the need of a good man's companionship. He turned his steps toward that distant village.

They had parted nineteen years ago, but his friend remembered him distinctly. Genuinely happy to meet again—so happy that they wept together—the two immediately talked of old times. It may be that their friendship remained pure because it was untouched by the sordid experiences that had marked Yonosuke's own life. As proof of the man's purity of thought, he showed Yonosuke a talisman of the goddess of mercy—said to have been the work of the Abbot Jikaku—which Yonosuke himself had given to him at the temple in Nakazawa as a pledge of friendship. The man had kept it firmly on his person, with undying faith, and Yonosuke was deeply affected.

This man was a samurai, but his ties with his former lord were no longer effective. His income had ceased. For all practical purposes he was a *ronin,* an unemployed warrior. He was so poor that he had no one to take care of his home. All he had was a portable cooking stove and a teakettle. For firewood he waited for the morrow's dead leaves to fall. Aside from some brown taros scattered on the floor of the kitchen, there was not even a bean-curd strainer. A broken fan held together with a piece of paper string, a paste spreader, a sprig of red pepper, and a piece of straw rope hung on the wall.

Yonosuke asked: "How did you manage to live during these many years?"

"I dealt in spiders to catch flies with. They are quite the thing in Edo nowadays, you know. I also carve toy halberds for children. They sell for one *mon* each. Ah, well, you have been so good as to come all the way here to see me. We must drink together. . . ."

Hiding an empty jug in the folds of his robe, the samurai was about to set out for the village wineshop when Yonosuke stopped him. Yonosuke knew that there could be no money in the house to buy saké with and that saké was a luxury his friend and host could ill afford.

"I have traveled a great distance without stopping, and I am tired tonight," Yonosuke said by way of dissuading him. "Let's go to bed early. Tomorrow we shall resume our talk of old times."

He lay down on the mat, using a whetstone for pillow. The samurai, embarrassed but taking the hint, fetched a wooden clapper and a bow from an old wicker basket.

"There are badgers running wild in the hills here. I shall go and catch some. They will make a fine feast for us."

So saying, the samurai went out into the night.

Yonosuke began to doze. But the night was chilly, even under a blanket, and he could not get warmed up. He was still tossing around, on the fringe of sleep, when a strange figure came crawling down the steps from the upper floor. The apparition had a woman's head, the legs and claws of a huge bird, and the scaly body of a fish. In a weird voice that sounded like waves crashing against rocks, the apparition said: "Have you forgotten me, Yonosuke-sama? How could you? I, Koman, the woman who kept shop in Ishigaki-cho selling carp, will take revenge upon you now for what you did to me."

Yonosuke sprang to his feet, seized the sword lying beside his pillow, and ran it through the apparition. The apparition vanished.

The next instant another woman, with the body and beak of a huge bird of prey, attacked him from behind. "I am the spirit of Ohatsu, daughter of Kichisuke of Kobiki-cho. You deceived me after pledging me your eternal love, so I chose death. Now *you* shall die!"

Yonosuke swung around and ran his sword through this apparition too.

A third monster, elongated, with the face of a woman and hands and feet resembling a maple tree, sprang upon him from a corner, and her words came to Yonosuke like the whine of a whirlwind: "I am the wife of Jirokichi. You lured me to Mt. Takao to see the maples, pledging me your love. For you I gave up the man to whom I had been devoted all my life. When you left me it was, to me, like swallowing poison. My husband refused to take me back. So I *did* take poison. You *do* remember me. Oh, yes, you do!"

The monster bit into Yonosuke's flesh. Desperately he grappled with it and threw it to the floor in a furious heave. But by this time he felt groggy, exhausted, and bewildered. He thought his end was coming.

Turning, he saw still another vision. This one swooped down upon him from the ceiling: the head of a woman and a body in the shape of a huge twisted straw rope. Yonosuke had barely enough time to snatch up his sword. "I, a nun preparing for heavenly duties in a temple in Daigo," shrieked the vision, "was hoodwinked by you into renouncing my vows, and you shall pay for it now. I won't let you get away from here alive. I am going to kill you!"

With that the vision flew straight for Yonosuke's throat. But in the nick of time he stepped aside and stabbed the twisting menace.

"This is the end," thought Yonosuke. He went down on his knees, gasping, trembling, and penitent. Renouncing all evil thoughts, he began to pray to the Lord Buddha for deliverance.

Some hours later his samurai friend and host returned from the hills. He found the matted floor spattered with blood and Yonosuke lying unconscious in the middle of it. "Oh, how horrible!" he shouted.

He spoke into Yonosuke's ears and shook him back to consciousness.

When Yonosuke had regained enough of his senses to think and speak coherently, he told his friend about the ghosts that had assailed and tormented him.

"Impossible!" cried the samurai.

But for all its obvious incredibility the samurai felt awakening suspicion. Could it be that the badgers he had chased in the hills had crawled into his house to perform those tricks? For badgers were known to have the power to bewitch human beings. But then he'd had a talisman of the goddess of mercy with him. And that led him on to consider another possibility. It must be spontaneous black magic, he decided.

He crept upstairs to where Yonosuke had left his few belongings. And there, sure enough, littered on the floor were the four amatory pledges which Yonosuke had induced those women to write and sign when he seduced them. They were torn to bits except for those portions that bore their seals.

Verily, thought the samurai grimly, one should never trifle with seeming trifles. One should never persuade women to swear to their love in writing. There is no fury like a woman deceived—especially *after* she is driven to suicide.

PRICE OF CHIVALRY

ONCE again Yonosuke was in Edo, the shogun's capital. Refreshed but aimless, he found security at last—and a new preoccupation—as the protégé of a wealthy, chivalrous man about town called Token Gombei. How he did it must be laid down to similarity of interests, tastes, and habits, and Yonosuke was never known to have passed up an opportunity.

Token Gombei was an amiable district leader, and he had many followers. There might have been rivals too, and enemies. And chivalry was a new privilege, a new indulgence, a new vogue. To have dashing young men in one's camp, with money to spend—money to achieve popularity, to help the needy, to dispense pleasure and the spirit of camaraderie—was a rising sign of the times.

Yonosuke looked handsome enough in his brilliant new robe. In order to hide the scar on his temple his long hair was necessarily fixed in a style different from the prevailing mode. And that made him a dandyish standout in any crowd. Altogether, one might say, an attractive figure that instantly caught the eye—and perhaps the heart too —of a passing woman, innocent or sophisticated.

While strolling in this manner on Sakai-machi he paused in front of a fashionable theater. The smooth-tongued barker at the entrance was clapping a pair of boards and shouting: "Here, here . . . here is where you can see and hear the only true *Tango joruri.*" He was announcing the performance of a ballad-drama that had originated in the province of Tango. "Come one, come all! The show is just about to begin."

Yonosuke bought a ticket and was about to enter the playhouse when a young girl looking like a maidservant accosted him from behind: "*Moshi moshi,* there is a woman who wants to speak to you privately."

He could think of no woman in this section of the town who might wish to converse with him, privately or otherwise.

"Who is she and what does she want to see me about?"

"She is waiting for you there." The girl avoided his question and directed him to a woman standing a few paces away on the street.

As Yonosuke approached wonderingly, this second woman said in a whisper: "I must beg your pardon for disturbing you in this way. I am a maid in waiting to a wealthy widow. My dowager mistress has been highly impressed by your physical appearance—so strong and handsome. She has a favor to ask of you. Only today she discovered the one who is regarded as her family enemy and on whom she must take revenge. She must kill that one. But being a woman, she cannot do it alone. She craves your assistance for the duel. Won't you please help her so that her mind can be set at ease?"

It was an appeal to his sense of chivalry, and to perform such a task was implicit in his new role. Besides, he could not very well ignore or spurn a request so desperately put to him, even by a stranger, even though he was not of the warrior caste and the enemy might be.

"This is a crowded place," he said. "Let us go somewhere near where we can have some privacy and discuss the whole thing."

He led the two women to a nearby tearoom. "Wait here for a while. I shall be back shortly."

Hurriedly Yonosuke returned to his quarters, put on armor for the sword duel, tied a white sweatband around his temples, picked up his sword, examined the sharpness of its edge, and in a few minutes more was back at the tearoom.

"Now tell me all about it," he said.

But the older woman, the rich widow's maid in waiting, seemed in no hurry to give Yonosuke the full details: who the widow was, where she lived, where he could meet her, the name of the family enemy, where that enemy was likely to be found, and for what particular offense the widow must kill him. Instead, she placed before Yonosuke a small brocade bag containing a mysterious object.

"Open it, please," she said. "When you see what it contains, I am sure you will understand what I mean." Then she hid her face behind her flowing uplifted sleeve.

Yonosuke untied the silken strings of the bag and opened it wide. His eyes bulged out in amazement. What he saw in there was an implement carved in an unmistakable form. Anger brought the blood to his face.

"You have deliberately deceived me!" he stormed. "I refuse to be caught in your web of intrigue. Go home and tell your mistress she can roast in hell for all I care. I am ready and willing to help anyone in jeopardy, even at the risk of my own life. But it must be for an honest cause, honestly approached. You have tried to make a fool of me. And I detest lies!"

Now the woman clung to him in mingled shame and appeal. "I . . . I can well understand your anger and distrust. But please believe me. My mistress is not to blame. This is my own scheme. She does not know about it. Still . . . still that thing in there is really her enemy. She asked me to buy it for her—a menace to her own life. Please . . . please help her conquer it." Yonosuke made no move to draw his sword on her, as perhaps he might or should have done. Again he was in torment.

The woman saw the hesitation, coolly disengaged herself, rummaged in her mirror bag. She slipped a number of gold coins to him. "We shall expect you, then, on the evening of the sixteenth of the seventh month."

She left the widow's address on his lap and departed hastily with her younger companion, leaving Yonosuke in a state of angry bewilderment.

"A male concubine!" he cursed to himself. But he knew he would keep that appointment. That was chivalry too.

NOTHING TO TELL

THERE was a man in Edo called Musan—a very, very rich man. The money was a legacy handed down to him through seven generations of shrewd, parsimonious ancestors. Something must have gone wrong—perhaps the gods were angry—when the eighth generation was born. For there was nothing clever or stingy about Musan. He excelled only as a playboy who knew how to spend the huge fortune lavishly. But not even he, play as he would, could make a dent in that glittering pile. Money begets money, and Musan's inherited gold kept on multiplying.

By day he went on merrymaking picnics, excursions, or flower-viewing expeditions on river boats, in mountains, in parks, depending on the season. To make these outings really merry, he took along with him a huge retinue of men and women entertainers. The nights he spent at teahouses, drinking and amusing himself with the whirling antics of dancers keeping time to the rhythmic drumbeats of a popular Kaga song. These lasted until the small hours of the morning. Apparently he rarely slept.

To him—to this fabulously rich "good timer"—Yonosuke, the much traveled expert on promiscuous women, their ways, and their specialties, was dispatched by the chivalrous Token Gombei as friend and confidant. It was Yonosuke's function to recommend new sources of pleasure, but he was getting a bit homesick for his home town.

"I should like," he told Musan, "to pay a visit to Kyoto. You have not seen the dancing maids of Kyoto yet, have you?"

"No, I have not. But wait," Musan worked up an enthusiasm for the as-yet-unseen dancing maids, "I shall go with you. Besides, I should like to explore the city of Kyoto and see for myself what it has to offer in the way of amusing a man with time and money on his hands."

And so, with the management of Musan's worldly goods entrusted to competent and faithful retainers during his absence from Edo, the two started out for the imperial capital.

111

Upon reaching Kyoto they secured a spacious house in front of the Chion-in Temple and hired a maid to do the housework by day. At night she could be a free companion.

Here Musan gathered ten dancing maids, at Yonosuke's suggestion, paying them one *bu* a day. They danced for him.

"Tell me about these girls," Musan said. "I am interested in them as representing a special group or profession—how they are brought up and trained."

Yonosuke explained: "They are first chosen for their natural-born beauty. From early childhood they are carefully brought up like boys—in their mode of living, their habits, their postures. Then from about the age of eleven to fifteen they are allowed to wait even on women guests at entertainment houses. After that the forepart of their heads is shaved and they are trained to imitate male voices. They wear the silk-lined *hakama* and walk along the streets in quite a pompous fashion. It is deliberately assumed. For what reason I don't know. Their feet are encased in sandals with thick straps, and their heads are covered with wide basket-shaped straw hats, the sort worn by strolling flute players. Usually they are accompanied by footmen or sandal bearers. Quite a sight, I assure you."

"And as they grow older?" Musan asked.

"For that," said Yonosuke, "we must rely on the confession of one who has graduated from their class. Let us ask the old grandmother who brought these girls here."

The white-haired old woman smiled obligingly. "As they grow older," she said, "they are called *ai-no-onna*— 'in-between' girls, you see—neither teahouse servers nor courtesans. Later they almost always end up as wives of masters of assignation houses. Still later they become simply old hags like me, useless and neglected. One must have youth to amount to anything in this trade."

Yonosuke said: "Tell us what you know about these assignation houses."

Musan urged: "Yes, you must have learned a lot about their secrets in your day."

"Well,"—grandma was not altogether reluctant to divulge what she knew—"there is this place called Snow Retreat with a Secret Passage. It is on Shijo-dori. There a widow of good family makes her home with her chambermaids and a number of other servants. She was once a dancing maid, and she married a rich man who died much too early in life. Men of wealth or position go there to do things with women which they cannot very well do freely and at leisure in other entertainment houses. Whenever someone happens along from whom it might be discreet to hide their identities, or if a minion of the law should come snooping around, a convenient secret passage leads the patrons out into the open without anyone discovering their flight.

"Then there is a place called Secret Closet. There, too, you will find a secret passage. Men patrons are first led into their very private rooms. Their women friends join them later.

"At the Raised Mats there is a hidden lane beneath the private rooms, and when things look bad for the patrons, for one reason or another, they can easily slip down unnoticed and out into the street, and breathe a sigh of relief.

"Also, at the Love Robes for Pretended Sleep there is a small tunnel-like room. A dowager's robe is provided here, together with a great cotton hood and a tasseled rosary. This room is for widows. A male patron is first led into it. He puts on the robe and hood and pretends to go to sleep. When no one is seen in the hallway, the widow slips gently in.

"A very beautiful woman is made up as a Buddhist nun in black robes at the Enticement to the Future

World. She stands at the door and calls to a likely-looking customer passing by: 'This is where I live. Won't you come in for a brief visit?' Then she as much as drags the indifferent man in.

"The technique at Sign of Bedazzlement is somewhat different. A man who wishes to keep a secret appointment with a woman ties a small red kerchief to the front doorway curtain of the tearoom and waits for her inside. A woman comes along, observes the sign, and pretends to have become suddenly ill. 'Kindly let me rest inside . . . until this dizzy spell is over,' she asks the proprietor, and she is ushered all too eagerly into the house.

"There are a number of other establishments, some forty-eight in all. Each has a special secret contrivance. Mostly they are in the trade to provide a meeting place for women who, for some reason or other, want to have secret affairs with men."

Oh, what a dreadul story! Hide the truth from innocent wives and daughters! To them we say: There is nothing to tell—nothing to tell.

PASSING SCENE IN KYOTO

As MIGHT have been expected, vast changes have taken place in Kyoto, the floral capital. The throngs on Shijo-dori and Gojo-dori are now thick throughout the day. Even the view of Higashiyama has been altered. The Chomeiji Temple has been transferred there. The river banks have been lined with rock walls, with houses strung along them to a place called Makuzu-ga-hara, which Priest Jichin once celebrated in a verse.

While sitting on a bench outside a tearoom called Namiya, Musan, the millionaire visitor from Edo, mused:

114

"After all, the only women with whom I should like to have love affairs are the maidservants of this region around Kyoto and Osaka."

Suddenly he pointed to a long line of some twenty-five women walking past some distance away and exclaimed: "Look! Aren't they pretty? They are so different from country girls."

They were all of about the same age, wearing outfits bewitchingly similar: pale green inner garment and dappled purple robe silver-embroidered with the word *ho* that sparkled at five spots, and a lavender sash tied at the back, its edges weighted with lead. Their hair was tied with colored paper strings, and their faces were protected by black satin hoods. Nevertheless their necklines, white as snow, were clearly visible and alluring. On their heads rested wide-brimmed wicker hats, while their feet were encased in red-and-white *tabi* socks and straw sandals. And trailing them was an escort of several men and women.

"And who might they be?" asked Musan.

"They are harlots," Yonosuke replied, "who are at the beck and call of a palace here. A lady palace official is said to be in the group, but she is difficult to identify. Every day these women go on a picnic like this, to enjoy the view of the Higashiyama range. Rather odd and whimsical, I think."

"No, very charming indeed," Musan commented. "An actor called Matsumoto Nazaemon who specializes in female impersonations once told me he slept with one of these palace harlots. Anyhow, it seems to me far better to have you, an expert about these things, to get someone with whom one can have a good time right away, rather than see, hear, or dream about women who are beyond one's reach." So saying, Musan ordered a female clerk from a fan shop to bring samples of the then fashionable paper handkerchiefs.

He looked over the submitted samples and frowned. "No," he said, "these may serve one's purpose on rainy days or when visiting the Koya Monastery, but after seeing the sort of things that are used in Kyoto, one cannot be satisfied with such shoddy material."

In the end Musan told Yonosuke: "We might as well pay a visit to the Shimabara gay quarters."

Thereupon a man called Zenkichi, who was also well versed in such matters, said with what seemed like overweening self-confidence: "I am sure even Yonosuke-sama is a novice in the gay quarters. Why don't you two men come with me, do as I do, and emulate my ways? I can show you a few tricks."

Complying gracefully with his suggestion, both Yonosuke and Musan set out for Shimabara, with Zenkichi leading. They were all big handsome men, accompanied by two youthful servants: Zenkichi's traveling-box bearer and a personal manservant. Lifting high the hem of their robes, they paraded into the gay district like dandies.

It was the sixteenth of the first month, and the annual exhibition and sale of dolls was in full swing. Every courtesan and prostitute was happily buying dolls priced at from ten to fifteen *ryo* each, which proved to be embarrassing to their patrons for the day, who had to provide the money. Curiously enough, even such droll grimacing dolls as Toroku, Kensai, and Mugima for once stood out conspicuously and were eagerly bought.

It seemed that Zenkichi, now in his most vigorous age, possessed a quality unknown to men that attracted women. The story was that a lesser courtesan in the Yoshiwara district of Edo once fell deeply in love with him. People talked about their love affair, and the courtesan, determined to perform some devotional feat which other women would hesitate to do, is said to have seen him off to the Great Gate early one morning, barefoot in the softly falling snow and holding aloft a parasol for him until her arm ached. It was a truly unprecedented act, and it became the talk of the town. The courtesan's employer, knowing that such gossip would hurt his business, remonstrated with her for this unseemly exhibition of devotion to one particular patron. Yet he could do nothing to separate the two lovers. In fact, the courtesan became more and more attached to Zenkichi.

By now Zenkichi was well known in practically all of the country's gay districts. But apparently not yet in Shimabara. Pausing in front of the Marutaya teahouse, he told the servant carrying his traveling box to put it down. Then, sitting on the box, he peered into the interior of the Marutaya and saw a number of pretty courtesans drinking saké all by themselves. Soon one of these courtesans, Sekishu by name, emptied her cup, called her *kamuro*—her little girl attendant—and instructed her: "Go out there and offer that stranger a drink or two with my compliments."

Zenkichi gracefully accepted the cup and drank two cupfuls, then dried the cup and returned it, as was the custom. "Thank you," he said.

Next he took out from the box on which he was sitting a six-stringed, ebony-necked samisen, handed it to the girl, and said: "Please offer this to the gracious Tayu-sama with my compliments." Then he ordered his servant: "Sing, Detchi!"

As the servant began to sing a passage from "Rosai," the courtesan Sekishu played the accompaniment on the proffered samisen. The singing voice was beautiful, and so was the accompaniment—perfectly matched, in fact. All the lesser courtesans inside the Marutaya, impressed by the whole proceeding, praised Sekishu for her discovery. The upshot was that Zenkichi was invited by them to go inside. The women all but pawed him with affectionate attention and canceled their engagements with other patrons so as to spend the day with him. There was no reason indeed why Zenkichi should object to such favored treatment.

Yonosuke, looking on silently, felt chagrined by the fact that even second-rate courtesans had failed to notice *him*. He told himself, if with a touch of envy not unmixed with hurt pride, but with confidence in himself: "I am not the sort to dally with women by playing up to them, no matter what happens. Some day I'll make women come to me of their own accord, without my putting on an act. This isn't the end by any means."

SUDDEN WEALTH

FROM the depths of a building on a narrow street in Kyoto came the tinkling sound of gold coins being scooped up and weighed on a *tembin* scale. "It has a vulgar ring," Yonosuke thought, quite without envy. He told himself: "No matter how much money I had, I would never be such a miser as to hoard it. I would spend it beautifully. Indeed, I would make all the courtesans in the country roll their eyes in wonder. Were I to lift my finger to summon but one of them, ten would come to me ecstatically at once."

But his conscience disturbed him. He reconsidered: "My father, however, is determined never to see me again. I cannot hate him for that, even slightly. The evil things people have said about me have come to my ears too, and I feel their scornful accusations to the very marrow of my bones. Perhaps ... with due humility ... I should retire into a mountain hut and, by practicing abstinence there, overcome these worldly temptations."

In this penitent mood Yonosuke thought of the hermit

118

who lived in the province of Kishu, on the desolate banks of the Otonashi River. This man too, he had heard, had dissipated his life on women, finally turning to the Buddhist faith in order to rehabilitate himself physically and spiritually. "Yes," Yonosuke decided, "I should seek the guidance of that living saint."

With this good intention he set out for the hermit's hut one day, passing from one coastal village in Senshu to another—from Sano to Kayoji to Gada. These were fishing hamlets noted for the loose morals of wives and daughters of fishermen while the menfolk were out at sea. They all imitated the prevailing city fashion by wearing purple cotton hoods. That made them appear incongruous in these rustic surroundings. No one seemed to censure them for their promiscuous habits. When their menfolk returned from the sea, these erring women stood up the family oars against their homes as a prearranged warning signal to male visitors from the cities.

Toward evening Yonosuke reached the shrine of the goddess of Awashima. Here he devoutly said his prayers. Before him stretched the Yura-no-To Sea, and he recalled how he had once read a poem,

> Lo, the boatman's oar pauses here,
> Crossing Yura-no-To Sea,

suggesting to himself that he had not been the first to feel *mono-no-aware,* the sadness of things.

Like the boatman, he decided to pause on his journey along this coast. But that inevitably stirred up a chain of complications. Within a day or so the profligate wives and daughters sought him out clandestinely. Rivalry for his company, jealousy, recriminations marred an otherwise pleasant sojourn. Determined to remain an ascetic, he called them together to an inn and treated them to a feast by way of restoring general harmony. There was much drinking and telling of gay stories. Then he invited them to a boating excursion on the sea. The merrymaking continued on a number of rowboats gliding side by side.

Unfortunately it was the end of the sixth month, and menacing clouds quickly gathered. Before the boats could put back to shore the storm broke. Rain fell in heavy drops, lightning flashed, the thunder rolled. Frightened occupants of the boats pressed their navels as a counteracting spell. Desperately they prayed for deliverance from imminent destruction. But the spell failed to work. A fearful gale now blew up from the south. Mountainous waves swept the boats to no one knew where or swallowed them up. Yonosuke's boat, buffeted about for some two hours, crashed ashore at a place called Fukei-no-Ura.

Thoroughly weary and nauseated, Yonosuke fell unconscious on the sandy beach. He might have perished there but for a lone passer-by poking around in the semi-darkness for flotsam and jetsam.

"A human!" cried the driftwood picker.

Under his vigorous ministrations Yonosuke came tiredly back to life. He could remember only one thing while hovering between life and death: that he heard the faint, ghostly cry of a crane.

The driftwood picker helped him along the shoreline until they reached the border of Senshu. By this time Yonosuke felt strong enough to plod on alone. Beyond this point, not far away, stood the town of Yanagi. In that town, on the main street, lived an old man who had once been in the employ of his father, and toward his house Yonosuke turned his weary feet.

The old retainer greeted him with mixed feelings. Happy to see again the wayward son of his one-time master, yet hesitant to break important news to him, he said at last: "We were talking and worrying about you these last few days. The truth is, couriers have been sent all over the country to search for you. Now just be calm.

It is just to tell you that your father, on the night of the sixth of this month, breathed his last."

"Died?"

That very evening a courier from Kyoto arrived with another report.

"Fortunate, indeed, that we followed you here," the courier told Yonosuke. "We heard you were traveling in Senshu, and when the storm sank the boats this afternoon we hoped you might have swum ashore somewhere along this coast." He paused for breath, then continued in a softer tone: "Your mother is terribly distressed by the death of your father. She needs you now. You must hurry back."

No sooner said than Yonosuke was hastened into a waiting palanquin.

At the Kyoto home on Kawara-machi his widowed mother, glad to have him back, acted quickly with the approval of the family council. All the keys to the family shops and warehouses were turned over to him, the heir apparent. Overnight Yonosuke became a changed man, a man commanding great wealth. As a final gesture indicating that all was forgiven and forgotten, his mother turned over to him ready cash in the enormous sum of 25,000 gold *kan*.

Sudden wealth turned Yonosuke's head. He reverted to his old sensual philosophy. "I shall dedicate this money to all the lovely courtesans of this country," he said in the form of a pledge. "It shall be made available to them whenever needed. My lifelong ambition will be realized. I shall purchase the freedom of all women in bondage to whom I have taken a fancy. At last I shall have all the famous beauties at my command!"

PART II

WOMAN OF QUALITY

A HAIKU poet once described the most admired courtesan that ever graced the entertainment halls of Kyoto in this fashion:

> Lo, our flowery capital
> Will never bloom again
> If death takes Yoshino away.

Yoshino had indeed earned the reputation of being an admirable woman because she was gentle and courteous and big of heart. No one could point the finger of scorn at her or complain that she was wanting in conduct or behavior. She was a good woman, liked by all who knew her.

Yonosuke had heard of her—her goodness, her refinement. And then one day he saw her on the street with his own eyes, and he felt great torment. This wasn't a case of casual infatuation with a common harlot or a woman of easy virtue. She was a first-class hostess, a woman of quality presiding in giddily high circles. It saddened Yonosuke to think that with all his newly acquired wealth she was inaccessible to him. He fell actually in love for the first time in his life.

Frustration begets humility, and Yonosuke started to earn money with his own hands—just fifty-three *me,* the price of admission to her presence for one brief hour of glorious entertainment. It was to be an expression of sincerity, unadulterated by any sordid urge. Daily he worked at the anvil of a smithy in Lord Kintsuna's studio. Every day he forged one small knife blade, earning one *me* for his labor. In fifty-three days he had amassed the needed fifty-three *me*.

And every day thereafter he waited for a chance to be admitted to Yoshino's table. But the keeper of the teahouse in the Shimabara district would not let him see her. She was barred to anyone unknown to the keeper as a man of wealth, position, and probity. Yonosuke refused to reveal his true identity, and those who had heard of his past misdeeds shunned him. His sincerity proved to be of no avail.

So then one night when the festival of the forge came around, he went secretly to the same establishment to pour out his woes to a woman attendant. "I'm mortified," he told her.

"I can well understand it," the woman said sympathetically. "I shall let Yoshino-sama know secretly anyhow that you are here."

When Yoshino heard about Yonosuke's plight and lament, she said without hesitation: "Of course he can see me if he wants to. Bring him into my room, please."

Unable to believe his ears, Yonosuke crept through the dark hallway into her dazzling presence. He felt humble and ashamed.

"But at least I am sincere," he said pensively. "I have come to you with love in my heart, knowing you will reject me."

Yoshino was greatly surprised and excited. No one had ever spoken to her of *sincere* love. "Tell me all about it," she invited.

Yonosuke made a clean breast of everything. "That is all," he concluded. "I must thank you for letting me come here to see you. Now I am satisfied. I shall always carry the thought of your generosity in my heart." He rose to go.

"Wait!" Yoshino cried, seizing his sleeve. "Don't go yet."

126

But the secret could not be kept. When the keeper of the establishment on the following morning heard what Yoshino had done on her own initiative, he complained sternly and bitterly.

Yoshino protested: "But I have not done anything that would ruin the reputation of this house or anyone else here. I have nothing to hide. You may not know the man who came to see me because he came as a poor and humble man, without displaying the privilege of wealth. He is Yonosuke-sama. He impressed me greatly with his simple, unadorned sincerity."

Nevertheless it seemed as if Yoshino had committed an indiscretion that could not be excused.

"It is against the rules of the house," the master insisted.

While her career thus hung in the balance, Yonosuke himself dropped in, now through the front door. When the master told him pointblank that he would not tolerate such clandestine defiance of rules and that in any event Yoshino's future was as good as ruined thereby, Yonosuke said: "Very well, I shall hold myself responsible for her conduct. She has done no more than what a generous-hearted courtesan would do. I will never let her suffer for it. In fact . . . I will pay ransom to secure her release from your contract. As of today she shall be a free woman."

And with Yoshino's glad consent he paid the ransom and took her home as his wife.

Pride and prejudice hurt the establishment, and sincerity was richly rewarded. For Yoshino proved herself to be a model wife. Wise and gentle in her ways and speech, she quickly familiarized herself with the affairs of her new environment and adapted herself to its manners and peculiarities without a trace of condescension. She joined the Buddhist church to prepare herself for the future world, the same as Yonosuke. She gave up smoking her long-stemmed pipe when Yonosuke confessed aversion for the ill-smelling weed. Yonosuke was pleased in every respect.

But his family and clan of relatives came forth to voice objections. Whatever she might be now, Yoshino was once a courtesan, a dishonorable profession in their eyes. She could not be entered in the family registry. "Get rid of her," they demanded of Yonosuke.

Yoshino was heartbroken. Yonosuke stood resolutely by her, but the clan council refused to budge too. Relations became strained all around. Finally, after discussing the matter sorrowfully with Yonosuke, Yoshino asked for separation.

"I shall be content to be your mistress," she said. "Please let me stay in a separate house for servants, and you can come to see me whenever you like."

"That won't do at all," Yonosuke replied. "I will not consent to any such arrangement."

"Then I shall make a final appeal to your clan council. I shall try to persuade your relatives to change their attitude toward us."

"How can you convince them when even Buddhist and Shinto priests have tried in vain to intercede for us?"

"Well then," Yoshino was persistent, "I have a scheme. Please write an invitation to all of your relatives. Tell them you are sending me away tomorrow, so please come to renew the former pleasant relationship. It is to be a feast of reconciliation, between yourself and them. The cherries in the garden are just about to bloom. Tell them to bring along their servants too and enjoy the day together here—the whole clan. And leave the rest to me."

"Whatever you wish," Yonosuke agreed pleasantly enough, and the letters were duly dispatched by messenger.

The clan members came, all of them—children, servants and all—in palanquin after palanquin, for they

128

bore no ill will toward Yonosuke. There was feasting and drinking in the great family hall overlooking the garden and in the pavilions overlooking hillocks, ponds, and flower beds.

At the height of the festivities Yoshino went before the revelers and bowed low with both hands on the mat. She wore a pale blue robe, a red apron denoting the status of a servant, and a kerchief on her head. She addressed the older members of the clan: "My name is Yoshino, and I was once a courtesan on Misuji-machi. I feel I am unworthy to appear before this family gathering. Today, however, I am to be sent away from this household as an unwanted wife. I should like, if you will let me, to serve and entertain you as my last act here."

Thereupon she began to sing a song of olden times. Next she entertained the guests by playing a haunting musical piece on the koto. Then she brewed ceremonial tea, serving it to the guests in a charming, well-bred way. And she recited poems. She arranged flowers in trays to brighten up the hall.

She did all these things serenely in a way that suggested they were not something merely to be enjoyed by men at first-class teahouses. She showed that they were accomplishments that any wife, in any home, might freely and profitably exercise for the enjoyment of her family.

After that she mixed easily with the guests as a hostess should, looking after the children's disheveled hair, making up a twosome for the game of *go,* going back and forth from the kitchen for more drinks and delicacies. She looked after the guests' every need, far into the night. And the guests unconsciously accepted her as the hostess herself. They forgot that the time to leave was long past due.

In the small hours of the morning the many clan members finally left for their homes. The womenfolk said: "We must never let Yonosuke get rid of such a fine wife. Even we women have never felt so pleasant as in her company. No one need feel ashamed with a bride so gentle and wise and capable." Then they told the menfolk: "Please forgive her for her past and let her become Yonosuke's legitimate wife."

The menfolk nodded their heads vigorously in affirmation. "She is a fine and lovable woman," they agreed emphatically. "Who said they must part?"

THE SPIRIT IS RESTLESS

BUT A WIFE is one thing, a man's prerogative quite another. Or so ran the thought to which the forever footloose Yonosuke instinctively fell heir. Before a year had passed, he felt no compunction whatever in straying from the home-fire *hibachi*. Domestic bliss is at best routine. The spirit is restless, lured by recurrent visions of fresh adventure.

Now it came to pass that Yonosuke acquired a like-minded friend and companion called Kanroku. This adventurer said: "With all the money in the world to spend, I have never yet gone to see the famous Shibaya-machi. Have you?"

"No," replied Yonosuke.

"The more the pity, no matter how you look at it."

"It must be a strange place. They say that in ancient times the sweet potatoes along the banks of the nearby River Nagara turned into eels. Some kind of magic there."

They laughed together over that.

"Well," said Kanroku, "There is no reason why we should not go now."

"Let's go!"

And so two palanquins squeaked their way rhythmically toward the town of Otsu, along the highway thick with travelers. Soon they entered the town from Hatcho Street.

A woman's teasing voice rang out: "Are you not looking for lodgings?"

Promptly the two men yielded to her invitation and got out of their palanquins. They were given a large clean room at her inn.

"Tell us, girls," Kanroku addressed the smiling maidservants, "who is the most popular attraction here?"

The maids snickered. "The goddess of mercy," was the sardonic reply. "You will find the goddess at the Ishiyama Buddhist Temple."

Kanroku made a wry face. "You think you are witty, don't you?"

Later he repeated the same question to the innkeeper.

The innkeeper deprecated the thought. "You had better get the idea out of your mind," he said. "You cannot visit harlots here for a mere six or seven *me* as you do elsewhere. And high-class courtesans . . . well, they are out of the question for *yabo* like you."

Kanroku gnashed his teeth in suppressed rage. "If we look like tramps," he said acidly, "it is because we are looking for secret adventure. Why should we travel in style, with manservants and all, and attract attention? We are not *yabo;* we are only disguised as such."

Yonosuke thought it was all very funny. "Show him your gold coins," he said laughingly.

From the kitchen came more voices of teasing ridicule: "Ah, Kanroku-sama is going to visit the prostitutes tonight! Oh, yes, he won't!" And fingers of loud laughter were pointed at him.

Yonosuke, bored by this mysterious taunt, went casually out into the street. There, beneath the eaves of shops row on row, a curious jabbering crowd had assembled.

"Here comes the splendid troupe of pilgrims," someone yelled.

131

Three gorgeously caparisoned pack horses came to a halt in front of the inn. On closer inspection of the crests on the horses' equipment, Yonosuke recognized them as Kurobune of Osaka, Sazanami of Fushimi, and Hankai of Yodo. Seated on each of the pack mounts was a girl of about twelve years of age. Yonosuke recognized them as *kamuro,* the little attendants at well-known courtesan establishments.

The long flowing sleeves of their right arms were of a different color design from those of their left arms. Their sedge hats were lined with red silk, with red-and-white tassels around the chin holding the broad headgear in place. They were singing the then popular Komuro-bushi song as the pack-horse leaders began to remove the bridles.

One of the girls recognized Yonosuke as he gazed smilingly up at them, and called: *"Moshi moshi,* we are making a pilgrimage to the Grand Shrines of Ise. Why are *you* staying here?"

That was an embarrassing question. Yonosuke lifted them down from the horses' backs, and they nestled up to him. "I am here only as Kanroku's henchman." He evaded the question without telling an outright lie. "Kanroku wants to visit the gay quarters. But I have a headache. Won't you please give me a gentle massage?"

The three girls giggled, grouped around him, and began to massage his head, his shoulders, and his back with their little hands.

One of them said: "We stopped here to visit the much-talked-about Shibaya-machi. Won't you take us to the place? We want to tell the Tayu-sama all about it when we return to Kyoto."

"Oh, no!" Yonosuke was horrified. "That is no place for little girls like you to visit."

But they begged and nagged him so charmingly that finally he said: "Well, all right . . . if you insist. But only

132

to pass down that street. Let's go." They entered Shibaya-machi from the south side.

What they saw was a strange and ugly vista. Prostitutes exposed themselves to view in front of their apartments, speaking in loud shrill voices. Heavy coatings of liquid powder made their faces look repulsively ghastly. Some of them were twanging the samisen in all stages of jarring unproficiency, singing with heads held high without regard for their ugliness. Those walking the street wad-dled hurriedly on large ungainly feet.

Worse, the men who came to gloat at them were a rough and quarrelsome lot. It was they who, more than the prostitutes themselves, gave a notorious character to the street. Pack-horse leaders, boatmen from nearby Lake Biwa, fishermen, wrestlers, playboy sons of rice-cake dealers, wayward clerks of fancy-goods shops—they were tough men of all ages, utterly without sentiment or mod-esty. There was a casual sense of camaraderie within certain groups and a strong, deep-seated rivalry against others for pre-emption of the favored prostitutes. It was as though the street were a gathering place to sound the tocsin for gang warfare.

Furtive male eyes sought out male rivals approaching. Before long they began to taunt, abuse, and insult each other. Sleeves were rolled up, hoods removed from shaggy heads. Quick hands fished out hidden weapons from hip sashes. Sharp blades flashed in the sunlight. Suddenly the street became a bedlam of little groups here, there, and everywhere, cursing, knocking, kicking, slash-ing. . . .

A horrible street indeed. No one who valued his life, thought Yonosuke, would venture to enter it at night. No wonder the maids at the inn had ridiculed Kanroku! Hurriedly he shepherded the three little girl pilgrims back to the inn.

That night Yonosuke and Kanroku gave a party for

the little girls, attended by such well-known local courtesans as Hyosaku, Kodayu, and Toranosuke. The next day farewells were solemnized with still more drinking. Yonosuke, feeling tremendously at peace with the world, what with the saké tingling in his veins, told the three girls: "If there is anything you want for the trip to Ise, tell me frankly and you shall have it."

The girls talked it over among themselves. One of them replied with becoming modesty: "We don't need anything, really. Except . . . except that traveling on pack horses is not fun. We . . . don't like it because it separates us on the road. We should like to be together, on a flat platform, so that we could talk freely among ourselves and lie down, and even maybe toast *kakimochi* to munch on the way. We should enjoy that very much."

"A tall order," thought Yonosuke. But he did not bat an eye. "That ought to be simple enough," he said.

Forthwith he ordered two huge palanquins to be clamped together side by side, with the middle walls where they met removed. A portable charcoal stove was placed in the center of this makeshift conveyance. Even a small shelf and a towel hanger were added. A handy folding screen was placed beside the pillows.

The three girls gleefully got in, and all in all the conveyance looked like a small portable house, borne by twelve stout men.

"Anything is possible," Yonosuke commented as the queer procession squeaked away toward Ise, "if you set your mind to it."

"Not with me," said Kanroku ruefully. "What did I come here for?"

COURTESANS in this country first began to thrive in two obscure communities in the western provinces of Koshu and Banshu. These were the coastal towns of Asazuma and Murotsu. Since then the tide of this gay profession has spread pretty nearly over the whole of this bored, gaiety-loving nation. But for some time now the glittering lights of the courtesans' quarters in Asazuma have been extinguished, and only dilapidated houses in a row remain, like scarecrows, to greet the casual visitor. Now the women weave cotton cloth at home, and the menfolk go to sea with long dragnets. Drab indeed is life there at most, poor and forlorn.

Not so in Murotsu. Here, in the largest of the western seaports, the courtesans are said to be superior to any that flourished in olden times. Their manners and accomplishments, it is also claimed, are no whit inferior to those of the courtesans in the big progressive city of Osaka.

To Murotsu, therefore, Yonosuke decided to pay a visit. Putting worldly affairs aside, he persuaded Kinzaemon of the house of Utaya to accompany him on this jaunt. Thus, two people with a common predilection for things droll and alluring set out in a fast rowboat, reaching the port late in the afternoon. As they dropped anchor the sun hung low, flooding the sky and hills beyond with the last golden splash of a summer sunset.

It was the fourteenth of the seventh month. All half-yearly debts had been paid, collected, or angrily written off on the previous day, and the town had already shed its prosaic business. As evening fell, a grand holiday air pervaded the streets, for this was the night of the annual

135

Bon lantern festival, when the spirits of the dead would once more join their loved ones upon this earth.

The crowds surged toward the great arena where the festival dance was already under way. The men wore little jauntily fashioned decorative straw hats, a symbol of the festival, and the women had towel kerchiefs on their hair. The huge drum atop the central platform beat out the rhythm, a male singer shouted his familiar *ondo* song, and the dancers swung gracefully into line, round and round in an endless throbbing circle.

Yonosuke and his friend Kinzaemon stood on the sidelines watching the merrymakers. But the spirit got into them too, and they joined the native dancers, feeling quite foolish and perfectly willing to appear foolish. Soon they discovered, from the pungent smell of perfume around them, that they were dancing among exotic, glamorous women.

They followed the scent as the women left the line to return to their quarters. They found they were being led to such establishments as the Tachibana-buro and the Choji-buro, and they went their separate ways. These were not high-class courtesans' quarters but plain brothels. Yonosuke entered the Hiroshima-buro.

Having been lured thus far, and just to see for himself the "pleasure women" of this town in their natural setting, Yonosuke asked his host Hachibei to conduct him to the three adjoining houses of Maruya and Himejiya and Akashiya.

All together he looked over some eighty women. Out of these eighty he casually picked seven pretty ones, including those of *tenjin* and *kagoi* ranks. Not that he felt particular interest in them, one way or another. He merely wanted them to join him in a drink or two in the reception room.

"However," he whispered in a jocular manner to his host, within earshot of the seven women, "if I should find one that pleased me, I might want to have her as my companion during my visit here."

Immediately, to Yonosuke's intense amusement, each of the seven women began to touch herself up—her hair, her robe, her eyes.

When the drinking was at its height, Yonosuke, by way of sobering up the atmosphere, produced a small incense holder from his sleeve pocket and dropped a pinch of the scented wood into the Chitosegawa burner. A thin haze rose from the burner, clearing up the stale air with its delightful aroma. Then he passed the burner down the line so that each of the women might inhale the burning incense, express her pleasure, perhaps comment on its quality, and even try to identify the type—as one would if one were a woman of taste. One by one, however, the women looked at it hastily and as quickly passed it down the line without exhibiting interest or curiosity.

The last one to receive it wore a robe open at the side, indicating that she belonged to a lower professional order —a newcomer. But her underwear, revealed slightly where the outer garment folded at the bosom, bore a *jizo* family crest. Yonosuke was surprised, as much by the presence of the crest—a hallmark of distinction—as by the calmness and refinement that suddenly characterized her posture. She took the incense burner gently in her hands, inspected it closely, inhaled the thinly smouldering incense, then tilted her head as though to recall something subtly associated with the scent. She inhaled again, sighed, put the burner tenderly down on the mat, and said softly: "Now I remember."

Excited over this gracious response, Yonosuke asked: "What do you know about this scented wood?"

"It is called *morokazura*," she replied. "I am quite sure of it."

"Right! I congratulate you. I must say you are well informed."

Yonosuke was about to produce another variety of aloeswood from his bosom when she stopped him. "No, no," she said hastily, "I am not well informed on different scents. Really I am not. But . . . but hasn't this one some kind of association with Wakayama-sama of Edo?"

"Indeed it has. It was given to me by Wakayama himself as a parting gift."

"That explains it. When I said 'Now I remember' a while ago, I had recalled a happy thought. I once met a gentleman from Fukuyama, in Bingo Province, and he did me the honor of making his presence agreeable to me by infusing a whiff of this scented wood into his sleeve. He said he received the wood from Wakayama-sama. I cannot forget that experience."

Greatly impressed by that delicate reference to her past and the quality of her feeling, Yonosuke said: "I am sure you cherish his memory. I envy him."

Then he realized for the first time that she was very beautiful.

The next day, as a parting gift to this extraordinary woman in a brothel, he rummaged in his long folding wallet, took out some forty pieces of silver, wrapped them up in soft paper and shoved the package into her sleeve pocket.

A few minutes later a mendicant priest came to the door, asking for alms. Casually, to Yonosuke's utter amazement, the woman took the package out of her sleeve and gave it to the alms seeker. The mendicant took the package, grunted perfunctory thanks, and walked away.

Soon he returned with a surprised look. "I did not ask for a *fortune,*" he complained, and threw the package back on the mat. "I merely asked for one or two coins." Then he walked off again, muttering to himself as though he had been insulted and resented it.

Yonosuke was mystified by the woman's indifference

to money. There must be something in her past, he thought, that should explain her character. Secretly he conducted an inquiry and learned that she was the daughter of a high official in Tango Province. For some unexplained reason she had drifted into this brothel. Taking pity upon her, Yonosuke paid his host a ransom to release her from her contract and sent her back to her Tango home.

What happened to her after that, Yonosuke never quite found out.

ALMS FOR THE GREEDY

"MOSHI, MOSHI," a woman's voice called. "Will you come back here a moment, please?"

Yonosuke, strolling on the street with a group of friends, looked back and saw that it was a maidservant of the Takashimaya teahouse. Wondering what possible message she could have for him, he retraced a few steps.

The woman whispered in his ear: "This is from a certain courtesan" and shoved a scroll letter into his sleeve pocket. Without further ado she hastened away.

No name appeared at the head of the letter, neither the sender's nor the addressee's. Yonosuke could think of no urgent reason why anyone should write to him in this puzzling fashion, unless . . . "Oh, yes," he thought, "this may be the answer I have been expecting from Takigawa, the courtesan."

He had recently acted as intermediary for a certain wealthy man who had become infatuated with Takigawa, and she had promised a written reply. He felt he could hardly wait until he reached his lodgings to find out her decision. At the intersection of Junkei-machi, beside a lantern post, he began to unroll the scroll letter and read it.

No, it could not be from Takigawa. The letter was filled with passionate, erratic phrases, indicating the writer's lovelorn, confused state of mind. "I am madly in love with you," it said at one point. "What do I care if I were to lose my soul? I shall risk giving up everything for you. For you alone."

"Well, well, whoever she is," thought Yonosuke proudly and elatedly, "she must really be in love with me!"

"Listen to this," he told his companions. "Here is what I call an easy victory. Usually a man makes love to a woman, and he rarely succeeds in the beginning. But this woman—this anonymous woman and a courtesan at that —confesses her secret attachment to me. Why, there are many desirable young men available these days, and yet she chooses me. After all, my hair is still thick and black. Aren't you envious? Why don't you try to emulate my ways?"

His friends laughed derisively.

"Why should I lie to you?" Yonosuke frowned. "Read this."

"No need to," said Sanshichi. "I have a distinct idea whom it is from. It could be from none other."

"How should you know? Explain yourself."

"Calm down, Yonosuke. It is this way. She is a woman of bad repute. You are not the only man she has written to so passionately. Just the other day, for instance, she wrote to the special friend of another courtesan and even to Satsuma-sama's inamorata. Her specialty consists in trying to steal other women's men. That isn't love by any stretch of the imagination. Besides, she insinuates herself into the pleasure of only wealthy men—those who appear to be excellent catches.

"And she cares little about how a man looks. To prove it, I might mention how, with her usual tactics, she snared the headman of Kawachi village, and this man has a deformed nose. For some time she made him pay all her expenses—costly robes and silk undergarments. She slept with him—or so she told her intimates—with her eyes averted. In the end she told him she disliked his looks and made it plain that she was through with him. And so they quarreled. At least *he* did.

"The man said: 'You talk as if you have only now noticed my deformity. You knew perfectly well all the time, but you were scheming to get everything you could out of me, and you merely pretended you didn't see it. You told me to prove my sincerity by presenting wheat to the matron here, and just today I had two whole bags of ground wheat delivered to you. You said your parents in the country needed raw cotton, so I had a hundred *kin* sent to them four or five days ago with all the seeds removed.

" 'You wanted dried turnip and melon and eggplant delivered elsewhere, and at great expense I had them forwarded to the distant addresses you mentioned. You got them for nothing from me, and you were trading them for money.

" 'I did everything to please you, but you heard that the Ninnaji dam burst this summer under the strain of swirling torrents, and you believed my paddy fields had been flooded and ruined. That is why you are casting me off now. It isn't my nose. You think I myself have been ruined. You were after my money only. . . .'

"Well, Yonosuke, more than one person saw and heard this quarrel, and they say the village headman wept as he left for his country home, feeling he had been willfully taken advantage of and cheated. I tell you frankly she is a vicious woman."

Yonosuke flushed with anger. To think that he, too, had been singled out as victim of her trickery! "What a hateful creature," he thought. "But when the time comes I shall turn the tables on her!"

He found out her identity at the Takashimaya teahouse and replied to her letter, flattering her in extravagant terms. Then he started to patronize her, without paying a single silver coin. One night, as he entered the same teahouse where she was entertaining a rich visitor from Bungo Province, Yonosuke received a brief note from her: "Come to the rear, please."

Curious about what she was up to now, he decided to play up to her whims. He went to the rear of the teahouse and waited for her in the woodshed. By craning his neck a little, he could see her entertaining in a guest room that opened out on the backyard. He saw her lifting the wine flask in a very crude way. Suddenly her hand shook, and she dropped the flask. Then she doubled up in a paroxysm of pain.

"Why . . . what is the matter?" said the alarmed patron, the wealthy country gentleman from Bungo Province.

"I have the cramps," she cried. "In my stomach."

Hastily the Bungo visitor fidgeted with his *inro* medicine case and gave her several kinds of herbal drugs to swallow. She kept the medicine in her mouth, tottered out of the room, and spat it out into the yard.

"Stay here," she told her little *kamuro* attendant, who followed her with a lighted torch. "And close the sliding door." Then she ran to meet Yonosuke in the woodshed.

"I like this sort of hazardous adventure, don't you?" she told Yonosuke, embracing him. "It is so exciting."

The unsuspecting country gentleman opened the sliding door and saw the little girl standing guard near the porch. "The courtesan," he said, "seems to take a long time. Is she still in pain?"

"She will be back soon," the girl replied, innocently.

In the woodshed Yonosuke and the courtesan lay among messy bales of charcoal. After a while Yonosuke rose abruptly and left. The courtesan sneaked back to the teahouse, into the central room, and let her maid brush off the dirt and bits of straw from her robe.

"How exasperating!" she cried. "My robe is ruined."

Everyone present in the room surmised from this that she had not enjoyed her liaison in the woodshed, that she had sacrificed her robe for some secret purpose. But she didn't care what people thought or suspected.

Still keeping her Bungo patron waiting in the guest room, she sat down in front of the household shrine and began to eat her supper of boiled rice mixed with tea, cowpeas, and strips of dried codfish. After that she took out her purse and made mental calculations of her earnings.

While she was in the midst of these calculations, the Bungo country gentleman, bored by being left alone, walked into the central room.

"I see," he said, without reproach, "that you are well enough now, even to be able to count your money. I am glad it wasn't so serious after all."

Still to all appearances innocent of her duplicity, he settled his account with the teahouse proprietor and took his leave.

The courtesan felt no qualms of conscience, even then. There is no need to reveal her name. Sooner or later she will be exposed for what she is.

Now she summoned a young man who happened to be entering the room and asked: "How much in the way of daily interest can I get for loaning small sums of money?"

Yonosuke had occasion to see her a number of times after that, and one day he received another letter from her, this time begging for money. She needed the money, she wrote, for new robes for New Year's. Yonosuke replied:

"Your letter asking for a large sum of money has been duly read. You must know that when a man visits the gay quarters he chooses the women he likes—not vice versa—

and pays for their services. You have acted all along as though no payment need be involved. Whatever your ultimate aims may be, I shall nevertheless remember to dispense some alms to you when we meet again. Allow me to tell you in the meantime that you had better look elsewhere for a victim. Then, when you are ready to loan the money you have thus accumulated, I may be able to help you find customers among beggars. But just now I am very busy and shall have to close this letter here."

FANTASTIC TRICK

IF RICHES and unceasing adventures among women had earned anything for Yonosuke beyond a kind of enviable notoriety, it was the homage paid him by a group of professional jesters. *Massha* they were called—sycophants all, who sought his good graces and were rewarded with paternalistic affection. Their function was to liven up parties and do squire's work at the various teahouses where first-class courtesans held court. Naturally partial to handsome smooth-tongued patrons who spent money liberally, they had easily gravitated toward Yonosuke, looking up to him as a hero among habitués of the gay quarters.

They were sedentary men who had never gazed upon anything more fascinating in the way of landscapes than the dull mountain range that reared its naked form behind the city of Kyoto. To them, therefore, Yonosuke decided to give a treat by taking the group on a trip to the seashore town of Sakai. There they might at least feast their eyes upon chanting fishermen hauling in dragnets in rhythmic motions and upon thousands of live fish snapping in the meshes of the net like silver sparks. But the main thing was, of course, to lodge them for the night in a suitable inn where the men, for once, could enjoy the role of being guests instead of second-rate auxiliary entertainers.

After the beach excursion Yonosuke led them past the Sumiyoshi Shrine and, at the north end of the street, to those sections that catered to pleasure-seekers: Naka-no-Cho and Fukuro-machi, noted for brothels in the Koshu district.

Brothels served almost the same purposes as inns (or vice versa for that matter), and Yonosuke took the group into one of them. He asked for a number of harlots—it made no difference who were chosen, so long as the required number were present—to be brought to the table spread in the upstairs reception room. But the innkeeper was uncommonly particular. "Name your choices according to rank," he said, "such as *tenjin* and *ko-tenjin.*"

"That is a lot of bother," Yonosuke snapped. "You don't seem to have any great beauties anyhow."

"But the cost. . . ."

"I'm footing the bill, if that's what is worrying you."

Anyhow, as the jesters, nine of them, sat down at the table, and the harlots, one for each guest, began to serve rice wine, a woman attendant came up and said: "Another guest has just arrived and asked for Kazuraki, so we shall have to borrow her for a while."

And Kazuraki, one of the harlots, rose from the table and left.

Soon the attendant returned and said: "Now it is a special call for Takasaki."

And Takasaki left the table.

These calls were repeated, one after another, for all of the harlots over and over again, so that they were constantly leaving the table or returning. In two hours' time each of them had left five or six times at intervals of about ten minutes. Now not a single one remained.

"I must say," thought Yonosuke, "this is a popular house indeed. I have never seen or heard the like of it before. They must have a good many steady patrons here, each demanding his favorite." Curious, he went out into the hallway and peeped down the open stairway into he waiting room below.

A puzzled look crept into his eyes. Then he frowned. There was not a single man to be seen, least of all one who might look like a customer. All the harlots who had been called from his table were reclining here and there on the mat, using their arms for pillows, looking bored and sleepy, yawning incessantly, drinking strong tea to keep themselves awake.

"Don't go up any more," the matron said. "Let them think you are all busy. Let them sleep it off."

It was a fantastic trick!

And it did not take long for Yonosuke to solve the riddle. Most likely, customers were extremely few and far between, and it was probably the custom here, whenever a group arrived, to give the opposite impression—that business was brisk and thriving. Hence the constant pretended calls for harlots to other tables. The innkeeper was no doubt trying to build up a reputation of popularity so as to draw the reluctant trade.

Returning to his room, Yonosuke saw that his men, deserted by the harlots, had quit drinking. To while away the rest of the boresome evening they were fussing with the straps on their traveling hats or with their ivory medicine holders. Or they were drawing pictures of houses with India ink.

"The women," he told them, "seem to be determined to remain down there for the night. They won't perform any further duties. Maybe they are afraid of catching cold up here. Maybe not. But I shall certainly have a funny story to tell when the time comes for me to write about my reminiscences. Let's go to bed."

146

The jesters, sorely disappointed, slid into bed and found the blankets much too short. Their feet and legs stuck out, and this made them cold all over.

LOVELORN MAN IN A TREE

"Truly there is fun in playing with young actors."

Yonosuke finally yielded to this importunate suasion and visited the Ryosan Temple in Higashiyama.

But the Noh drama rehearsal was already over, and after everyone had left, there was not a sound save the sigh of the evening breeze among the pines and the sizzling of the wheat-gluten cake called *fu* being fried in deep oil in the temple kitchen. The frying of *fu* signified that a humble feast of abstinence, a vegetarian repast, was being prepared, which in turn called for abstaining from saké drinking.

"This is indeed going to be a test of humility," said Yonosuke. "What will we do now? I'm ready for anything."

His host gave an order to a servant: "Go and fetch Tamagawa, Ito, and four or five others from Miyagawa-machi. We'll have a different group this time."

Forthwith swift-traveling palanquins were requisitioned, and in no time at all, as it were, the good-looking youths arrived.

"Here they are! Who can resist them?" was the general exclamation.

Yonosuke's host put it this way: "Dallying with these youths is like seeing wolves asleep beneath scattering cherry blossoms, whereas going to bed with prostitutes gives one the feeling of groping in the dark beneath the new moon without a lantern. Truly," he continued, "that *is* the difference between the two types of indulgence. Almost every man is bound to be bewildered in either situation."

Forgetting their age, the assembled men played all sorts of indoor games with the youths, as though they themselves were boys again, until they became soaked with perspiration. To enjoy the cooling breeze, they all moved to the porch with a southern exposure. It was a night in May, and the moon was hardly bright. A Zelkova tree stood in the shadows, and from the thick foliage of its lower branches came myriads of leaping lights, like some bright glittering objects. Taken aback by this vision, the men ran back helter-skelter into the temple kitchen and administrative office, as though they had lost their minds. One of them, however, a husky chap with great muscular powers, fetched a bow and arrow and was about to leap out into the garden when Sansaburo Takii, one of the handsome youths, seized him from behind.

"Stop it!" said Sansaburo. "There is nothing up there that you should shoot at."

But when Sansaburo walked to the foot of the tree and looked sharply upward toward the leaf-laden branches, he saw a black object moving darkly against a starry background.

"Who are you?" he demanded, "And what are you doing up there?"

A voice from the treetop answered: "Mortifying! This is indeed mortifying! If I had been shot to death by an arrow, I would never be suffering like this. But you, Sansaburo-sama—you, out of your goodness—stopped it, and my agony has increased twofold. I feel as though my bones were cracking—a living hell, I tell you." Hot tears flowed from the eyes of the man in the tree as he said this, and he now wiped them with his sleeve.

"Well then," Sansaburo asked, "are you in love with someone?"

"You're making it harder for me when you ask me that," said the man in the tree. "It is you I have watched every day at the Noh play. How many times, indeed, have I followed you secretly to the gate as you left the theater! Really, I felt like dying when I heard you speak. Today I heard the sandal bearer Kongo and others whispering that you were coming out to Higashiyama again, and I wanted desperately to see you. So I came here and climbed this tree with the intention of forsaking this world by hanging myself. Now that I have had the good fortune of speaking to you, I have nothing to regret. If you have any pity for me, please burn incense for me after I am gone." So saying, he threw down the loose crystals of his broken rosary.

Sansaburo said: "I, too, have felt right along an emotion for you. Now that you have confessed to me, I am very glad. The feeling, I assure you, is mutual. How can I deny your wishes? Wait for the dawn, and your wishes shall be fulfilled. Come to my house in the morning."

The other men at the temple, ignoring this passionate confession of two homosexual males, surrounded the tree and, despite Sansaburo's pleas, dragged the man down from the tree. To the amazement of all, they found him to be a priest living at this temple.

When Yonosuke learned the truth of their attachment, he said: "Splendid!" and himself made arrangements so the two lovers could embrace each other in privacy right away.

The rest of the story came to Yonosuke's ears long afterwards in Edo at a gathering of men devoted to love among homosexuals—a gathering at which confessions were freely made. On that occasion Sansaburo made a clean breast of his life with the priest. He even had the word *Kei* tattooed on his left arm as proof of his devotion to the priest, whose name was Keisu. This, therefore, is not fiction but a true story.

THE VOYAGE down the Inland Sea was smooth and pleasant. It was the sixth month, warm and rippling and green. Yonosuke and his two companions Kanroku and Kinzaemon, together with his manservant Katsu-no-Jo, debarked at Miyajima with considerable luggage. A huge crowd had assembled from nearby towns and villages.

"What is the excitement about?" Yonosuke asked a passer-by.

"Excitement? Oh, you mean this crowd. I believe they came for the country fair."

It was a motley crowd smitten by the holiday spirit, noisy, reckless, hungry for amusement. Groups of young townsmen were flirting with peasant girls sheltered in the enormous hall in front of the Miyajima Shrine. Country youths were admiring good-looking actors or were being led away. Still others were arguing about the best way to handle prostitutes.

Some of the inns of Miyajima had shallow fronts, and a passer-by could see pretty nearly everything that harlots waiting for trade inside were doing. They wore summer *yukata* and exposed parts of their innermost garments in very indelicate fashion. Yonosuke decided they were fly-by-night amateurs. He heard them twanging samisen noisily and singing clumsily a popular song, "Okazaki Joro Shu," and a local Arima ditty about the bored look of a brothel's front. They twanged and sang as though they had just learned those pieces. It was all very disgustingly gay. Yonosuke and his two companions decided to lodge in one of these establishments, however unprepossessing it seemed.

150

"Introduce us," Yonosuke told the innkeeper, "to a snappy, smart-looking woman who appears to have enough guts to thrash a man."

That was meant to be mere blandishment, a commentary, as it were, on the coarseness of these provincial women. Imagine his chagrin, however, when just such a prostitute did presently appear at their table, flanked by two female attendants. She looked superior enough, at least in size and bearing.

Yonosuke whispered embarrassedly to his companions: "We should have changed our robes."

The prostitute looked disdainfully at them and refused to serve drinks. She gave her attendants a knowing confidential look. "They are probably poor slum menials," she said, sniffing.

At this point a hawker on the street outside came crying his wares: "Apples . . . apples for sale!"

Yonosuke, quick to seize the opportunity to establish his own sense of dignity, threw a few pieces of copper at the prostitute. "Go outside," he ordered, "and buy some apples for us."

The prostitute refused to budge from the comfortable position on her cushion. With a superior-sounding laugh, she said with mild contempt: "Is that the way you tried to buy a woman here last evening?"

"All right," thought Yonosuke, "so this is going to be a battle of wits." Aloud he said, "What do you think we look like?"

"Human beings."

"That is old stuff. What would you say our occupations were—our social rank?"

The prostitute smiled condescendingly. "I would have to judge you men as patrons of this establishment. Let me see. I would say"—she decided to be tactful and charitable for the sake of business—"yes, I would say you were all common sedentary men from a big city brought up on the *tatami* floor mats. That man there," pointing at Kinzaemon, "is probably a shop hireling who sells writing brushes. And you," gazing straight at Kanroku, "you are, I think, a peddler of sewing kits whose boss is an exacting taskmaster. But you," and she looked disdainfully at Yonosuke, "you no doubt wait on old women to sell gaudy-looking obi."

Kanraku and Kinzaemon looked somewhat surprised, for the prostitute had guessed right, at least in the type of goods their huge self-owned wholesale houses dealt in. But Yonosuke did not take kindly to the prostitute's low estimation of himself.

She should judge, he thought, by visible evidence. Anyone could tell a man's occupation and place in society by the kind and size of *inro* medicine case he carried with him on his sash, or by the shape and condition of his hands and feet, no matter how misleading the garments he happened to be wearing might be. She had also ignored the fact that he had brought with him his manservant Katsu-no-Jo, one of the most correct and fastidious of his kind in Kyoto. Katsu-no-Jo was sitting sedately and respectfully in the background. No one boasting such a manservant could conceivably be a mere shop menial.

Ignoring the laughing prostitute for the moment, he told his two companions in an apparently extraneous fashion: "Let's put on a puppet show here. Katsu-no-Jo," and he turned to his manservant, "fetch the dolls. We'll show this woman what a high-class amusement is like."

The dolls were removed from Yonosuke's mass of luggage and displayed on the mats. And as the comic play progressed, with Yonosuke singing the *joruri* accompaniment, the entrance of the doll portraying Shinta's wife drew a surprised comment from one of the prostitute's attendants: "That doll is an exact image of Komurasaki, a noted courtesan in Yoshiwara!"

"At least *you* have a discerning mind, or memory, as

the case may be," Yonosuke praised her. "Yes, I had it made in the image of that charming courtesan."

Then he smiled and said suavely: "That reminds me. Komurasaki is an example of how bright a true courtesan can be. Let this be a lesson to you prostitutes in Miyajima. Once a young lord went with two of his servants—all three disguised but dressed alike to hide the lord's identity —to seek clandestine amusement at Komurasaki's table in the house of Ichizaemon in Yoshiwara.

"The lord asked the courtesan: 'Can you guess who among the three of us is the master? Pass the wine cup to him first.'

"The courtesan replied: 'I would not know offhand because I am not a god. Just a moment, please.'

"And she went into the kitchen, whispered instructions to a little girl attendant. The girl released a pair of caged nightingales, went out into the garden, and yelled excitedly: 'Look, the nightingales are here!'

"The young lord and his two servants rushed to the side porch, slipped their feet hurriedly into wooden clogs, and went out into the garden to look at the birds.

"When all three returned to the drinking table, the courtesan passed the wine cup to the young lord.

" 'How did you find out?' the lord asked, amazed.

"The courtesan smiled and replied demurely: 'You alone among the three fidgeted longer than usual with your footgear. You are not used to action in a hurry, or undue excitement. You have poise. *You* must be the master.'

"And that is showing good judgment, good taste, and respect for a worthy patron. You country prostitutes have a lot to learn."

THERE WERE other gay districts Yonosuke had not yet seen, but he had already tired of dallying with provincial women of pleasure. The weather along the seacoast was fine, and he decided to go up to Osaka. As the boat approached the reedy banks in the delta and docked at the Sangenya, he felt a pleasurable sensation.

There had been women of pleasure in this port town in the old days, and he remembered, as if carried away in a far-off dream, the songs they used to sing about "the deer that went back and forth to Awaji Island" across the Inland Sea.

The winds of early spring blew over the reeds in the brackish water, and very important young men-about-town were cruising in the bay on luxury boats, with flutes and drums filling the air with cacophony in unrestrained fashion. Among them were Koyama Sennosuke, Kojima Tsumanojo, and Kojima Umenosuke. Yonder were Matsushima Hanya, Sakata Kodenji, and Shimakawa Konosuke drinking and exchanging huge wine cups. The waves piling up on shore and breaking were a beautiful sight. The rocking of the boat seemed to add to their pleasure. On the opposite bank Matsumoto Tsunezaemon, Tsurukawa Somenojo, Yamamoto Kantaro, and Okada Kichijuro were fishing with bamboo poles. This, too, was beautiful to behold.

On the cruising boats were makeshift bathrooms and barrels of sea bream and sea bass. The men scribbled on fans and set them adrift in the water by day and exploded fancy fireworks in the sky by night, as if heaven itself were on a drunken spree.

154

Verily, there is more fun in this pleasure-boat cruising than in playing in the mountains of Kyoto. Yonosuke felt a momentary wish that he could show this to the court ladies. The most that the ladies could taste in the mountains of Kyoto would be the forbidden repast prepared by the yeomen of the guard. There is nothing tastier than light watery sea food aboard a cruiser, but this is probably unknown to a non-drinker. Yonosuke liked his wine, and he allowed himself the luxury of thinking that he would perhaps like to spend a day here with those men, and he felt envious of the view before him, without realizing why.

"Aren't you Yonosuke?" came a voice from across the water.

"Who's that?" Yonosuke shot back.

"I'm the man you loved at Ogura."

"What are you doing now? Haven't you gone up to Kyoto?"

"I have a lot to tell you. Come into this boat."

When Yonosuke got into the boat, he found the group in it to be all past acquaintances. Noisily they started drinking from wine cups he vaguely recognized. Before long the boat reached Yottsubashi.

"Let's go."

Yonosuke, following the others out of the boat, asked: "Where to now? The bad places, as usual?"

"Y . . . yes, let's look the place over before going home. This, too, would be like enjoying 'the night flowers of Yoshino.'"

And so they entered the Shimmachi gay quarters from the eastern side, and went into the Yoshidaya, the ninth establishment in the row.

Yonosuke went out to the kitchen, and there he saw an old man in colorful robes summoning the female attendants. The man questioned Onaru, the woman in charge: "Who is that?"

155

Onaru replied: "He's the papa of this house."

Strange, thought Yonosuke, that a man who has been coming here off and on for some three years should not be known by sight. It was, of course, because Onaru managed everything here herself, a capable woman.

"Anyhow, tonight," the man said, "I'll be satisfied with any prostitute who is physically normal." He directed that all the women uncommitted for the night be summoned.

This was what Yonosuke had been wishing. Himself looking over the women, he picked out a woman of the *tenjin* class, saying he knew her well.

Upstairs in the big entertainment hall, the moonbeams entered from the south. It was here that Yonosuke used to meet Kaga no Saburo in times past. It was here that the courtesan Ichihashi used to reign. The room seemed to have lost its former splendor. What was once of golden design now boasted only of the lower panels decorated with Minato paper. In those days there was a splendid four-foot writing table with an inkstone, writing brushes, and incense boxes on it. Even if one's foreign-made article was forgotten here, no one so much as picked it up to examine it. Now there were not even enough wooden pillows. Guests stole the tobacco from the tobacco boxes, and the long-stemmed pipes disappeared from time to time. Surely, no one would run off with a wig forgotten by a bald-headed man.

While these lugubrious thoughts were troubling Yonosuke, the matron Joharu brought in a samisen.

"Oh, I understand," said Yonosuke sardonically. "Aside from some gold coins, is there anything else you want to wheedle out of me?"

He continued: "Why hasn't the prostitute come? I'd send her back after looking at her face, even before she could sit down."

At this moment the woman Yonosuke had chosen came

in. It seemed she'd already had a few drinks at another table. She was considerably on the tipsy side.

Bedding was meanwhile prepared for the night. The woman said: "I haven't slept for a long time, so I'm going right to bed," and promptly slid into bed without even taking off her outer garments.

While she was seemingly fast asleep, someone yelled from the garden below: "Get up!"

Thereupon the woman awoke and said: "I'm going home, too."

Apparently she was still drunk and while prone on the bed she refused to engage Yonosuke in conversation. Yonosuke tried to keep himself awake by remaining standing and puffing at his tobacco pipe.

The prostitute suddenly pushed out her buttocks from underneath the bedcovers. As Yonosuke stared at this in wonderment, she let loose a volley of smelly gas in an explosion that seemed to reverberate to the four corners of the room. So then Yonosuke bent down and pressed the bowl of his tobacco pipe on the spot from which the explosion came. If the explosion was deliberate, it was a sad state of affairs indeed. But if it was spontaneous, beyond her power to prevent, then even the Lord Buddha would perhaps condone it.

LOVE OF A COURTESAN

YONOSUKE's interest in women had on the whole been wide and discriminative. Always on the search for new faces, from one end of the country to another, it had hardly occurred to him to settle down to the habit of visiting one favorite house of entertainment. Seldom, for he could not afford it in his earlier years, had he patron-

ized a first-class courtesan. But for some time now he had felt irresistibly drawn to the Osakaya, a teahouse operated by one Gonzaemon, in the city of Osaka.

Gonzaemon was the hard-grained, inflexible type of master, meticulously mindful of the rules governing the conduct of both the courtesans in his employ and the men who paid for their services. His main preoccupation was to keep his business running smoothly and profitably. In fact, he lived strictly for business. He was a man notably devoid of human feeling.

Ironically enough, the leading courtesan in his employ was a woman of deep feeling. Her name was Mikasa. She was one of those physically graceful beings who seemed to have been born to the profession. She knew how to adorn herself too, and she had both poise and dignity—so much so, indeed, that she stood out distinctly even among the smart-looking younger set. Men were afraid of her at first. No one dared to accost her on the street.

Yonosuke, on the first evening spent at her table, felt immediately attracted to her. There was wit, gaiety, and laughter at her table.

"Very charming," he complimented her.

"I am sure," she replied, "the admiration is mutual. You are . . . shall we say, very handsome and you have . . . distinction." She gave him a shy look, rather unbecoming for her, but there was warmth in it. "You will visit me often, won't you?"

He did. And he discovered the softer, generous side of her nature. Mikasa was constantly looking after the comfort of her attendants, her servants, even her palanquin bearers. On cold nights she would see to it that the palanquin bearers keeping vigil outside the establishment got enough wine from her table to keep their bodies warm. The strictly business-minded proprietor Gonzaemon might sternly forbid such extravagance, but Mikasa managed somehow to have the hot drinks taken out to the palanquin bearers without his knowing it. If her female attendants got into trouble with the men-servants, Mikasa intervened or hushed up the affair so as to forestall ugly rumors. If the little girl waitresses and kitchen maids dozed on their jobs late at night, she would smile sympathetically, would never scold, would even go to their defense if their elders tried to chastise them.

But Mikasa, perhaps because of her warmheartedness, was extremely indifferent to money matters. Some patrons at her table were behind in their payments, and when Gonzaemon insisted that she induce them to pay up, she said:

"Let them pay when they can. Trust them."

"I will hold you responsible!" Gonzaemon threatened.

Meanwhile she fell into a pensive mood when Yonosuke neglected her even for a day or two. Then she sent for him. Their relationship went beyond that of patron and entertainer.

"I feel sad when you stay away from me too long," she confessed. "I . . . I love you, very much. Don't be cruel."

Yonosuke was now in the prime of life, gallant enough to respond wholeheartedly to her tender wishes. But he had to visit her secretly, for continuance of such ties—he being a family man—placed him in a compromising position. It was all very well to patronize teahouses where courtesans reigned, but to become intimately attached to one particular courtesan was quite another matter. He was now seeing Mikasa at the Osakaya not as a patron but as an invited lover.

Gonzaemon demanded payment for all such visits. "Strictly business here," he insisted.

"That would be very awkward," Yonosuke said. "Not that I'm a miser."

Gonzaemon turned on Mikasa. "Collect!"

"But . . . but Yonosuke-sama is now a very dear friend of mine, not a guest."

That taxed Gonzaemon's patience. "I forbid you ever to see him again." Then he glared at Yonosuke. "You are no longer welcome in my establishment. Get out!"

Barred at the entrance of the teahouse, Yonosuke walked the street alone at night.

When Mikasa was obliged to leave by a side door for a distant assignment, she sent word to him by one of her attendants. But he could never, never trace her palanquin in the dark.

Finally Mikasa herself, longing for him, arranged to meet him secretly on the street outside the teahouse. And in this way they saw each other in the moonless night, speaking tenderly and sometimes with amusement during those precious stolen moments. It was a far cry from the bright shelter, the comfort, and the gaiety of the teahouse drawing room. She would slip her hand inside the sleeve of his robe and pinch him to let him know she was there with him. But all too soon there would be a business call for her from the house within. She would hurry back into the establishment in tears, promising to see him there again the following evening.

Late one night she came crying out to him.

"This may be our last meeting," Mikasa said bitterly. "Gonzaemon-sama introduced me to a man called Kichichiyo, from Kishu Province, who wishes to make me his mistress, and . . . his intermediary, Shichi-sama from the house of Takeya, demanded that I break off relations with you at once."

In the end, however, she succeeded in spurning the offer in spite of the stern insistence and remonstrances of Gonzaemon, who had anticipated a fat commission on the deal. But Gonzaemon would not let it go at that. Because of her known attachment to Yonosuke, from which he could draw no profits, he was also losing lucrative business that might have come his way. He decided to break her spirit. He resorted to humiliation.

He demoted her from the highest-ranking courtesan to plain kitchen maid. Daily he sent her out in miserable patched robes to do the marketing, especially for bean-curd refuse, the lowest form of food in any household.

Seeing her fallen so low, some people who secretly envied Mikasa's beauty jeered at her. But proudly Mikasa performed even this menial task. "For *his* sake," she said to herself. "For his sake I would stoop to do anything."

That made Gonzaemon angrier than ever. "Stop your nonsense with Yonosuke," he demanded, "and I will put you back into your former position." But Mikasa vigorously shook her head.

Things came to a head in the eleventh month, when the first snow of the year fell. Gonzaemon ordered his menservants to strip her naked from the waist down save for her innermost garment. Then her hands were tied behind her back. Next she was strapped standing up to a willow tree in the garden, her back against the tree.

"In this way," said Gonzaemon, "you will be exposed to cold and ridicule until you change your mind. Think it over."

She thought it over for a whole week, standing out there in the snow, a half-naked prisoner, refusing the food brought to her.

"Now will you promise not to see Yonosuke?" Gonzaemon asked.

"I would rather die."

The other courtesans, attendants, and maidservants, though sternly warned not to go near her, could no longer endure the agony. They stole out in a group early one morning when Gonzaemon was still asleep. They saw Mikasa weeping. They wept too, as much out of sympathy for her as in protest against Gonzaemon's cruelty.

Mikasa told them: "It is not the humiliation that brings tears to my eyes. Or even the suffering. That is nothing.

But surely Yonosuke-sama must have heard about this. Why does he not come?"

A few minutes later a dealer in sweet oils named Tauemon sneaked in upon the scene to offer his sympathy. The courtesan knew that this merchant was a frequenter of Yonosuke's household.

She said: "Come to think of it, I have done Yonosuke-sama an injustice. Will you kindly untie my hands for a few moments? I promise you I will not try to escape and thereby put *you* into trouble. I just need the use of my hands to write Yonosuke-sama a note. I shall ask you to strap me up again when I have finished."

As soon as her hands were free, Mikasa tore a strip from the only piece of garment she was wearing. Then she bit off the tip of her right little finger. With the blood oozing out slowly and the silken strip of rag serving as paper, she wrote down her thoughts.

"Will you, then, be good enough to deliver this note to Yonosuke-sama?" She handed the message to Tauemon. "Now, tie me up again before Gonazemon turns his anger against you."

Tauemon strapped her hands to the tree as requested.

An hour later Mikasa, giving up all hope, was about to end it all by biting off her tongue when Yonosuke came rushing up. He was robed in white, the emblem of death, apparently meaning that he had decided, if death must come, then Mikasa should not die alone. This brought the entire horror-stricken household out into the garden. There were cries of "It's going to be a double suicide!" and "No, no! Stop them!"

Gonzaemon came out with blood in his eyes. "Stay away, every one of you," he stormed. "Let them die if they want to."

"No, no, no, no!" There was great commotion, arguments, pleas. "The law . . . the law!"

"The law is on my side!" Gonzaemon shouted. "She is

under contract to me. Remember that. No officer will interfere. If she prefers to die rather than fulfill her obligations to me, then I won't stop her. It's her penalty for insubordination. And if this . . . this man Yonosuke wants to go along with her, it is his privilege. He has hurt my business. His going will be a good riddance."

Yonosuke, calm in his majesty of white, and with dagger drawn in readiness for the suicide rites, confronted him. "I can easily put *you* to death with this dagger, Gonzaemon," he said.

"You wouldn't dare!" Gonzaemon cried, his lips atremble.

"That way," Yonosuke continued, "I could save her."

"You have no right!"

"I have the moral right." Then Yonosuke smiled sardonically. "But you needn't shiver in your sandals . . . yet. Save that for afterwards. You see, Gonzaemon, I am not inclined to take the life of another. You will see why. Not with a dagger anyhow. I shall give you one more chance to be human and reasonable. Now . . . this is not a question of contracts. It is a matter of conscience . . . and humanity . . . and honor. *If she dies, I die.* I cannot honorably do otherwise. You will then have the blood of both of us on your hands. Remember that. Have you ever seen ghosts, Gonzaemon? Well, I have. So I speak from experience. We will haunt you every night. We will never let you sleep . . . ever! We will drive you mad with fear. We will drive you relentlessly to your own suicide. We will . . ."

Gonzaemon turned white with fear. "All right," he said hoarsely, "set her free." Then he fled back into the house.

It was a yearly custom at the Ikudama Shrine, on the eleventh of the seventh month, to cut all the lotus leaves in its sacred pond, so that new shoots might rise resplendently from the old roots. Boats plowing through thick clusters, sharp sickles severing the huge flat leaves floating on the surface, the general disturbance in the water— all this caused a tremendous hubbub among the fish, the frogs, the turtles, and the waterfowl as they swam or leaped or fled in dismay.

At the southeast corner, where a small neck of land jutted out into the water, a group of five men had been sitting since early morning. They had come to witness this excitement, making a regular picnic of it, drinking and singing popular songs. Cronies all, they were men of wide experience.

There was the proprietor of a fan shop on Echigo-machi, another shopkeeper who owned the Sumiyoshiya, a comic actor named Dempachi from Sado Island, and a man called Hei, the head *banto* of the Yoshidaya. And there was, of course, Yonosuke.

Soon the excitement in the pond was forgotten, for the five men—as it always happened when such cronies got together—had begun to exchange reminiscences. All of them, as if by prearrangement, had brought along in their sleeve pockets a number of love letters addressed to them. These they showed one another. They were amorous confessions written by high-class courtesans with whom the five men had at one time or another carried on clandestine affairs. None of the letters had been answered.

165

The talk of the five men then drifted to telling each other frankly about the authors of those epistles of feminine devotion. First there was the courtesan called Seyama.

"She is small of build but no longer young," explained the fan dealer, "and that is regrettable. She has a pretty face and form, though by nature she is rather imperious. She manages, however, to be amiable most of the time. A clever woman, that."

Then there was Ohashi. "She is tall and slender," said the master of the Sumiyoshiya. "She has a bright-looking face, though her eyes are dark. Unfortunately, her mouth has a mean look sometimes, especially when she complains. At the entertaining table she is the quiet type, not very sure of herself: a poetess, one might say, who is shy at reciting her own verses. Usually her young girl attendant prompts her along."

And there was Okoto. "Ah, there you have a woman with a homely face, almost repulsive," said Hei. "But the curious thing about it is that there are men who prefer such a woman. What is more, she is a resourceful courtesan, much too efficient. One feels she is the greedy sort. Worse, she has a scar along her neckline, which can hardly be said to improve her looks. Yet at the entertaining table she always shows good judgment. I have never known her to commit an indiscretion that might have embarrassed either her patrons or her employer. Somehow, with all her faults, she manages to display manners and mannerisms that distinguish the high-class courtesan from the ordinary prostitute."

And Dempachi, the comedian, said about Asazuma: "She has a long slender torso and fascinating hips. A very beautiful profile she has too, for her nose is well shaped. But her nostrils! Oh, how black they are! They look as if they were chimneys filled with soot that had never been swept. That is her only fault. On the whole she is the frail sort with a mild disposition. But she can really be stubborn. The frail and mild ones usually are. I ought to know."

Now the five men talked about the model courtesan. What should she be like?

They agreed that she must be the sort who looked charming and presentable even if she did not comb her hair meticulously. Her face should look pretty enough without liquid powder. Her fingers and toes must be slender, yet full-proportioned. She should have a graceful figure, with just the right amount of bulge at the right places. Her eyes should always look calm and cool. Her skin should be white as snow. She should know how to drink. She must have a good singing voice and be capable, in addition, of playing well on the koto and samisen.

Such a woman must be a good literary composer, they agreed, and write charming letters. She should never think about receiving gifts but must be generous in giving to others. Always she must have sympathy and understanding. Above all she must use discretion.

Yonosuke laughed. "If such a courtesan does actually exist," he asked, "who among those you have known comes closest to this ideal?"

His four companions were unanimous in their judgment: "Yugiri, of course."

"Tell me something about her."

Well, the four agreed, Yugiri was most of all sympathetic and discreet. Those men who became desperately infatuated with her she would politely but firmly hold off by explaining the public nature of her own duties and their obligations to their wives and children. If embarrassing rumors cropped up, she would hush them up in order to protect the family men involved. It made no difference to her who came to drink at her table. Be he fisherman Chobei or farmer Goroshichi, she would let him hold her hand and entertain him with charming words and looks.

At first the four men spoke about Yugiri in loud words of unstinted praise. But gradually, as they began to divulge their own frustrated experiences with her, their voices dropped and a sad look came upon their faces. It seemed that Dempachi, the clown with a light heart who made people laugh, had fallen most mournfully in love with her.

Yonosuke, hearing all this, felt a sudden desire to see Yugiri and satisfy himself as to what manner of woman she really was. He feigned a headache and left the spot ahead of the others. In his room he composed a long artful letter to her, detailing the matchless account he had heard of her, praising her virtues, asking for a private meeting. Then he dispatched the letter to her by messenger.

He received no answer. So then he visited her house nightly, in wind and snow and storm, but still he received no welcome to enter. He decided she was deliberately avoiding him.

On the twenty-fifth of the twelfth month, however, when everyone was busy at home preparing for the year end, Yugiri, apparently moved by Yonosuke's persistence, addressed a brief note to him: "Come and see me secretly tonight."

She named the teahouse and waited for him in a small private room. They were not to be disturbed, she told the mistress. In the center of the room a small charcoal brazier was left burning in the deep hollow of the matted floor—the *kotatsu* foot-warming hollow—with a low table and coverlet spread over it. At this table they could sit facing each other, their feet dangling beneath the covered table in the warmed-up hollow.

Yonosuke was duly admitted into Yugiri's presence. But they had barely begun to converse when suddenly

Yugiri summoned a maidservant. "Put out the charcoal fire in the bottom of this hollow," she said.

The fire was put out, and the *kotatsu* hollow went cold. Yonosuke looked surprised, for it was a freezing winter's night. But he did not ask Yugiri why she had ordered it.

Yugiri's prescience was well founded. A maid soon came in excitedly to announce that Gonshichi-sama had crashed the front door and demanded to see her at once.

Yugiri did not bat an eye. Apparently Gonshichi was one of those persistent infatuated patrons who annoyed her by jealously trailing her everywhere, demanding her undivided attention. Calmly she asked Yonosuke to dive into the hollow, for there was no other place in which to hide, and no time either, and there might be trouble. Just in time, too, for as Yonosuke settled himself uncomfortably in the cramped hollow underneath the covered table, Gonshichi stormed in. Now Yonosuke knew why Yugiri had ordered the maid to put out the fire. He might otherwise have been scorched or suffocated to death.

Yugiri stood up, took out a letter from her bosom, and started to leave for the kitchen.

"Who is that letter from?" demanded Gonshichi, obviously jealous and angry. "Let me see it!"

"Oh, no you won't," Yugiri replied. "Besides, I have told you time and time again not to follow me or interfere with my personal affairs."

Then she slipped past him into the hallway.

Gonshichi followed her out. "Let me see it, I tell you!"

Yonosuke crept out of the hollow and dashed out of the room. For he had wits enough to understand that Yugiri had deliberately contrived that opening for him to make his escape—if he cared to avoid a nasty fight with that jealous brute. Out in the vestibule he could still hear them quarreling in the kitchen.

"She is *not* the ideal courtesan," he decided, "but maybe the most harassed."

MORE than anything else, Yonosuke loved his freedom. His wife had finally tired of his roving infidelities and left him. There was no mourning either way. Things just faded away. Courtesans who were seriously in love with him tugged at his heartstrings for a while. But only for a while and through no fault of their own. He refused to be manacled by amorous ties to any woman, however tenderly clinging, for any length of time. This was Yonosuke—always on the way from one place to another.

And so, this bright New Year's morning, he was on his way to Tambaguchi in his two-man palanquin, the bearers shouting rhythmically to keep their steps in unison as they trotted along. At the entrance to the gay district Yonosuke ordered them to halt in front of a tearoom. "The nest of the nightingale," he said, "is not far off."

Shoroku, master of the tearoom, came running out to offer his holiday greetings.

"Today," Yonosuke told Shoroku as he alighted from the palanquin and sat down on the welcome bench outside, "I have come to see the special ceremonies at which Hatsune, 'the nightingale'—or so I hear—will exhibit herself. I wouldn't miss the show for all the world." Hatsune was a noted courtesan whom he had never yet seen.

While he was sipping his holiday tea that Shoroku's wife had brought, a solicitor from an entertainment house came up to him.

"Won't you come over? Come over, please," the solicitor invited.

"Where are you from?"

"From the Tsuruya, the house of Denzaemon."

"Does Hatsune perform there?"

"Oh yes, she is our reigning beauty."

"I shall be there."

As Yonosuke approached the establishment, he saw that the exhibition rites were just about to begin. He saw three breath-taking beauties.

"This is Kodayu, the courtesan," explained the master of ceremonies, pointing and bowing to the woman on display closest to him. "And that is Nokaze-sama. Over on the other side is Hatsune-sama."

So that was Hatsune! Yonosuke went forward for a closer look. She was wearing a sky-blue inner garment, exposed at the neckline, a white satin midgarment of plum-blossom design, and a gorgeous robe of five-colored damask with brilliantly etched gems, battledores, and bows and arrows against a background of vari-shaped leaves and the sacred *shimenawa* rope. Over all this she wore a lavender *haori* coat on which a hand-painted nightingale sang from a plum-tree bough. It had scarlet decorative tassels. And in this splendid New Year attire Hatsune paraded past with her train of attendants, light of heel and very alluring.

Yonosuke recalled that his friend Mataichi once said a good courtesan must appear to be lighthearted and yet be inwardly firm and shrewd. Men could see that on the women's faces. The rule seemed to fit Hatsune very well, Yonosuke thought.

But his disappointment was great when, upon starting negotiations, he was told that Hatsune had already been booked full for the next twenty-five days.

"Then could you let me have the twenty-sixth and twenty-seventh days?" Yonosuke asked.

That was all right, he was told.

"I am going to give a party," he said. "My friend Kinzaemon will be there."

But at the first party Yonosuke realized with something like horror that he was no match for this astute courtesan in witty conversation over the festive board. From the very outset, in the exchange of greetings, Hatsune took the initiative, reversing the order of formal compliments. She gave him no quarter. He could not put in a brilliant word edgewise. Kinzaemon likewise felt embarrassed.

"I have had the pleasure," Hatsune told Yonosuke with a beaming look, "of seeing you off and on before this. Really, I must say, your manly ways have impressed me as being the quintessence of a gentleman of good breeding. I do not know the woman whom you are patronizing regularly, but honestly she is to be envied."

What could Yonosuke say in reply to such elegant flattery? Obviously she did not mean it. It was a tour de force designed to keep him silent—to show who was the acme of brilliance, the shining star here. The polite, conventional tribute he had intended to pay this celebrated courtesan died on his lips. For all his bountiful experience with women of her profession, he found himself on the defensive, uttering inanities. He fidgeted with his robe out of uneasiness lest his personal appearance fall below the high standards she had gratuitously attributed to him. He was doing precisely what she had subtly driven him to do. He felt the cold sweat on his hands. Everyone at the table became tense.

By way of worming himself out of his embarrassment as best he could, Yonosuke called for more drinks. He drank copiously. He called for the incense burner. He burned precious incense copiously. He looked about him and saw that the ceiling needed repairs.

"You cannot leave it as it is," he told Denzaemon, the proprietor of the establishment, who was sitting sedately with him at the now none-too-festive board.

"No, I suppose not," replied Denzaemon. And he too shut up like a clam.

Yonosuke even offered to contract the job. Then he paid compliments to Denzaemon's wife, who was also present at the party. She said thank you and that was all. A woman attendant of the courtesan picked up a samisen and began to sing at random. Yonosuke took up the rhythm, beating time with his hands to encourage her.

His companion Kinzaemon's embarrassment deepened as he saw his friend behaving before the courtesan as though he were a plain novice paying a visit to a common whore. He tried to divert attention to himself with the cleverly uttered jokes of the not-too-inebriated, playful drunk. It failed to draw the anticipated amused applause.

It was Hatsune who restored cheerfulness to the room. "Men are such charming creatures," she said. "I like them when they throw off all formalities and act like boys again. So natural, so guileless and simple."

Yonosuke leaned over and whispered to Kinzaemon: "By that she means men are fools."

"Yes," whispered back Kinzaemon, "and she intends that no man shall make a fool of her."

"Yet I have heard it said that if her guests were honest beginners she would say pleasantly funny things to make them feel completely at home. She knows we are experienced men and her tactic evidently is to smother in advance those who, she suspects, may try to act smart in her presence."

"Vain?"

"Clever, I am afraid."

"She is putting on a front, an armor, so to speak."

"Well, she is succeeding . . . unpleasantly perhaps . . . but let us admit it."

When bedtime came, the choosing of rooms and room-mates at the establishment—a common practice—usually was a give-and-take affair. There were many rooms, many likes and dislikes. Guests and entertainers alike were accommodated. Hatsune showed no preferences.

"Tonight I am really tired and sleepy," she said. "Any small room will do." Then she went off to do her toilet.

Curious Kinzaemon followed her into the kitchen and found her gargling her throat industriously. She patted her hair into place, perfumed the sleeves of her night robe with two different burning scents, and then soaked the hem in the fumes of an incense she picked out of a box bearing the sign Muro-no-Yashima. Critically she examined her own profile in a bronze mirror.

As she approached the small room in which she was to sleep that night, Hatsune asked the elderly chambermaids to draw apart the sliding doors that shut off the adjoining room. Yonosuke was already in bed in that room. Then she dismissed the maids and called for her little girl attendant. A lighted paper lantern stood at the head of her bed.

"Spider!" she cried, as if in alarm. "What a strange spider!"

That awakened Yonosuke in the adjoining room.

"Oh, bother!" he muttered. He was about to get up to help her chase the spider out of her room when Hatsune hurried over, seized him and said: *"I am the spider!"*

Baffled by her trickery, Yonosuke tried brazenly to embrace her, but she pushed him off. "Don't be rude," she said, laughing. "And don't misunderstand me."

Early the next morning, as she walked past the foot of his bed, Yonosuke thought she deliberately kicked his blanket.

DRAWN like a moth to a flame, Yonosuke was back again
in Edo, the shogunal capital, to look over the upper
bracket of the Yoshiwara gay quarters. If he had not
yet heard, he was soon to learn—and bitterly—that the
courtesans of Edo differed markedly from their refined
contemporaries of Kyoto or those of uninhibited Osaka.
They possessed an ingrained quality typical of the city
that could not be so easily trifled with. Verily the pride
of the Edo courtesans was an amazing trait. Yet it was
kept well under control, as exemplified by the rising star
Yoshida, known for her skill in the art of *kuzetsu,* or what
was popularly called "lovers' quarrels" in gay circles.

Not that her behavior was any the less circumspect
than that of the gentle Kindayu of Osaka. She wrote
just as beautiful a hand as the artistic Nokaze of Kyoto.
But she also had a talent for composing verses, and in
this she had no peer. What gave distinction to her talent
was a quality of challenge, subtle and facile.

Once a poet called Hinyu paid tribute to her charms
by composing only the first half of a *waka* verse:

> Cool is the evening as
> Along the festive board
> Lovely Yoshida reigns . . .

and promptly Yoshida responded by adding the daring
second half:

> Then lo, the wandering firefly
> Leaps into her warm bedding.

175

It showed she had her wits about her. And when the dormant pride of such a woman is assailed, then alas for the assailant!

Inevitably it remained for Yonosuke to explode that smouldering inner fire. Her reputation as a daring wit represented, to him, a very pleasant challenge, and he finally secured an appointment. He was no longer young —well along in his prime, as a matter of fact—but one appointment led to another, and this was a tribute to her. He became so persistent and so generous with his money that Yoshida could hardly frown upon his visits. She even had to refuse appointments requested by other men. Believing Yonosuke's attentions were sincere, she soon became seriously attached to him. Thereafter she thought of him as a lover, not a mere patron.

But intimacies rarely call for the exercise of one's wits and, as usual, the moment he had secured what he wanted, Yonosuke's interest in her palled. Ever seeking new faces, he found the charms of another Yoshiwara courtesan much more appealing. This meant that he had to sever his relations with the unsuspecting Yoshida.

Out of consideration for her feelings, he hesitated to declare his change of heart openly. He gave her hints instead: fairly obvious and brusque indications that his mind was already roving elsewhere. But she failed to take the hints, seemingly with sublime innocence. She showed no distress, no resentment.

So then one evening Yonosuke took Shohei of the Kozukaya along with him to the house of Ichizaemon. "Today," Yonosuke told Shohei, "it must be final. I am going to be very rude to Yoshida, so rude that she will never want to see me again. I can then visit the other courtesan freely. So you must bear witness and help me along. Let's hurry."

Three was indeed company among intimates, and the impertinent behavior of the two men at last seemed to convince Yoshida that she was going to be jilted. Yet she betrayed no anger, made no recriminative remark. She drank no more, no less than she had always done. She was imperturbably cool.

That confounded the two men. They gulped down their saké, cup after cup. In their nervous excitement they began to feign drunkenness, the better to infuriate her. Shohei overdid it, knocking down the wine flask and spilling its contents. He tried to stop the flow of the saké on the mat with his paper handkerchief, but to no avail. There was altogether too much of it. Just as it was about to soil the courtesan's immaculate robe, one of her girl attendants mopped it away with her own brown-and-black robe, soaking it up clean. The robe had to be discarded.

And then, just as the flowers in the garden were being lighted up by lanterns, Yoshida excused herself in order to go to the kitchen. Halfway down the exposed corridor, as she stepped firmly on an apparently loose floor board, there was a curious explosion of sound about her, loud enough for the two men watching her in the room to hear. Without any show of embarrassment, however, she proceeded on her way.

"What an interesting sound!" Shohei exclaimed. Yonosuke nodded, laughing. "That gives us a splendid chance to make her really angry with you. When she comes back here we shall hold our noses, and if she does not take the hint . . . well?"

The courtesan took a very long time.

"She must be embarrassed," Shohei surmised.

Before the two men got through laughing, however, they saw her coming back up the corridor. She had changed her robe and she carried a sprig of cherry blossoms. She paused, sidestepped the spot where the sound had occurred, and frowned at it. Then she re-entered the room.

Her singular coolness awed the two men. Shohei hesitated to hold his nose. Yonosuke stood up and went out for an elaborate inspection of the corridor. He stepped vigorously on the floor boards, but no explosion resembling the previous sound could be heard. Just a small squeak. He, too, re-entered the room, silent, with a significant nod at Shohei.

It was the courtesan's voice that now exploded, with cold fury. "For some time now," Yoshida said, glaring at Yonosuke, "you have been acting very rudely. I have known your intentions right along. It was understood that we would keep up our relationship until one of us got tired of the other. Well, let me tell you now that I am fed up with you. Absolutely. I never want to see you again, ever!"

Without giving Yonosuke a chance to reply, she marched out of the room and down the corridor toward the front of the establishment. There, just as cool as ever, she began to play with a little dog. Totally taken aback by this unexpected reversal of the jilting process, the two men left forlornly by a side door.

Worse, the true account of this incident soon spread through the Yoshiwara district, and there was general condemnation of Yonosuke's behavior. The upshot was that the other courtesan for whose charms Yonosuke had tried to desert Yoshida refused to see him.

Later Yoshida called together the mistress of the establishment, the head man Shigeichi, the matron Oman, and all the courtesans to explain her action without equivocation. She said: "I purposely had the floor board loosened just a little at one spot so as to produce a sound when one stepped on it. If the two men were to assume —as I expected they would—that the explosion was of human origin, I would have confessed that such was my contempt for them. But when, upon returning to the room, I sidestepped the spot on the corridor floor, they were completely fooled. It was very, very funny. So I had the last word. Of course the sound did not come from the floor board."

DEFIANT HEART

IN THOSE days there was one courtesan in Kyoto whom all men admired. Her professional name, Takahashi, was derived from that of an ancient practitioner illustrious in her own time.

"She has a fine figure, a charming face, and bright sparkling eyes," said one of her admirers. "She has something else besides."

Whatever that "something else" might have been, it was the way she comported herself that drew men to her. Graceful and mild-mannered, with hair done up in alluring style, she became the model of all aspiring Kyoto courtesans. But there was fire too behind that gentle spirit, intractable and firm.

One morning, as the first snow of the year turned the garden trees into a silvery fairyland, Takahashi's fancy turned importunately to thoughts of tea. She decided the day was much too beautiful to be spent in idleness. The tea ceremony with its refined trimmings should be just the thing to match the white loveliness outside. So thinking, she had the upstairs rooms of the Hachimonjiya prepared for a party. Her only invited male guest would be Yonosuke, lately returned unsatisfied from Edo. Three young courtesans from the Kambayashi completed the group of five. This was to be holiday relaxation, not business.

Yonosuke, curious and interested, saw suspended on the wall a number of blank picture mountings. "There must be some hidden meaning in them," he told himself as he tentatively contemplated the blank scrolls.

The tea utensils bore the crest of the mandarin orange. Tea delicacies were seen on dainty doll-festival plates. Everything seemed new, to be used for this purpose only. "Very charming," Yonosuke said. He was aging, his mood mellowing.

At the tea brewer's seat sat the courtesan Takahashi as hostess, her hair in bangs, brilliant with a golden ornament. Her inner garment was of plum-red sheer, her robe of white satin embroidered with the crest of the Sambaso, a symbolic theatrical design. Her over-robe displayed an irregularly spread pattern of a long-tailed fowl and vermilion tassels.

Presently an attendant brought word from the kitchen: "Kyujiro has returned from Uji."

That meant, Yonosuke knew, that Kyujiro had been sent all the way to the Uji brook to fetch pure water for the tea. Although it seemed to be a mere trifle, the thought behind it—the desire of the courtesan to obtain the purest water possible for the tea, for *his* pleasure—was no trifling matter.

When the rites were over, Takahashi began to wet a number of ink slabs. "All this beauty of the snow spread outside before us," she said, "should not be wasted by our just looking at it. We should all compose verses and preserve the impressions forever."

Now the intention behind the blank picture mountings became clear to Yonosuke. Everyone, including himself, took up writing brushes to fill in the blank spaces with tributes in verse, not drawings, to the sparkling snow. Some of those present composed their poems in the seventeen-syllable haiku, others in the thirty-one-syllable *waka*.

In the adjoining room there was the lively samisen music of the lion dance. As the guests returned in high spirits to the tearoom they found bamboo vases suspended on the walls, with no flowers in them. But it was no surprise to Yonosuke. "Ah," he told himself, "this day's festivity is an assemblage of beautiful courtesans—beautiful flowers in themselves—so why fill the vases?" Despite the aging process, his romantic feeling was as youthful as ever.

After tea came relaxation. Ceremony was dropped. All strove to be comfortable in natural ease. Rice wine was brought in, with tidbits and food. Gaiety brought relief to taut nerves. Yonosuke drank more than he should.

In this inebriated condition, obeying his customary instincts, he took out his huge wallet and poured out piles of gold and silver coins on the mat. Then he scooped up the coins in his two hands and offered them to Takahashi, his hostess and courtesan.

"Take them," he said. "They are yours."

Now that was a queer thing to do. He was the honored guest of the courtesan at a private holiday party. Obviously it was unethical to offer payment. The other guests, the three young courtesans from the Kambayashi, snickered and then frowned, as if to say: "He's drunk, but that's an insult, you know."

But Takahashi smiled suavely. "Indeed I shall accept them," she said and received the coins on the tray lying beside her. "There is no difference between accepting the money here in your presence, ladies, and my getting it secretly after nagging him in a letter."

She handed the coin-filled tray to the little girl attendant sitting beside her. "Take it away for safekeeping," she said. "It is one of life's most precious necessities. Some day Yonosuke-sama may need it, though I hope not."

In this manner, in whatever she did or said, Takahashi proved to be unpredictable. The day sped much too

181

swiftly for the guests. But toward sunset a messenger arrived to summon her to the house of Maruya. A wealthy visitor from Owari Province, he said, had been waiting for her there for some time.

It was a business summons, and Takahashi was loath to go. "Why should they call me on this day which I have set aside as a holiday?" she thought rebelliously. But the Maruya messenger was insistent. "It is the man's first visit," he said, "and we must entertain him promptly and properly."

Business was business, and for the first time the courtesan was saddened by the inexorable demands of her profession.

With tears in her eyes, she told the young courtesans: "I suppose I must go. But I shall offer an excuse and come back here as soon as I can. Please look after Yonosuke-sama and keep him entertained so he won't be lonely for me."

She started to leave, but at the gate she paused and then returned to the room upstairs and told the young courtesans: "Please offer him drinks and make him comfortable while I am away." She even left her little girl attendant with Yonosuke and proceeded alone to the Maruya.

But instead of going upstairs at once to entertain the wealthy visitor from Owari, Takahashi went into the Maruya kitchen. There she began to write a letter. It was an affectionate letter, addressed to Yonosuke. Evidently she was in love with him, and she poured that love endlessly into the letter.

The Maruya master and mistress, concerned for the guest upstairs, used every known device to cajole and wheedle her into going up. "Please," they pleaded together, "if only for a few minutes. He is waiting for you." But Takahashi turned a deaf ear.

The worried jester-attendants of the house came down

with haggard looks. "Please go up," they begged. "Food will be served."

Suddenly Takahashi showed anger in her face.

"You jesters," she scolded, "ought to know more than anyone else about the sort of women we are and the kind of life we lead. On second thought, I don't think I would care to meet a guest who is so impatient. I am going back."

With that, she returned forthwith to the Hachimonjiya. The Maruya messenger followed her there to entreat with her, but to no avail.

Yonosuke, now sobered by her obdurate defiance, tried to plead with her. "It is best," he urged, "that you go. It is your duty as a courtesan, an obligation of your profession. You must not keep him waiting alone."

Takahashi replied: "You know as well as anyone else, Yonosuke-sama, that the ethics of my profession call for leisurely entertainment and enjoyment. Nothing hurried or forced. I don't like that man. He seems to be hungrily impatient for something." She added: "The gods of this country forbid it. I won't go."

Yonosuke feared the consequences for her. "You must use your good sense in a case like this. That man may not meekly accept this rebuff by twiddling his thumbs. Are you prepared to defy him when he forces himself in here with a drawn sword?" Then he added: "He may cut you up," and laughed good-naturedly, "leaving your head here and taking your body along with him."

"I am prepared for anything." She smiled. "Come play for me."

She pillowed her head on his lap while he played for her on the samisen. Entering into the mood of the music, she sang snatches of a popular song about a woman's sad life.

Suddenly there sounded a tremendous hubbub downstairs. Up the stairs the hubbub continued. The next instant the outraged Owari visitor burst into the room with a drawn sword, just as Yonosuke had predicted he would. Takahashi ignored him and kept on singing. There was not even the semblance of a tremor in her voice.

Yonosuke sprang to his feet, and so did the three young courtesans. Seizing the intruder, they strove desperately to prevent him from swinging his sword.

"Let me go," he shouted. "I want to kill that woman!"

"Calm yourself," Yonosuke said. "She hasn't done anything to you to deserve death at your hands."

"Oh, yes? She shall pay for insulting me. Take your hands off!"

"You can't kill anyone without getting killed yourself, sooner or later. Remember that."

"A man must be willing to risk his own life to fight for his dignity. Let me go, I tell you."

"Oh, nonsense. She isn't fighting you. She is ignoring you. She doesn't even know who you are. Only the worst kind of a fool would strike an innocent unresisting woman."

"Get away from me, I warn you!"

The would-be killer struggled vainly to free himself. He raised such a din that the attendants downstairs had meanwhile summoned the police. The officers arrived in their formal *hakama* to placate the maddened intruder. Servants from the two houses, the Maruya and the Hachimonjiya, added their conflicting shouts of recrimination and angry apologies.

In the midst of this noisy brawl Kizaemon, the master of the Hachimonjiya, came rushing up into the room. "Stop!" he commanded. "As her master, I have the right to settle this case. Neither you," and he pointed to the Owari intruder, "nor you, Yonosuke-sama, shall have the pleasure of her company henceforth."

Thereupon he seized the calmly defiant courtesan

Takahashi by her hair and dragged her out of the room. But she, forever the strong-willed woman, put in the last word fondly:

"Farewell, Yonosuke-sama. Farewell."

BIZARRE TO THE RIDICULOUS

As TIME passed with not much else to do, the rich *daijin* and the first-class courtesans of Kyoto made a gala affair of their appointments. Visitors to the gay district glittered like brilliantly groomed dandies on parade. Showy styles in dressing set the theme. Extravagance was carried to extremes. But the courtesans were the greater offenders.

Among those noted for such extravagance was Kaoru, the leading courtesan of the Kambayashi, whose prosperous air was mainly due to her presence. Priest Sosen once wrote that the splendor of splendid material things is pleasing to the eye—as much as to say, no matter what you may think about the soul's need for it. And Kaoru, taking her cue from that otherwise sage ecclesiast's earthy sermon, decided that there was no splendor so pleasing to the eye as autumn's burnt-colored blooms.

First she commissioned the renowned artist Kano Yukinobu to paint a picture of flaming autumn on plain white satin. Eight court nobles were next asked to inscribe vignettes in verse, in black decorative calligraphy, on this gorgeous design. The result was a picture of breath-taking beauty, admirably suitable for a hanging scroll. But Kaoru had no idea of putting it to such trifling use. She had it made into a robe for herself.

Such luxury would seem to have been almost sacrilegious. People who went to see her in this bizarre attire—

men who could not be easily amazed by anything in this mundane world—reported that it could have happened nowhere but in Kyoto. Only Kaoru could have dared to conceive it.

The rich men who patronized her table—and they were readily recognized about town—vied with one another to match this outfit with dashing robes of their own.

"The gay district is no place for the struggling poor in old washed-out robes or dirty loincloths," commented Ichibei of the Fujiya teahouse with barbarous contempt. "It is all very well to economize and save your money, but men must die sooner or later, and you might as well spend what you have while you can."

"Right!" agreed Yonosuke. *"While you can.* We're no longer young."

His undergarment, tastefully exposed at the neckline, was of spotless scarlet, despite his age. His robe was of yellow crepe de Chine embroidered with the fancy crests of his favorite courtesans. His sash was light gray. His *haori* coat was made of black camlet, with golden borders and lined with striped satin.

On his left hip was a long sword, the kind that was popular with men about town, with a sharkskin-covered hilt and a short sharp blade as an accessory. Dangling from his sash was a tiny *netsuke* wood carving inlaid with agate. His folding wallet was of colored leather, and his flat medicine case had gold and lavender braid. In his hand he carried an ukiyo-e hand-painted mousseline fan mounted on twelve slender ribs. His feet were encased in cotton drill *tabi* socks and sandals. His sandal bearer carried his walking stick and parasol.

Along with him as he paraded down the street in this flashy attire was his retinue of jesters from the Hachimonjiya. Anyone seeing him could tell at a glance that he was headed for the gay district. Perhaps—but of course!—to the Kambayashi, where Kaoru reigned in bizarre splendor. Again, however, he paused to think of others. Of people who could not afford such luxurious living. Of the jesters accompanying him, for instance. There were nine of them. Why not give them a treat and let others entertain them for once?

"Men," he told them, "we are *not* going to the Kambayashi today. Let Kaoru enjoy her own splendor alone for once. She likes her mirror best anyhow. And she is too exacting and fussy. We'll go to the Hachimonjiya."

As the gaudy parade arrived at that teahouse, Yonosuke told the jesters: "Today I shall be in the background and you shall take the stage. Consider yourselves patrons here for the day—at my expense, of course. Enjoy yourselves."

The jesters trouped upstairs with a whoop, changed into carnation-design bathrobes, loosened their topknots, and raised a great din. Anything could happen when such rough comical characters were given free rein.

Courtesans interested them not in the least.

"For once," comedian Yashichi said, "we can do the things we have always wanted to do but couldn't. Let's go."

They began, in rollicking fashion, to tease, jeer at, and challenge the other courtesan establishments across the way and to their right and left.

Yashichi fetched a hemp broom, pasted white Shinto shrine paper pendants on the handle, and shook it like a mailed fist from the second-story balcony at the Maruya across the street. *(It was a playful accusation that the Maruya was unclean, maybe a whorehouse, and needed purifying.)* *

* Interpretations of these symbols are the translator's, in his own idiom, closely approaching the meaning and spirit of the originals. The author's text contains no explanation, presumably because such symbols were easily recognizable to the readers of his time.

But the jesters at the Maruya were hardly less resourceful. Soon they responded by brandishing an Ebisu god-of-wealth statuette at the Hachimonjiya. *(You're jealous. See, oh you paupers, how blessed we are with riches!)*

Jesters at the Kashiwaya, to the right, witnessed this symbolic exchange of epithets and joined the fray by flaunting pieces of choice dried carp. *(Yes, and we have plenty of fancy dishes here. You must be famished!)*

Tokozaemon cleverly took up the cue for the Hachimonjiya by clanking a baking pan that had a long cluster of beard attached. *(You poor fish! We cook well-seasoned, substantial food here. Yours must be old and stale.)*

From the house to the left, the Marutaya, its jesters followed by flashing a sheaf of oracles from the Three Shrines at the Hachimonjiya. *(We predict dire things for you. Repent!)*

Maruya immediately brandished a hammer. *(That's right. We're coming over to inflict dire things upon you.)*

Kichibei the Parrot, from the Hachimonjiya, displayed a lantern. *(We dare you and offer a light so you won't stumble to your own doom.)*

Maruya responded with a kerchiefed statuette of the Buddha. *(Thank you. We didn't stumble. We crushed you. You're already dead. Peace be with your soul!)*

Hachimonjiya exhibited a cutting board. *(You're crazy. See, we're very much alive. In fact, we're going to cut you up. Be prepared to die like the carp, resigned and unflinching.)*

Kashiwaya from across the street at the right renewed the symbolic fight by swinging a wooden well bucket. *(It's you who are dirty. See, we're going to give you a bath!)*

Maruya added a bunch of vegetables. *(Yes, and avoid eating meat; it's sacrilegious.)*

Hachimonjiya responded with a salmon, a toothpick in its mouth. *(Ha! What's sacrilegious? We like meat and who's going to stop us?)*

Then the challenges flew thick and fast, back and

forth—a cat *(Still alive? You must have two lives!)*; a grocery account book *(Hell, our credit is good!)*; a noble's headgear *(Be careful of your language; we're not common trash!)*; a package of jingling small coins *(Oh, yes? You're nothing but beggars. Here's charity for you!)*.

Finally the jesters at the Hachimonjiya accused the three other teahouses with a dismounted paper sliding door bearing the legend, "Abortion drugs sold; also the service of midwives." *(You're nothing but a bunch of whorehouses.)*

The challenged houses exchanged friendly signals, agreed on a common reply, and brandished a wooden pestle. *(Say that again and we'll pound you to death!)*

Hachimonjiya laughingly exhibited funeral ornaments. *(Drop dead!)*

The street outside was meanwhile thronged with people. It seemed that everyone in the district—courtesans, patrons, shop attendants, servants, loiterers, passers-by —was out there watching, rooting, jeering, laughing. The jesters, having nothing more to exhibit, paused for breath, and the crowd shouted: "We want more! We want more!"

Easily flattered, the jesters were also versatile. Now they trouped downstairs, out into the street, mingled with the crowd, and told them funny stories. The crowd roared with laughter, bent with convulsions.

Anger rose from the empty teahouses. This sort of foolish merriment was bad for business. One teahouse keeper, his patience taxed to the limit, cried to another: "Isn't there a way of stopping this nonsense right now?"

"I know of a way. I shall show you. I shall have my pages scatter coins into the street. That will divert the crowd's interest and they will forget about the jesters. Watch them pick up the coins!"

That was the master of the Kambayashi speaking. Kaoru, the lovely, magnificently robed courtesan, sat bored and neglected in her upstairs boudoir.

The pages of the Kambayashi came out with a huge package of copper coins, scooped up handfuls, and threw them into the crowd. The coins came down like scattered showers. But no one stooped to pick them up. All interest continued to be centered on the jesters' jokes. The pages threw bigger handfuls.

"Stop it, you fools!" someone in the crowd demanded.

Chilled by this rebuke, the pages withdrew into the Kambayashi.

Later, as Yonosuke watched with an amused smile from the balcony of the Hachimonjiya, hordes of rubbish pickers came creeping up among the laughing crowd, picked up the coins, and returned like runaway thieves to their miserable hovels.

DISTANT ENCHANTMENT

DEEP autumn was the season of the year when the courtesans of Edo paraded through the Yoshiwara district in the most gorgeous robes. Above all, it would be a treat to see the peerless Takao and her train of attendants in this setting.

So deciding, Yonosuke set out from Kyoto, some 120 ri away, with his retinue of five jester-henchmen. Fittingly for such a journey, he was attired in a traveling outfit of shimmering maple design. His huge palanquin, borne by eight husky men, moved tirelessly over the mountainous route, night and day, ever eastward toward Edo.

It was a picturesque sight, this spectacle of the most celebrated amorist of the day riding in style and hurrying up the hazardous trails to see a pretty wench in a distant city—so dandyish indeed that one might have thought the god of love himself was nestled inside the swaying palanquin.

Soon the vehicle reached the village of Utsu in the hilly district of Suruga Province. Yonosuke was thinking of negotiating for a courier who might take a message back to Shimabara when he descried his friend Seiroku, master of the Kameya on Kyoto's Sanjo-dori, heading homeward from Edo astride a pack horse. No sooner had the man dismounted than there was a swift exchange of greetings and information.

"Well, well, how is your Chinese goods shop doing?"

"How have you fared in your makeshift meeting with Komurasaki in Edo?"

"If you have a toast for the pretty women of Kyoto or Osaka, I shall be glad to convey it back for you."

"Yes, one moment," said Yonosuke and forthwith scribbled a note on a paper handkerchief, indicating that though his heart was now set on Edo, he still felt the lure of Kyoto.

"I have just met Seiroku in this country lane," he wrote. "He has seen how gaunt and weary I have become from continuous traveling. Nevertheless I long for you in the deepest way. If our lives, meantime, do not vanish like the dew, we must see each other again. This hurried note is being written as proof of my assurances."

Yonosuke handed the note to Seiroku. "Give this to Kindayu, please."

His five jester-henchmen also wrote sad messages to their loved ones back in Kyoto. One of them called out: "Oh yes, I almost forgot. Remind the matron Oman at the Kambayashi, if you please, not to forget to wash her neck." And so they parted at last with shouts of resounding laughter.

As the palanquin worked its way precariously down the moss-covered, ivy-bordered trail, the austere, primitive beauty of the reed-thatched huts on the slope seemed to

Yonosuke singularly restful. Even the mountain wenches peddling home-made dumplings looked charming to him. He waved to them as his palanquin trotted past. At length he arrived at a place called Tegoshi where a wineshop and the home of a man he once knew stood amid a cluster of quaint decorative pines.

Crossing the River Abe, he heard someone beating time, palm on palm, and singing, " . . . He doesn't come, making me wait—the bitter feeling."

"Well, well, the gay quarters, even here," Yonosuke cried to his companions, slipping out of the palanquin. "This we must see."

They saw, and Yonosuke said acidly: "It was like a bouquet—before we saw it."

At a place called Mishima, Yonosuke inspected the ruins of what was once a brothel, then crossed the Hakone barrier, where even women were inspected closely. Finally he arrived safely at Heikichi's dyeshop, which boasted some connection with the "amorous flower of Musashi plain," the courtesan Komurasaki.

"What is the latest from the Yoshiwara?" Yonosuke asked.

Heikichi showed him a newly published album of beauties. Yonosuke read: "The maples are for the courtesans of the Miuraya," and his five companions, gazing at the alluring forms, cried: "Let's go before a pitiless storm scatters the crimson leaves."

And so they went, skirting Mt. Kinryu and down along the banks of the River Asakusa in puffing double-quick time. Passing the Komagata Hall, the palanquin swept past Asaji-ga-hara and Kozuka-hara and finally entered the flat land of the Yoshiwara.

In a teashop at the Great Gate that led into the gay district, Yonosuke and his companions changed from traveling robes to fresh town outfits. Then they went straight to Seijuro's establishment.

"Guests from Kyoto!" the porter cried, and the master himself came out to greet them.

Seijuro said unctuously: "The name Yonosuke-sama I have often heard, and knowing that sooner or later I should be playing host to you, I have awaited your coming with these preparations," and forthwith opened sliding doors that led into an eight-mat room bearing the sign, "Reserved for Yonosuke-sama of Kyoto."

Yonosuke was even more agreeably surprised when he saw that the wine cups, wine jugs, and lacquered soup bowls all bore the scattered carnation design patterned after his own family crest. "I certainly appreciate your thoughtfulness," said Yonosuke. "Now, what about the courtesan?"

Seijuro rubbed his hands apologetically. "I . . . I regret to say that Takao is booked full for the rest of this year. She has already promised the ninth and tenth months to patrons at the house of Ichizaemon and the eleventh month to others at the Ryuemon teahouse. In the twelfth month she is engaged to entertain still other groups here in my establishment. She has even promised New Year's Day to someone else. I am grieved to say that she cannot spare a single day until the second day of the new year."

Yonosuke and his jester-companions stared aghast at him. "Who are those men?" Yonosuke demanded.

"Oh, they are men of no particular account, I assure you. They are all strangers whose occupations and social position are unknown to me," Seijuro said with a sniff, indicating that for all he knew they might be newly rich riffraff. "Why don't you rest here at leisure until the new year opens?"

"That's wasting time," Yonosuke said, irritation and disappointment showing on his pale handsome face. "I have brought a thousand *ryo* with me to spend on Takao, and I cannot wait."

In the end Seijuro, together with Heikichi, one of Yonosuke's jester-henchmen, went to see Takao herself to beg for a special appointment. They managed by sheer persuasion and persistence to have her spare just one night, the second of the tenth month. But it would have to be a secret backdoor rendezvous, for she had already committed herself to her promised patrons that she would entertain no other man during the period of their contracts.

At sundown on the appointed day Yonosuke went out into the street with Heikichi to steal a look at Takao returning from a day's work at Ichizaemon's. It had to be a stolen look because he must avoid recognition for fear that a meeting in a public lane witnessed by others might lead to suspicion and therefore to the anger of Takao's promised patrons.

And there she came: a brilliant figure in soft fawn-colored silks, with crests of flaming maple on her robe. Her obi was worn high above her hips, and she walked with firm steps, proud and straight. Silent like a statue on parade, she acknowledged the greetings of her friends and intimates with only a nod or two.

Trailing her were two girl attendants robed in the same flashing colors. Then came her matron, followed by her palanquin bearers. All wore her crest on their robes, so that as the courtesan and her entourage swung down the lane it looked as though little autumn hills crimson with maples were moving in unison.

That night, at Seijuro's, Yonosuke waited impatiently for her coming. He waited until the temple bells tolled the hour of midnight, and still there was no sign of Takao. Bitter musings over her possible default on her promise rankled in Yonosuke's breast.

Then all stirrings ceased on the streets outside. Lights went off. Silence, deep and thick as doom, brooded over the sleeping world. . . .

"I am going to bed," Yonosuke said angrily.

"It does not seem as though she is coming after all," Seijuro said, nodding sympathetically.

"Any courtesan who does not keep her word is not worth even a single *mon*. And to think I've brought a thousand *ryo* for her! Even prostitutes are mindful of their honor. I have come 120 *ri* to see Takao and waited for her a whole month while she . . . she cannot even walk a few blocks nor spare me a minute. Likely as not she is drunk and sprawled shamelessly on the floor with her clothes half off. Who said Takao was a peerless woman? I am going right back to Kyoto."

Suddenly there was light, just a pinpoint of fire on the street at first, as a ghostly palanquin approached. Quietly the palanquin swung off the street and moved up to the kitchen doorway at Seijuro's. A woman, faultlessly robed even at that late hour, stole into the kitchen. Takao had kept her word.

CONFESSION IN A DIARY

YONOSUKE decided to part from his one-night companion early that murky morning to catch the scheduled boat back to Osaka. He had come to this seaport town called Tokonai, in Dewa province, mainly on business: to order a huge supply of rice for his wholesale shop. The woman was glad to be rid of him quickly, and the matron fidgeted nervously in the hallway. Yonosuke was equally impatient, but for another reason. The boat had failed to arrive on time.

While he was thus nursing an irascible mood a thick letter was delivered to him by courier. Breaking the seal and unrolling the scroll, he found it was from the courtesan Washu of Osaka. This was in response to his own letters, and she had composed it in the form of a diary beginning with the first day of the third month. She wrote:

"*1st day:* I had guests at the Takashimaya teahouse from early in the morning yesterday: the manager of Uemon's salt house in Naka-no-Shima and his party. This was my first meeting with them. At night, with writing brush in hand, I started to reply to your letters, but I was so exhausted from my daytime work that I lay down to rest on the mat, with my arm for a pillow. I must have fallen asleep. I had a vivid dream about you, a very pleasant dream. I was still dreaming when someone rattling my sliding door jolted me into wakefulness.

" 'Get up!' a harsh voice said.

"I was so angry at this shattering of my dream that for some time I refused to answer the summons. The yelling continued, and even Yachiyo, the sleepyhead in the bed next to mine, awoke and called me. I told her to get up and take her morning bath first.

"The man outside my door heard our voices.

" 'I cannot wait that long!' he shouted angrily and left.

"Soon I heard the palanquin bearer's black dog barking at him and chasing him into a side lane. Good riddance, I thought.

"And that set me to thinking further. How different indeed is this attitude from one's feeling for a man one likes! Having felt the difference, I realized how desperate is my love for you. There seems to be no limit—dreadful extremes, I fear—to what the human heart can feel.

"At this point a messenger arrived from the teahouse with an appointment for me, and I left as soon as I could.

"A poor start, I must say, on the first day of the month, making a fuss over trifles.

"*2nd day:* I entertained for the first time a group of men from Yatsushiro, in Higo Province, at the Kawaguchiya.

Other entertainers were Kiriyama from the Yagiya, Yoshikawa from the Fushimiya, and Rihei from Kiyomizu. They sang the *joruri* ballad about the hero Michiyuki who longed for his paramour in faraway Edo. That surprised me, for I, too, was longing for you. There is nothing sad in *our case,* but just the same I felt the tears in my eyes. No one of course knew, I am sure, that the tears were for you and not for the tragic hero.

"At nightfall, as I left for my home, someone saw the carnation (your) crest on my paper lantern and said in a slurring tone: 'I see that you have not changed your paramour yet.'

"I thought I had heard wrong, so incredible it seemed, and I walked back a few steps to see who it was that had made the unkind remark. I found it was Mata-sama of Temma. He now asked in a less unfriendly tone: 'When is Suke-sama coming back?'

"This man, it seems, has incurred the displeasure of Lord Echizen and has kept away from the gay quarters for some twenty days, and, it is rumored, he is now frequenting the young men's section on the south side. A queer practice, I must say, this consoling oneself vicariously.

"By the way, your good friend Kichiya is getting to be a very handsome man indeed.

"*3rd and 4th days:* I went over to Choshiro's Sumiyoshi-ya. The patron was a visitor from Karatsu called Tokosuke. He is the man who performed the Lantern Festival dance for us last year. During the daytime he went to gather shellfish off Sumiyoshi while the tide was at a low ebb.

" 'I have soiled my robe before meeting you at the party,' he said, half apologetically, half in jest. A modest and gentle man, this patron.

"*5th day:* I had to entertain a repulsive man. He is someone you know. At his request, just for form's sake as part of my duties, I exchanged written pledges with him. Really mine is utterly without sentiment or sincerity. His, I am sending along with this letter for you to keep.

"*6th day:* I took a cauterizing moxa treatment and had a chance to rest my bones. I spent the day leisurely.

"*7th day:* I went to entertain at the Ibaragiya but was summoned to the Izutsuya to take care of a party from Mogami.

"*8th day*: Continued to entertain the Mogami party.

"*9th day:* This happened to be the thirteenth anniversary of Mother's death, and I had a tombstone dedicated to her at the Sennichi Temple.

"*10th day:* I made up with a patron from Itachibori with whom I had quarreled. Hachirouemon acted as mediator.

"*11th day:* Entertained a visitor from Aboshi, in Harima Province, at the Oriya. This man was really a regular patron of Kiriyama-sama of the Yagiya, but they had severed their ties for a legitimate reason. I had the case investigated thoroughly before I accepted him.

"*12th day:* The gold-lacquered India ink box which you so kindly ordered for me from Jisuke, the lacquer artist, arrived today. The embossed view of Waka-no-Ura on the cover is very beautiful indeed. It reflects your excellent taste. The pines in particular are so finely drawn that they look almost real. I like it very much, and I started using it in writing this diary to you.

"*13th day:* By the way, I happened to remember that you left one of your inner robes with me. Laughing to myself, I wore it, thinking of you. But at the teahouse, the patron from Karatsu, Tokosuke-sama, admired it when I told him it was yours and begged me to give it to him. I gave it to him ungrudgingly because he insisted so much. There is really no other consideration involved.

"Then he wrote to me, saying he was sending me a bolt of silk that he could spare. I also received a package containing fifty pieces of silver, but there was no sender's name on it. I was too busy to bother with the bolt of silk, so even without examining it I had it sent on to Sahei's tailoring shop.

"All sorts of sad things seem to be piling up since you went away . . ."

There the diary-letter faded into an inconclusive end as though Washu could not bear to write any further.

Sad things! As Yonosuke's mind ranged wistfully over these vicissitudes of Washu's daily life, so intimately told, a vision appeared before him as though it had materialized out of the unfolding letter. It was the image of Washu herself, vivid in his mind's eye. And the image began to weep, saying: "It has been decided that I should be transferred to Kyoto. I must leave Osaka alone day after tomorrow."

Then the image added: "They are sending me away just because I am no longer as popular as I used to be. It is cruel, cruel. I want to die. I should soon die anyhow if I were to leave Osaka."

The vision seemed so real that Yonosuke's heart went out to her. Then she walked away a few steps, sadly looked back once, and vanished. *Was she already dead?*

NO TOMORROWS

THERE was a merchant from Osaka who came up to Kyoto some time ago to order a fresh supply of silk materials. Yonosuke had helped the man establish a temporary home in Muromachi, but since then had neither seen him nor heard about his doings. Then one day he came.

"You are just in time," said Yonosuke. "This is Devotional Day at the Toji Temple here. My friend Kichisuke, the paper dealer, has invited us to a feast of abstinence in the temple courtyard. Why don't you come along?"

"Thank you. I will."

Cloth banners rigged up in the form of a small square near the temple's Gate of Beasts formed rippling walls of privacy. Kichisuke, the host for the day, had his caterer prepare a meatless feast spread for five men inside this enclosure.

Compassion for all animal life was the keynote of this quiet Buddhist festival. There was implicit repentance here, and tranquillity. The five men feasted on boiled spinach and mushrooms. They drank from the bubbling wine cup. Buddhist scriptures were recited and discussed. From animal to human life the theme revolved, inevitably, to the following sutra passage: "As the sun rises and sets, so does human life. None may escape this law."

But alas, there was no precept against drinking immoderately. Everyone drank his fill. What started as a humble religious observance thus turned into a merry, merry session.

"Before we leave," Yonosuke told the host Kichisuke, "do us the honor of accepting a parting drink. Permit me to offer you this cup. Here, allow me to pour the saké."

Kichisuke bowed, accepted the honor with thanks, and took the cup. Yonosuke tipped the jug. But no saké flowed. Not even a drop. Yonosuke screwed his none-too-steady eyes into the opening. "This is embarrassing indeed," he said apologetically. "I feel . . . I feel awful about it."

"Think nothing of it," the host replied. "It is all my fault. I should have been more thoughtful." And he forthwith ordered the caterer to fetch more rice wine.

More saké arrived, and a second round of drinking

began. Everyone felt properly and sumptuously drunk.

"It would be a pity to go home like this," said Yonosuke. "Let's all go over to the Shimabara gay quarters. That should be a fitting climax. A fitting climax!"

"Oh, how right you are!" everyone agreed.

And so the five men staggered merrily into the Hachimonjiya.

"Bring on all of your unoccupied women," demanded one of the group who was more visibly inebriated than the others. "A thousand of them, if you have that many!"

All, as requested, were assembled for inspection, and all of them were no more than third-raters, of the *tenjin* class, and not a bit pretty at that.

"Unfortunately," the master Kiuemon apologized, "all our first-class courtesans are engaged for the day."

"These won't do at all," said Yonosuke. "Myself I don't mind, but I happen to have a guest here from Osaka, and I should hate to disappoint him. Won't you try to get the release of a courtesan from another establishment?"

Kiuemon tried at several houses. "It's no use," he reported back. "No one is available."

Then his wife, herself returning from another negotiation, said breathlessly: "I have just come from the Maruya, the house of Shichizaemon, and he said that the courtesan Yoshizaki-sama of Osaka is making her debut there tonight. She is going to establish herself here in Kyoto. I asked Shichizaemon to let us have her for the debut. Something must have gone wrong at his house, for he was willing to let her go. It will cost a lot of money, but if she will do . . ."

"She will do," said Yonosuke. "Never mind the cost. I shall foot the bill."

Negotiations were renewed with the house of Shichizaemon, and an agreement was quickly reached.

A courtesan's debut of this sort was a rare enough event

and called for elaborate rites. A mammoth candle was lighted in the kitchen. The cooks changed into formal white robes and worked feverishly preparing fancy dishes. Here was an opportunity for them to display their skill with knives and pans and sauces and condiments and with turning fish and other sea foods into rare delicacies and converting vegetables of all shapes, sizes, and colors into wonders for the eye and palate. The cooks chanted rhythmically and vigorously as they worked, for the ritual began in the kitchen.

Over his kimono the master of the house put on a formal *kamishimo:* a jumper with broad winglike shoulders and a pair of skirtlike *hakama* trousers. The mistress wore a fresh kimono and a cotton hood.

Then four women arrived from the house of Shichizaemon to prepare the courtesan Yoshizaki's room for the ceremony. Twelve robes of all colors and designs were spread over the lacquered clothes rack. Sleeping garments and cushions were piled up in corners like brilliant little mountains of silk. A scroll painting was hung on the alcove wall and an incense burner placed below it. Gold-lacquered boxes, paper containers, tobacco sets, and small ornaments were ranged on the adjoining *chigaidana* tier shelves.

Presently there was a joyful shout—part of the ceremony itself—at the front entrance: "The courtesan has arrived, looking gorgeous and charming!"

The shout was repeated formally as Yoshizaki, holding a lighted candle, entered the vestibule at the head of a procession and mounted the stairway . . . slowly, silently, sedately. Proceeding to the huge reception room, she took her position near the alcove, toward the center of the oblong room, and sat down on a pile of cushions with an elaborate sweep of her flowing silken robe. Trailing her were eleven lesser courtesans and seventeen novices serving as her retinue. These two groups of attendants

203

ranged behind her, the first sitting down at the left, the second at the right. All wore colored robes with no designs signifying their special function for the evening's rites. Finally the main *hikifune* and girl *kamuro* attendants sat down beside Yoshizaki, like guardians of a temple goddess.

Thereupon the five principal guests, still more or less drunk, moved in, followed by the mistress of the house. Then, for the first time, a voice was raised: the voice of the mistress of the house greeting the courtesan. The formal introductions followed.

Yonosuke and his friend from Osaka were well acquainted with the courtesan, but still it was necessary upon an occasion such as this for all those present to exclaim in unison: "This is indeed a pleasant meeting."

Next the sacramental *shimadai* stand-trays, big golden plates with choice sea foods symbolizing felicitations, slender pottery jugs containing amber-colored saké, and lacquered wine cups were brought in by waitresses to initiate the rites. The wine cups were passed from guests to courtesan, from courtesan to guests, and toasts ritualistically sipped.

The courtesan's gifts to the house were next formally presented. This was followed by lively samisen music by her attendants and the showering of silver coins in the garden below. There was a merry scrambling of men and women servants, matrons, even prostitutes, for the coins. The commotion, a celebration shared by the lower strata, shook the house, and there was great rejoicing. Back in the upstairs reception room the formalities of the staid festive table were discarded, and the atmosphere turned to one of unrestrained conviviality.

Thus, what had begun earlier in the day as a humble feast of abstinence—without meat—in the temple courtyard ended up in a magnificent—with meat—display of unholy carousal. "As the sun rises and sets, so does human life. None may escape this law."

When his Osaka guest reminded him of the daytime session, Yonosuke said laughingly: "But there is no law against one's making the best of it before one's 'setting' time comes. There will be no tomorrows for us!"

FRIGHTFUL BET

A MEDIOCRE man, to all appearances a sedentary shop-keeper, dismounted from his pack horse at the edge of Sanjo Bridge in Kyoto and told his servant holding the reins: "See to it that my money bag is tied securely to the saddle. I shall be right back."

There was haste in his voice, and his legs carried him uncertainly to the front door of Yonosuke's mansion. Yonosuke saw that the caller was Juzo, master of a tailoring shop whom he had frequently helped along in securing business favors from the Shimabara courtesans.

Juzo said: "I have all of a sudden decided to go to Edo. It will be just a short trip, and I came to say good-bye."

"Well, that's fine. Take good care of yourself on the way," said Yonosuke and presented him with the usual parting gift of money.

But as Juzo started to leave, Yonosuke called him back. "What are you going to Edo for this time?"

"Well, I . . . have made a bet. While exchanging blandishments with a certain man, I happened to make a careless remark. Come to think of it, he maneuvered the talk in such a teasing way as to goad me on to make that slip. Anyhow, I boasted lightheartedly that if I were to go to Edo and ask the courtesan Komurasaki for an evening's appointment, she would never turn me down.

'She would,' he retorted seriously. 'You're a nobody. I'll make a bet with you.' Well, I could hardly go back on my word and be damned as a coward, so I found myself compelled to say: 'You're on.' He said he would have his friend Uhei the 'Rat' of Edo be his witness. So you see, I am now obliged to go."

"What whimsical men you are!" Yonosuke said. "It is not so simple as that. He might win. Can't you denounce the bet?"

"I am afraid he would kill me if I dared."

"Why let him? Hit him back."

"Besides, my honor is involved, don't you see?"

"What did you bet?"

The tailor replied in a roundabout way: "A bad, scheming man, that. He insisted on naming the bet. If he lost, he said, he would give me his town house on Kiya-machi. I felt the stake was too high, for I had nothing comparable to offer—not for such a bet anyway. But he pinned me down to my promise. If I lost, he said . . . he said . . ." Juzo's voice trembled and ceased, and his face turned pale.

"Tell me the truth. Don't hide anything."

"I . . . won't. The truth is . . . if I lose, I must surrender to him something of myself . . . something which would not, perhaps, take my life but which is . . . at least *vital* to me. Allow me the dignity of not mentioning what it is. You probably have already guessed it. I suspect he demanded it with some vicious intention. Maybe to cripple me. I don't remember that I have, at any time, insulted him so seriously as to deserve such underhanded revenge. Oh, he is a devil!"

"What fools they are!" Yonosuke thought. "These men who stake their possessions and even their honor so recklessly on trifles. And how cruel!"

"Who is the man that imposed this frightful bet on you?"

"I promised not to reveal his name."

"This is a serious matter, perhaps the most serious in your lifetime. But since you have been caught in his trap, you might as well face it with all of your wits and resources. Komurasaki is the hardest of all Edo courtesans to get. Keep your rosary constantly in your hand. Don't hesitate about using all your money. You have no one to leave it to anyhow."

That seemed to fill Juzo the tailor with overwhelming doubts about his ability to stave off defeat and misfortune. He said goodbye again, but the tears came to his eyes and he stood there forlornly, unable to move.

"Wait!" said Yonosuke. "I'll go with you. I'll help you win the bet."

And so, to Juzo's immense relief and delight, Yonosuke ordered his own pack horse, and the two set out together for Edo.

Upon arrival in Edo, at Yonosuke's branch shop in Yonchome, Nihombashi, Yonosuke gave Juzo the necessary instructions and urged him to go immediately to the Yoshiwara gay quarters and negotiate with Komurasaki for an appointment. They got in touch with Uhei, and the "Rat" went along as witness.

But Yonosuke, knowing that the famed courtesans of Edo were available only to men of great wealth and great names coupled with generous, agreeable, continued patronage, felt grave misgivings for Juzo. The tailor was just another man from another city, unknown and of no particular accomplishment or reputation. Yes . . . a nobody. Besides, Komurasaki might be booked full for months ahead. So he decided to appeal to Ryuemon, the master of the establishment where Komurasaki reigned.

Showing his own credentials as a privileged patron of the Shimabara courtesans of Kyoto, Yonosuke built up Juzo as a man of immense wealth and a fellow patron. The visitor, he said, could not tarry long in Edo, so would he, Ryuemon-sama, use his kind influence in securing a favorable answer from Komurasaki?

Juzo meanwhile returned crestfallen. Komurasaki had looked him over curiously but put him off indefinitely. "I am booked full now," she said, "and I cannot promise you anything. Come and see me again in a month or so."

But somehow Yonosuke's intercession seemed to have worked marvelously. Within four or five days a messenger arrived from Ryuemon. Komurasaki had consented after all to give Juzo an appointment. Overwhelmed with joy but still incredulous, Juzo exclaimed: "This is almost unbelievable!"

"Go and see Ryuemon and have them decide on a day," Yonosuke told him. Uhei the Rat suspected trickery and now *insisted* on going along. The appointment was duly confirmed and made.

As Juzo was about to take leave of Ryuemon, he presented the master with a gift.

Uhei was greatly offended. "You have no right to resort to bribery. If you want to reward the master, it should be done after everything is over. The appointment is still to be consummated. A promise can be broken. It is not fair at this stage."

Juzo laughed. "I know. But that package does not contain any money. Will you open it, please, Ryuemon-sama, to satisfy this man?"

The package was opened. It contained a rivet for making bamboo fans, a bamboo staple for holding together the skeleton of a fan, a needle, silk thread, glucose paste, and an ear scratcher to boot. In terms of money, they were worth no more than three skimpy *mon*.

"I just thought, Ryuemon-sama," said Juzo, "that you might be glad to make use of these articles as a pastime. Most people would. You can make a fan now."

Uhei, who least suspected that the setup was a joke on

him, frowned with disgust, as if to say: "Oh, you cheap-skate!"

On the appointed evening Juzo was very agreeably received by Komurasaki. A lavish table was spread before him, with many lesser courtesans and attendants present. Rice wine flowed freely. Juzo drank freely. And as if to drown out eagerly some fear that had not yet altogether left him, he offered with unsteady hands to pour Komurasaki a drink.

The courtesan accepted graciously, and he poured clumsily. The wine spilled over, soiling her robe from sleeve to waist. Juzo's face reddened and contorted almost comically with mingled chagrin and pain. He apologized hastily, but Komurasaki, taking no offense, stood up smilingly and said: "I shall wash up and change" and left for the bathroom.

Soon she returned to the *zashiki* parlor in a fresh outfit of precisely the same material and design: white under-garment, scarlet midgarment, and yellow robe. This custom of keeping on hand reserve replicas of outfits for just such an emergency was a luxury which only the courtesans of Edo boasted.

It was likewise the custom of courtesans here never to offer beds except to a lover. But as bedtime came, Komurasaki ordered a bed for Juzo and invited him into her boudoir.

The next morning Komurasaki took up her writing brush, spread out her short inner sash, and wrote on it:

"I spent the night with Juzo-sama.
This is the naked truth."

She signed it "Komurasaki" and affixed her seal. Then she offered the certified document to Juzo.

Uhei, upon seeing the incontestable proof, was greatly astonished. Juzo had won his bet. "There never, never has been a case like this," the Rat complained.

Even Yonosuke was mystified. He sought out Komura-saki. "Just to satisfy my own curiosity, why did you do it?" he asked.

And Komurasaki replied: "From Juzo-sama's uneasy attitude throughout the evening I sensed he was under some heartbreaking pressure or fear. Sometimes one comes across a case like that. I suspected that someone seeking sly revenge, perhaps for some trifling offense that Juzo-sama had already forgotten, had sent him to me on a dare and a bet, believing him to be an easy victim, with the stakes high or precious. Precious, no doubt, for money is hardly an inducement to such people for this sort of mischief. So suspecting, I felt pity for Juzo-sama and hatred for the other man—whoever he happened to be—for taking advantage of him. I hated the evil character behind the scenes so much that I willingly went out of my way to help Juzo-sama. I want to see evil punished thoroughly. Was I right in my guess?"

"You were," said Yonosuke, "and your heart is in the right place."

HOW WOMEN SHOULD AND SHOULD NOT BEHAVE

IT WAS a cold winter's night. Snow fell so heavily that the pine trees in the garden of Nizaemon's Kyoya teahouse in the Shimmachi gay district of Osaka—the garden in which he had taken great pride—cracked under its weight. All the guests at the party that night at the Kyoya drank heartily to endure the bitter cold and went to bed early, soon snoring heartily too.

In one room the courtesan Kindayu of the Atarashiya snored so loudly that the man sleeping near her, Mansaku of the mallet shop, was awakened from his sleep. Not knowing, of course, that he was laughing at her, Kindayu was already dreaming sweet dreams.

Meanwhile, in another room, the courtesan Mifune frowned and swore aloud in her sleep: "Prepare yourself for battle, Shichiza-sama. I won't let you go this time!" The next instant she bit the shoulder of Yonosuke, who was asleep beside her. The surprised Yonosuke sat bolt upright on his bed.

"You're chewing up the wrong man," he shouted. "I am Yonosuke. Remember?"

Mifune came out of her dream and opened her eyes wide. "Oh, I beg your pardon," she said. "I was dreaming that I met Shichizaemon-sama of the Maruya, with whom frankly I have been having an affair that gossip has made the most of. Abruptly he told me in the dream: 'Out of consideration for the public at large and the patrons of my establishment in particular, our love affair —you and me—must come to an end as of today.' I felt so angry—in the dream, of course—that I talked back to him and threatened to hurt him. That is why I behaved the way I did in my sleep. I am really ashamed of what I did to you."

She seemed so downhearted that Yonosuke had to use all his wits to soothe her. When she felt better, she told him without equivocation the story of her hard luck—an amazing story revealing a woman so good and true that her kind, he thought, would never be duplicated on this earth.

As Yonosuke prepared to take his leave, Mifune shared drinks with him, tending to his last needs and speaking gently to her departing guest in a manner that made the mistress of the establishment and even the maidservants happy. Accompanying him to the vestibule, she slipped on her own footwear noiselessly. Then she spread out a parasol for Yonosuke in the snow outside and saw him off to the front gate, unmindful of the snow falling on her own robe. Impressed by her graciously considerate attitude, Yonosuke impulsively said in a low voice as though to himself: "I wonder why they didn't promote her to a *tayu* in Kyoto."

A manservant accompanying them heard this remark and commented: "Well, with her looks . . ."

"You fool!" said Yonosuke. "High-class courtesans are not made by looks alone!" Then, as the last goodbyes were said and Mifune began to walk back to the teahouse, Yonosuke gazed long and admiringly at her receding figure.

As she mounted the stairs, Mifune saw that the harlots that had been hired as her attendants for the evening were grouped around the guest table, finishing off the remains of a sumptuous feast and gossiping out loud at the same time in such an uncouth manner that their mouths worked incessantly, with hardly a moment for rest between mouthfuls. Here and there on the mat were other indications of irresponsible conduct. A large lacquered plate had been broken in two and carelessly patched together. A samisen that had been stepped upon and broken at the neck was left in an obscure corner as though these women had had nothing to do with its condition. The whole disorderly scene was in fact so comical-looking that one felt the leftover dried cuttlefish and tiny sardines would momently rise from their carcasses and start dancing on the plates.

Soon Mifune's male escorts came to fetch her home. The group, changing into lighter attire, started to leave the establishment when they were surprised by melting snow falling on them from the edge of the roof. One escort, apparently the leader, cried: "What's the matter with Nizaemon, the owner of this place? Hasn't he sense enough to install a bamboo drain from the edge of the roof, at least right over the front entrance?"

Later, as the procession left the house, the leader of the male escorts started lecturing to Mifune's attendants: "A certain courtesan at the Yoshidaya is said to have demanded and extracted a rustic guest's crepe de Chine inner sash, and on the very next day she made drawers out of the material for her own use. Another courtesan is said to have held on tightly to her silken purse, and when one of her male escorts happened to notice a yellow-colored package hidden in the purse, she explained: 'When one is traveling late at night in these dreadful times, one must guard against robberies, and nothing worries me more than the thought that I might be robbed of this precious article.'

"These incidents have one thing in common: they indicate a detestable spirit. I have seen or heard about countless other cases involving similar indiscretions during the last five years, but I won't mention names out of pity for the offenders. Let me give you a piece of advice. Women should try to behave more discreetly when there is no one around than in the presence of others."

As the procession entered Echigo-machi, a sleepy-sounding voice came floating out of the latticed window of a teahouse on the north side: "Right now, I'd like to eat fresh sliced tuna."

The male escort leader said: "An interesting conversation seems to be going on in there. Let's stop right here and listen. Quiet, everybody."

Everyone pricked up his ears and listened, anticipating choice items of gossip to follow that appetizing lead. What actually followed was an outspoken revelation of other individual preferences at the moment for choice delicacies:

"I want to eat chestnut rice cake until I'm full."

"Me, I'd rather have boneless crane."

"Cooked yams for me."

"Wild pigeon is my favorite."

"Mine is fried watercress."

"I'd like some *aruheito* sweets right now."

"I'm dying for a boxful of broiled clams—in the sort of box they use aboard the Kawaguchiya sailing boat."

The eavesdropping group outside the window recognized the voices as those of well-known courtesans. "Now what do you think about their appetites?" asked the same male escort leader.

Tahei of Hatsune and four other men replied in a chorus of disgust: "Well, we've been treated to a fine repast—just to hear them talk."

"Matter of fact, we've just had about enough, so let's keep moving," the leader added as his opinion, and the group laughingly proceeded on their way.

Speaking of the appetites of courtesans, Yonosuke recalled later when the midnight incident was reported to him: "Last summer I treated Yoshioka to some fresh watermelon, and she ate it so ravenously that she unwittingly exposed all her protruding teeth. At another time I treated Tsumaki to some gelidium jelly and she said happily in her provincial dialect: '*Mumai, na!* It's very tasty!'"

Yonosuke also recalled how a notorious male gossip of Fushimibori once saw a group of harlots having a tea party in a back room of the Sumiyoshiya. "The women," the gossip said, "were roasting rice cakes—offerings taken down from the household shrine—over a *kotatsu* fire." He was particularly impressed by the fact that the women drank no wine, only tea, Yonosuke continued. "A very pleasant party, the only kind fit for women."

THE EVENING breeze came floating in from the dried-up
sandy stream below. As Yonosuke sat cooling himself on
the teahouse veranda in Kyoto, a man came excitedly
out of the reception room. He looked for all the world
like a lost soul. From one hand dangled a huge fan. The
other clutched a cumbersome ash tray and pipe holder.
His rolling eyes searched anxiously up and down the
veranda. It was Choshichi, the jester from Yanagi-no-
Baba.

"Well, well," Yonosuke called teasingly. "You certainly look funny. What happened? Is your new inamorata eluding you?"

Choshichi made no reply. Then, with a sigh, he pointed
laughingly, foolishly with his fan at a beautifully robed
woman and her two attendants coming up from the far
corner of the veranda. "My wife Haru," he said. He
added with a comical grimace: "And her entourage."

From all indications this was Haru's special day.
Choshichi had given her a new robe, fitted her out with
a maid in waiting and a maidservant, and brought her
here for a day's leisurely enjoyment. He himself was
acting assiduously, if clumsily, as her manservant for the
day.

"I owe it to her," Choshichi said, seriously now. "She
has taken good care of me without complaining, cooking
the meals at home, drawing water from the well for my
bath, feeding me at odd hours of the day. She washes my
clothes. My work keeps me out until late every night, but
never have I had to rattle my door upon returning. She
has always sat up and let me in quickly. And always she

215

has greeted me with a happy face, asking me gently how I felt, inquiring after my work. Really, Yonosuke-sama, a woman should never marry a jester. . . . She is dear to me, and today I am paying tribute to her in this way out of gratitude."

There was good reason for their mutual attachment, for theirs was a love marriage. Haru had once served as an attendant to a high-class courtesan in the Shimabara district called Fujinami.

Yonosuke said: "You haven't spent all the savings she brought with her at the time of your marriage, have you?"

"Oh that," Choshichi replied with a shiver, indicating the extreme hardships of making a living. "That has been used up long ago. Good thing, too, we don't have any children."

After Haru had come up and greetings had been exchanged, Yonosuke said: "Why don't you two come over to my house tonight? Let's spend the night talking over old times. There are things I want to show you."

At his mansion on Kawara-machi Yonosuke asked them to go into a musty back room. A strong odor suggesting lingering perfume but at the same time sharply remindful of oil of some sort permeated the room.

Choshichi sniffed the air with a puzzled look. "Haru, I cannot understand it," he told his wife. "What is this strange smell?"

Haru was no less puzzled. "I wonder what it is."

At this moment Yonosuke followed them in.

"Today," he said, "I am having some of my precious possessions aired in this and the adjoining room. That accounts for the queer smell. I asked you in here because I want to show them to you."

In one corner was a big paulownia box. "Open it," Yonosuke urged, "and see for yourselves what it contains."

The cover bore these characters in fancy script: "Box

containing tokens of fidelity. Dated from the second year of correspondence." The contents were letters from women addressed to Yonosuke and sealed with blood. They were one-sided love pledges, dated from the year 1653.

From the tokonoma post a line of *koto* cord was stretched across the alcove, and from this line hung separate strands of women's long hair in small clusters, each unit bearing a small tag with the name of the donor. These strands had been cut and given to Yonosuke by other women as similar pledges of attachment. Choshichi examined the tags and counted up to 83 names, but there were so many more that he stopped counting as a waste of time.

To the right, on the ornamental *chigaidana* shelves, Choshichi found countless close-clipped fingernails being aired on their crepe wrappers.

Yonosuke then led Choshichi and Haru into the adjoining room. Here the couple saw a woman's silk robes of all sorts: white background with love notes written on it, white background with dappled blood patterns, purple background with fox-and-geese designs.

"These are keepsakes," said Yonosuke, "which were presented to me by the courtesan Hanasaki-sama."

On the walls were life-size paintings of women mounted on *kyafu* and obi scrolls. Lying here and there were samisen with engraved crests, and countless other things—all given to Yonosuke as tokens of undying love by the women he had dallied with.

"You certainly have moved the hearts of a lot of women in your time, haven't you?" Choshichi said, somewhat cynically. "You have worried them to extremes. What happened to them and where are they now? But I suppose you cannot escape the consequences."

Before Yonosuke could reply to that prophetic remark, a strange thing happened. A toupee fashioned from the

217

strands of a woman's hair started to come apart on the tokonoma alcove. It expanded and it shrank, without any human hands touching it. Then it leaped into the air like a live thing, as if it demanded attention and desired to say something.

So frightening was it to look upon that Choshichi and Haru felt goose flesh appearing all over their bodies.

"What is the meaning of this?" Choshichi demanded.

Yonosuke said: "Perhaps Haru will recall what I am going to say. You remember, Haru, how one night I asked Fujinami, the courtesan whom you were then serving, to cut strands of her hair and her fingernails for me? Well, this toupee was made out of those strands and clippings. You can see that I have given it a high and honored place in my alcove. Sometimes I dream about Fujinami; at other times I see visions. At still other times I see her in that shadowy world which is neither sleep nor wakefulness. We then talk about her present inescapable ties with the man who, as her demanding patron, has come to dominate her life. In these trancelike talks we are always together as though in real life. We discuss things we hesitate to impart to others. Only last night she gave me a bolt of striped crepe, saying if I had a formal *haori* coat made from the material, I would look especially handsome in it. Even if that took place in a trance, it is still a mystery to me to find that dreamed-of bolt of crepe right here in this room. Here it is." And he pointed at the cloth on the mat. "As a matter of fact, I invited you both here tonight because I particularly wanted to show you this and tell you about it."

Choshichi and Haru expressed amazement over this mystic revelation.

"Even so," said Choshichi, as though to rationalize the revelation, "I suppose it should not be so surprising after all. Everyone familiar with the gay life in Kyoto knows the strong body-and-soul attachment which Fujinami, for reasons of her own, bears toward you."

Haru, on the other hand, had certain premonitions. Leaving the house at once, she hurried over to Fujinami's quarters in the Shimabara district. She reached there just as Fujinami was searching in her chest of drawers.

"I am sure I had a bolt of crepe in here," Fujinami said, "but I cannot find it."

Haru, awed by this inexplicable confirmation of the mystery, said excitedly: "I have just come from Yono-suke-sama's mansion. He showed us your missing crepe. He said you gave it to him in a dream. But he is still puzzled that the actual thing—the material out of the dream—is there, right in his room, for him to see, touch, and feel."

Fujinami burst into tears. "Yes . . . yes, I wanted so very, very much to give it to him. I . . . I think of him so much that I cannot keep him out of my mind, sleeping or awake. But I cannot go to him. I am pledged to another man. There is no sense . . . really no sense in my continuing my work and duties here." So saying, she picked up a pair of scissors and cut off her long black hair.

"I am going to be a nun," she told Haru with mingled passion and resignation. "I am going to renounce this world's cruel affairs. I am going to try to forget them in the seclusion of a Buddhist temple. The only thing left for me to do is to prepare for the next world."

ALL FOR HIM

CHRYSANTHEMUMS, petal-curved, sparkled from every doorway, white as snow, purple and golden like the sunset glow. Their deep scent, heavy with mystery, permeated the Shimmachi district. It was festival time in Osaka city, a yearly tribute to the royal blooms. And it was the gayest time of the year in the gay quarters. Everyone, courtesans and patrons alike, vied with one another in exhibiting the newest finery to match the beauty of the flowers. It was as if life itself had emerged from the wash-tub, perfumed and gaily bedecked.

Here was a well-groomed but aging man making the rounds of the teahouses, extending complimentary greet-ings. He wore a light yellow *kamishimo* over a silk robe embroidered with small purple crests. On his hip was a sword worn at a fashionable angle. But today, differing from others, he looked somewhat incongruously serious, like a man from another world—like Lord Yasaburo going a-visiting in the legendary land of Shaba. It was Yonosuke himself.

Even a nameless harlot peeping through the rattan blinds of Tahei's brothel felt faint stirrings in her heart. It was just possible that she might not have been so buoyantly moved had this not been a festival day. So much depended on the occasion.

Suddenly Yonosuke's eyes flashed with admiration. The gorgeous Takama was passing by with her young girl attendants. She was a courtesan at the Sadoshimaya, superior and sedate but certainly alluring. One could follow her all day and never tire, Yonosuke mused and then sighed, for he was no longer young and active.

Next he saw an oblong chest being carried out into the yard of the Izutsuya. Thin silver coins and coppers were scooped out and dispensed to passers-by. Even the ma-tron here received her share of the bright and shining metal, her face just as bright though far from charming. A heavenly city, this, thought Yonosuke.

Dusk was falling as he moved on to the Sumiyoshiya. There Yonosuke exchanged blandishments with the master, Shiroza, and bought sweet wine for Agemaki's attendants. He sat on a bench in front of the teahouses, watching lesser courtesans go by. Beckoning and teasing them with heartless humor and getting tongue-lashed in turn ("You decrepit libertine!"), he invited them one after the other to come sit on the bench with him. Reluctantly they sat, and he ordered saké from the teahouse. They sipped and felt much better. And he laughed uproariously.

The last in turn to enjoy his brief hospitality on the bench was a woman called Kenko. "Now I begin to understand," she said fawningly, "and to like the ways of old men who are not set against drinks."

"Let's go inside," teased Yonosuke, who really had another appointment to keep.

Stirred in retrospect by the more refined allurements of the courtesans of Kyoto, he quickly tired of these second-rate Osaka women. Suddenly he stood up, abandoned Kenko without ceremony, and hurried toward the thriving Dotombori section. There, on Tatamiya-machi, at the home of an actor friend, he ordered a palanquin borne on four husky shoulders. "On to Kyoto!" he said, and the vehicle squeaked into the night.

From somewhere in the dark came the tolling of a midnight temple bell. "We have reached the *tenjin* establishment of Sata," one of the front palanquin bearers said.

"Let's have a hot drink out here," Yonosuke urged. "All by ourselves, without benefit of harlots."

As he stepped from the palanquin the four men gathered brushwood from the roadside, built a small bonfire, and heated jugs of rice wine. For tidbits they broiled *miso* bean paste. "Very interesting, this primitive outdoor repast," commented Yonosuke and drank his fill.

The palanquin started off again in the pitch dark, trotting and puffing through the snoring villages of

Katano and Kinya and the narrow wooden bridge over the foggy River Yodo. "We have come to the Love Hill of Toba," a palanquin bearer shouted to the napping passenger within.

That roused Yonosuke from his nap. "Oh yes? Yes, I know."

The palanquin came to a stop in front of a wayside teashop at Yottsuzuka, and the four men pounded at the bamboo braided door. "Give us water to drink!" they shouted hoarsely. "We can't wait for tea to boil. We'll die by then."

Inside the palanquin Yonosuke, fully awakened by that cry, mused regretfully: "Come to think of it, this is the road through the forest region where one of my palanquin bearers died of sheer exhaustion last year. I should not have demanded so much speed on such a long run." He wanted to leave the spot immediately, and he could hardly wait for the blinking stars to vanish in the growing light of dawn.

The next stop was at the entrance to Kyoto itself, at Tambaguchi, in front of Shohei's teashop. Sleepy-eyed Shohei, waiting for his all-night guests to take their early morning leave, came out to greet Yonosuke.

"Well, well, coming back to Kyoto?" Shohei said. "What a surprise, at such an odd hour! Oh, by the way, only yesterday the courtesan Takahashi was speaking about you. She seemed to be waiting anxiously for your return. Go and see her right away. I shall send word ahead to her." And Shohei immediately dispatched a messenger to the Sammonjiya teahouse.

Dawn at last lighted up the sky, and Yonosuke was deeply moved by its fresh and lavender-tinted beauty. He mused: "Priest Saigyo could not have seen this. Else he would not have sung the praises of dawn over Matsushima or of nights in Kisagata."

And now the climactic thought flashed through his

mind: "Only last evening I saw Shimmachi in all its glory, and this morning I am already in matchless Shimabara—the gay districts in two cities so dear to my heart. Not even the gay adventurers of old China can equal this!"

He set out for the Fujiya, where paper lanterns were giving off their last sputtering light and the old pot was boiling. Hikozaemon, the master, had some fresh mushrooms put on the fire.

"This is exceptionally good," said Yonosuke and topped off his breakfast with two jugs of rice wine.

Just then the courtesan Kasen, her freedom purchased by a patron and now looking more like a housewife, emerged to leave the employment of Hikozaemon forever.

"It is *sayonara*, isn't it?" Yonosuke said. "Where are you going to retire to?"

"My home will be ... " said Kasen mysteriously. Then she left abruptly, with the unanswered question dangling as it were in mid-air.

Hikozaemon said: "She is hardly fit to go to Uji."

"Why, of course," Yonosuke agreed with an ungracious grin. "She will probably end up by going to the rear of the Rokkakudo, where newborn babies are left on the doorstep."

They had hardly finished this unkind comment when a troupe of messengers arrived from the courtesan Takahashi. There were three women in the group, themselves courtesans. And there was Jihei, representing the Sammonjiya teahouse, and a number of other men.

"Takahashi-sama," was their greeting, "awaits you, Yonosuke-sama, at the Sammonjiya. We have come to escort you there."

If this troupe of escorts appeared like a festival parade, it reflected the commensurate prestige of Takahashi, now at the height of her popularity and fame. And anyone watching this early-morning spectacle proceeding down the street might have thought that a great feudal lord, with his colorful retinue, was calling on his paramour.

Having traveled all night, however, Yonosuke went straight to bed to rest his tired body. Toward evening he awoke. The harvest moon rose big and round and golden. Benches and stools were placed in the teahouse garden. Here came the celebrated Takahashi, together with other noted courtesans such as Nokaze, Shiga, Enshu, Nosé, Kuranosuke, Tsushima, Miyoshi, and Tosa. Nowhere else could one see such beautiful women grouped together in one place. Perhaps no one but Yonosuke could have convoked such an assemblage. They were doing him special honor as the grand old patron of Kyoto's gay district.

"All for me, this lovely party of lovely women," the mellowing Yonosuke mused happily, and he drank much too freely. But the courtesan Takahashi was wise enough merely to look smilingly askance at his falling wistfully into a stupor. She wore her robe with such ease and perfection that on anyone else it might have appeared like an impediment rather than ornamentation.

As the night waned and the moon grew pale, she went indoors to prepare for bed. Yonosuke was awakened and helped to his room. The others followed Takahashi. She touched nothing. The quilts in three thicknesses, the special pillow, the soft sleeping robe—all were handled reverently by attendants. Even the last pinch of tobacco was stuffed for her into the bowl of a slender pipe. Gently the blanket was spread over her tired, restless body. And so she went sighing off to sleep, hoping at least to dream sweet dreams.

GRAY-HAIRED Yonosuke now felt his bones creaking, and he made a strange decision about his future. He began to give his wealth away. Curiously enough, his hitherto unregenerate mind turned wistfully to thoughts of religion, to the possible rewards and punishments of the hereafter. Yes, he must provide for the needs of Buddhist temples and Shinto shrines. He showered them with money to build pagodas and stone lanterns that burn all night. One must propitiate the gods, for one never can tell . . .

There were other poor folk that needed help, especially those within the periphery of his pleasure-seeking world. He bought homes for destitute actors and jesters. And he paid for the ransom of courtesans in bondage whom he had at one time or another befriended, so that they might be free to become common housewives or go to the devil as free-lancing harlots. But these charities made only a small dent in his fortune. A great deal more remained to be spent, and he was hard put to it to decide how he should dispose of it to the best advantage or to whom, individually, he might give it.

At this point a merchant friend of his came to him and said: "I am going on a buying trip to Nagasaki."

"That gives me an idea," Yonosuke said. "I shall follow you there. You will be doing me a favor by taking along this box of gold coins for me."

"What are you going to use it for? To buy foreign goods?"

"No, native."

"In the Maruyama gay quarters, perhaps? Well, well." There was mingled cynicism and blandishment in his friend's tone. "Very well, I shall wait for you with the money in Nagasaki."

And so the merchant set out for the southern port city where foreigners dwelled. It was on the fourteenth day of the sixth month, a day on which a festival began, and his heart was torn between longing for the moon over the gay Gion quarters, which he was leaving behind, and the lure of material gain that had beckoned him on to Nagasaki, which after all proved the stronger.

It was long afterwards, on the thirteenth day of the eighth month, that Yonosuke finally left Kyoto on his projected southern adventure. In ancient times the great scholar Abe-no-Nakamaro, while sojourning on the foreign soil of China, expressed in verse a powerful yearning for the moon rising over his native land—over Mt. Mikasa in Yamato. Yonosuke, however, as he started out on his journey, reversed that sentiment. He was already feeling the lure of the moon over the "foreign" port city. Taking a ferryboat down the River Yodo, he first set foot on the southern shore of Osaka and spent several days with some old actor friends. They treated him well, and on parting he presented them with 500 *ryo* in gold.

"We actors," said Heishiro on seeing him off to the ocean-going vessel, "are a really rootless lot, victims of a whimsical fate. Blessed today, destitute tomorrow—no one knows what the future will be. Like the drooping willows weighted with snow, we soon shed our good looks and become gaunt-looking. Sometimes, for pleasure, we take up cockfighting, or we become absorbed in *bonsai* dwarf trees. Soon we lose our popularity and are no longer wanted on the stage. We sell our homes and move from one city to another, from Kyoto to Edo to Osaka, like nomads without a real home. If we are innocent of desperation and wrongdoing, we are just as innocent of anything like owning money."

226

The sea was calm, for the wind seemed to have a heart and not even the sound of an angry wave could be heard. In due course the ship reached the great port of Nagasaki. As Yonosuke swept his eyes across the Sakura-machi waterfront, his spirits rose. Even before registering at an inn he hurried over to the Maruyama gay district.

People thronged the streets, and there was great hustle and bustle. There was prosperity here: crude, lively, far more flourishing than Yonosuke had heard or anticipated. Some eighty or ninety prostitutes exhibited themselves in one establishment alone. Foreigners, he was told, kept to their own brothels. Trade was brisk there, for—or so the natives said—they were of a tough breed. But their prostitutes were never exhibited to public view. Everything was done secretly, night and day, as if it were a shameful thing and must be hidden and its existence denied. The Dutch carried on on the little island of Deshima in the harbor, while other foreigners living in uptown Nagasaki took in prostitutes freely, without restrictions or segregation. Their stamina never seemed to wane. "Ah, these foreigners!" thought Yonosuke. He felt old, old.

But to his agreeable surprise, Yonosuke found a number of courtesans whom he had once patronized but who had since drifted down here from Kyoto's gay district. "Imagine seeing you here!" he beamed at them. "It really must be a small world, this."

"We shall make your visit a very pleasant one. How would you like us to perform some Noh dance dramas for your pleasure?"

"The Noh? But that is performed by men only. The stage is man's exclusive province."

"Ah, Yonosuke-sama, but why shouldn't women exercise their talent too? What men can do, so can women. We can do it just as well, even though tradition forbids it. You shall see!"

And surprised indeed was Yonosuke when he discovered their extraordinary versatility. Themselves planning, supervising, and erecting the Noh stage precisely according to pattern, the courtesans chanted, handled the percussion instruments, acted, and danced all the parts of three of Zeami's celebrated two-act plays, *Sada-ie, Matsukaze,* and *Miidera.*

"You did very well," he praised the courtesans after the performance. "Properly cadenced, beautiful and graceful. A happy talent indeed."

"Just for that, Yonosuke-sama, we shall honor you with a grand party. We'll show you that, though some of us have drifted away from Kyoto, for one reason and another, to this exotic southern port city, we have not forgotten the true art of entertaining. You shall see!"

And what he saw was a thing of sheer sumptuous delight. Great golden plates filled with strange delicacies were placed before him, and thirty-seven courtesans robed in varying shades of reddening autumn leaves put on a show based on the ancient Chinese wine-and-drinking poem called "Chiu Ko-sun." They wore scarlet net aprons, their sleeves girded up with golden sashes, sprigs of flowers in hand. They danced in wild abandon:

> Under the shade of pines ever green,
> Shall flow the wines of Iwai
> For ages eternal.

The food was luxurious. "I once paid 35 *ryo* for quail broiled over a charcoal fire, just to please a Kyoto courtesan," Yonosuke reminisced, very apropos. "But here . . . these foreign-looking delicacies cooked or baked in wonderful tasting condiments . . . everything is so . . . so amazing. And so delicious."

Some of the native Nagasaki courtesans said: "Speaking of Kyoto courtesans, we wish we could see how they look today. We are curious, and we may have a lot to learn."

"You shall," Yonosuke replied. "I knew you would, so I brought with me the very things which will satisfy you . . . at least from this great distance."

He ordered the 12 boxes he had brought with him as extra luggage from Kyoto be brought into the room. Opening them one by one, he produced 44 huge full-robed dolls: 17 likenesses of noted Kyoto courtesans, 8 of Edo, and 19 of Osaka. These he arranged on the Noh stage, attaching the names of the courtesans on whom each was painstakingly and accurately modeled. Each face, each posture, each colorful robe was different from the other. Collectively they gave the impression of the height of female grandeur and beauty. There was not a single hint or suggestion of vulgarity.

"Oh . . . oh! This is too beautiful for us alone to see!" was the general exclamation.

And so the huge dolls were placed on public view, and almost everyone in Nagasaki came to see and sigh over these wondrous things of beauty. They satisfied, even if vicariously, the secret yearning of every normal man.

NO RETURN

AT LAST the time of reckoning came for Yonosuke. For twenty-seven years, with his patrimony, he had ceaselessly devoted his mind and body to adventures among the gay quarters of the country, playing the part of the amorist for all it was worth. Now he was a gaunt figure, emaciated and fast deteriorating

Yet he had no regrets. He had seen everything and done everything he wanted to do with the 25,000 gold *kan* bequeathed to him by his mother to spend as he pleased. Both of his parents were dead. He had no wife, no heir, no legitimate children of his own, no family cares or obligations whatsoever. But how much longer, he wondered, could he continue wandering and losing himself in this mundane hell of the flesh, to be finally burned out by its all-consuming flames?

Ah, but he would soon, next year perhaps, enter into a state of second childhood. He was already hard of hearing. His legs were weak and wobbly, and he leaned heavily on a mulberry staff as he walked.

His once handsome face had gradually become withered and ugly. But he was not alone in this creeping decrepitude. All the women he had known intimately were now crowned with snow-white hair. Their once lovely faces were shriveled and wrinkled with age. Young girls whom he had gallantly helped into palanquins, parasol in hand on rainy nights, had turned into prosaic housewives—the sort that hold the affection of unexciting men.

Verily the times had changed irretrievably since his youth. That, perhaps was to be expected. "Even so, how could the world have changed so radically?" he mused.

He had never prayed consistently for salvation in the next world, accepting resignedly the incontestable belief that, after death, he would willy-nilly be torn by the punishing demons of hell. Even if he were to embark on a change of heart now, it would not be easy, he knew, to be saved by Buddha's mercy. Yes . . . yes he would have to accept whatever punishment awaited him for his ignoble life upon this earth. He gave away most of his remaining property.

Then, in a final ineluctable flight of fancy, he buried 6,000 *ryo* of gold coins deep in the woods of Higashiyama, with the following epitaph engraved on a small stone monument:

Here lies the glitter of 6,000 ryo,
Hidden under morning-glories
That bloom in the shade of the setting sun.

And he planted morning-glories over the "grave."

Quickly the story of this strange, whimsical burial symbolizing his own life spread through the city of Kyoto. But no one has ever been able to discover its location.

Later Yonosuke gathered together six of his cronies who had from time to time shared his unbridled life of pleasure. Then he had a ship built on a tiny delta island near Osaka. He named it *Yoshiiro-maru* and hoisted a white sail made from the silken inner garments that had once been those of Yoshino, the courtesan who had at one time been his lawful mate.

Curtains for the ship's cabins and decks were fashioned from the robes given to him as keepsakes by other courtesans with whom he had dallied and whom he had abandoned. Sitting rooms were papered with the written mementos of still other courtesans. And the great ropes for the ship were braided from the thick strands of hair that had been presented to him by yet other women, in years past, as pledges of undying love.

Tubs filled with fresh-water fish were placed in the ship's kitchen. Fresh supplies of burdock, yam, and eggs were buried in boxed soil. Into the hold went other foods, household drugs including rejuvenating stimulants and painkillers, bedside pictures, copies of *The Tale of Ise,* paper handkerchiefs, loincloths, and numerous other articles that gratified men's needs and desires, such as leather strips, tin plates, clove oil, and pepper. Even swaddling clothes—signifying second childhood—were taken on board.

"We may never return," said Yonosuke, "so let us drink to our departure."

"Not coming back here?" His six bosom friends were amazed, baffled. "To what distant land, then, are we to accompany you on this ship?"

Yonosuke replied in an even tone: "All of you pleasure-seeking men have spent your lives in seeing and experiencing all there was to see and experience among dancing girls and wanton women. There is nothing else for you, or for me, to get excited about here. We shall leave with no regrets. From now on, we are going to cross the sea, in search of the isle of Nyogo, an isolated body of land inhabited solely by women. There I shall introduce you to a different type of female: the aggressive sort who will come to seize you and sweep you off your feet."

"Well, that's different!" his cronies responded gladly. "Even if we might turn to ashes there, we should feel content, for are we not destined for the amorous life forever?"

And so, with fanciful sighs, Yonosuke and his six companions lifted anchor and set sail, first for the Izu Peninsula. Then, on a clear day at the end of the tenth month in the year Tenwa 2 (1682), the ship with its human cargo of forever gay adventurers embarked on an ocean voyage, steadily toward the limitless horizon, from which there was to be no return.